# STUDFINDER

# Studfinder

## L.B. DUNBAR

HeartEyes Press

Editor: Melissa Shank
Editor: Jenny Sims/Editing4Indies
Proofread: Karen Fischer

# RITA

"You," I hiss, glaring at the most annoying man I've ever met, and I've met plenty of annoying men. Of course, not all of them were hunky, smirky, sexy silver foxes, but that was neither here nor there. I am standing here, and he is sitting there. "You are in my spot."

This is the third time this week he's encroached on my couch in the Busy Bean Café, and three strikes mean you're out, handsome.

Taking a moment, the offender blinks before narrowing his bluest-of-blue eyes and glares back at me. For a second, I wonder if I have something on my face. Maybe chocolate in the corner crease of my lips or lettuce in my teeth from lunch.

*What the frick is he staring at?*

Then he blinks again and slowly leans forward. His arm porn-worthy forearms rest on his wide-spread thighs as he glances up at me. Since I think he's about to stand from the place where he's perched, I speak.

"Thank you." My mother taught me manners, even if I some-times lack the use of them. Especially on this occasion, *where a hunky, smirky, sexy silver fox who is the most annoying man I've ever met* is sitting in my spot on the plush peach couch in my favorite coffee shop.

He stops moving at my gratitude and turns his head slowly left to right. Then he swivels at the waist right to left, exaggerating his motions as if he's searching for something over his shoulders. Did he forget something? Did he drop his phone? His hand moves to his side and smooths over the velvety cushion, stroking it like the soft texture is a pleasure fabric or a preferred pet. My mouth waters for some reason because his movements might match that of him caressing a woman, taking his time to sculpt along her thighs. Maybe glide over her backside. Stroke the inside of her legs and . . .

"Just what are you doing?" He's taking too long to move it.

"I'm looking for a sign that says this seat is taken." Turning that edgy face upward, beaming those blue headlights at me, he crooks the corner of his mouth in the smirkiest of smirks. "But as I don't see one, nor do I see your name on this couch, I think I'll stay."

He falls back against the couch as if he's dropping onto a mattress, tossing himself down into the fluffiest of pillows to catch his hard body in a cushion of heaven. His arms stretch wide to encompass the length of the couch back. He even sighs. A long, lush, deep groan of pleasure emits from him while his eyes close for a second. Then he inhales. When his lids flip open, he spears me in place. That does not stop my mouth.

"Look, handsome, this is my spot. Everyone knows it's my spot. Think Norm in *Cheers*, where everybody knows his name. This is where I sit." I shouldn't have called him handsome. He probably already knows he is. In fact, I'm certain he knows he's good-looking. I don't know how he even faces himself in the mirror every morning. He's *that* good-looking.

"I'm curious if everyone is always glad you *came* . . ." His eyes narrow at me, and I ignore the emphasis he's put on a certain term. I will not fall for these kinds of wordplay games, nor will I falter under the curl of his sassy mouth. Even the crinkle of his nose as he annunciated that word was hot.

"Of course, they're always glad I'm *here*, occupying my spot." My voice hardens as my fists clench at my sides. I've had a day, and I just want to sit in my happy place and sip some coffee. Is the Busy Bean the most convenient spot for me to haunt? No, it is not, but I've been to worse places—been there, done that—and I will not be going back. I live halfway between Colebury and Montpelier, where my law office is located, and coming here is out of my way most days. But today is one of those days when I need my spot and a good cup of dark roast, and I do *not* need this hunky, smirky, sexy silver fox glaring back at me or his fine backside taking up residency on my couch.

*Get a grip, Rita.*

Technically, I don't own the couch or the right to claim this space as mine. The Busy Bean Café is owned and operated by Audrey Shipley and Zara Rossi, both excellent businesswomen. They've taken this quaint location on the old gin mill property and made it into something special. With brick-red walls and chalkboard painted beams overhead, the creaking wooden floors and eclectic mixture of furniture begs a person to come in and linger, which is what I do—often. Not to mention, the coffee is divine. The dark roast is a special blend introduced to the place a while back, and the addition of delicious cupcakes on the menu from Oh, For Heaven's Cakes makes this place more than just a coffeehouse. It's heaven in Vermont.

It's *my* heaven, and the devil himself is sitting here.

Jake Drummond is his name, actually, but that's semantics to me. He's quickly becoming a huge thorn in my side.

"What are you even doing here?" I snap although I might know the answer. The local Catholic church hosts an AA meeting soon, and perhaps he'll be attending it. Internally, I bitterly laugh at the thought. This man does not take Alcoholics Anonymous seriously.

Jake peers around the room, exaggerating his observation once again before lifting a coffee mug. "I'm enjoying the local brew."

My eyes narrow at him, and I try to ignore the sharp edge to his cheeks. Plus, the layer of scruff that is a mix of gray and black blended to perfection against the cliff of his jaw. His short-cropped hairstyle matches that stubbly facial mixture. Despite his face looking young, the crinkles near his eyes and the tightness to his mouth give away the fact he's easily over forty like me.

In comparison, the wrinkles on my neck and the graying strands of hair weaving their way through my mousy brown mop make me look older than I am some days. While the indents near my eyes are often called laugh lines, I'm well aware their presence is from stress and glaring at people, like this man, who knows he's handsome, full of charm, and giving off a vibe that makes me want to tackle him to said couch and have my way with him.

A shaky hand comes to my forehead. What I really need is to get laid, but it's been so long I don't know what that is anymore. Why do we even call it *getting laid*? I can do it standing up. I can do it on a bus. I can do it against a door. I can do it on the floor. I can . . . stop rhyming in my head like a sexually deprived Dr. Seuss fan.

His sapphire eyes stare at me, and silence lingers as if he asked me something, and I've taken too long to answer.

"Did you say something?"

"Nope." He pops the p-sound and lowers his lips for the brim of his coffee mug, taking his time to sip at the heavenly dark roast. As I'm easily distracted by the scruff surrounding his mouth, I notice the rich red color of his lips and wonder if they taste as candy sweet as they look.

Probably more like a red-hot cinnamon drop.

"Fine," I grumble, turning away from the plush peach couch I long to sit on and step back to the counter.

"Roddy, give me a dark roast to go and one of those Dark Horse Mochaccino cupcakes." I glance back at Jake, who is watching me. Turning back to Roddy, I add, "Better make it a double on the cupcakes. I need something sweet to rid the bad taste in my mouth."

I glare back at Jake, squeezing my entire face like a child sticking out her tongue at my nemesis. I don't know what it is about Jake, but *something* about him raises the hackles on my neck and dampens my underwear at the same time.

As Roderick pours my coffee and sets my cupcakes in a bag, my foot taps impatiently. I'm a bundle of nerves and need to get out of here if I can't sit here to relax.

"Two Dark Horse Mochaccino cupcakes and a dark roast for the plush peach couch defender." Roderick winks at me, before eyeing the man hogging my spot.

"Next time I come in here, he better not be taking up space in my place."

Roderick laughs. "Now, Rita, as much as we love you, you know we can't reserve you a spot, nor will we kick patrons out if they sit there first."

Jake can hear Roderick from his seat, and he lifts his mug to salute Roddy's words.

"Well, we'll just see about that," I snap, preparing for battle over a set of cushions in a coffeehouse.

"I look forward to the challenge," Jake mocks from his seat on said couch, and then he has the audacity to wink at me. *He winks.* Quickly, I turn my back on the hunky, smirky, sexy silver fox and strut across the wooden planks to exit the Busy Bean. Only as I use my backside to push the door open, I glance back at Jake Drummond once more and find him watching me with those cinnamon hot lips quirked up on one side, and I realize he's going to be difficult to ignore as he recently started to work with me.

# 2

## JAKE

That Rita Kaplan is a pain in my ass. Not only would she not sign off on my meeting sheet a week ago, but she is the supervisor where I work, and now she's staking claim to some antique piece of furniture in a coffee shop. She's insane. And something about her makes me want to push all her buttons. Push her and her buttons right up against a wall and fuck some sense into her.

*Jesus, Jake.* I swipe a hand down my face and fall back on the cushions, not realizing how tense I'd been in her presence. The tension is due to my absence on the sex scene and the need to expel some seriously pent-up energy soon. Only problem is not many women are interested in an ex-arson investigator, ex-convict, and ex-husband. The final ex doesn't really define me, but it fits with all the other things I've been ex-ed out of in the last decade.

With a shaky hand, I lift the coffee mug of dark roast to my lips and sip. In my opinion, people do not appreciate good coffee enough. I get it they'll pay exorbitant amounts for a decent brew, but do they actually savor the flavor, the satisfaction, and the downright joy of drinking a good cup of coffee? I know I didn't until I had to live with the piss-poor sludge served in the state penitentiary. As far as prisons go, it wasn't the worst. It wasn't riddled with gang warfare and boyfriend swapping like I've heard of in other places. This was Vermont. We're all grunge-happy, ice cream royalty, organic farming, and woodland animal safety. Cue the bitterness of being trapped like an animal for seven long fucking years.

Taking a deep breath, I remind myself I'm free. I'm liberated from schedules and constraints, and someone telling me when I can shower, shit, and watch television. I'm able to be me, only I no longer know who that is. I'm also not one-hundred percent unshackled. I still have the mandatory parole period, including enforced work-placement and required AA meetings. It's a cross I'll bear to get me to the other side—true freedom and possible escape from Vermont. As soon as I've done the remainder of my time, *I am outta here*, said with all the lackluster gangster in me. I want to be so far gone from this place, this state, and all the haunting memories.

The thought saddens me as I'm finally able to see my brother without a partition between us or a supervisor watching over me as we sit at a folding table in cold chairs. Soon, I will see my nephew, who is no longer a teenager but a grown adult. Rory has come far despite the fumbles and foils of two men trying to raise a reckless boy into a good man. Just this summer, he'll be graduating from law school. My heart fills with pride while bittersweet over Rory's accomplishments. So much had been sacrificed to ensure he became more than his father or myself.

Willing away thoughts of things I cannot change, I brush my hand over the velvety worn material on this ugly couch and chuckle. Rita returns to my mind. *Who does that woman think she is? Thinking she holds the rights to a piece of furniture in a public coffeehouse?*

The first time I met Rita Kaplan was at an AA meeting a week ago. The local church hosts them in their basement, and as part of my parole, I must attend. It's bullshit if you ask me, and my behavior illuminates my attitude about attendance.

*"We have someone new with us tonight. Would you like to intro-*

*duce yourself and tell us a little bit about your story?"* Rita's cheerful voice was like nails on a chalkboard, but it was her eyes that scratched me. We'd only crossed gazes, but it felt like she saw into the depths of my soul, or maybe it was just the glare of her eyeglasses under the fluorescent lighting. At least, that's what I told myself after her bright blue eyes pinned me to the folding chair.

*"Yeah, I'm not ready to share,"* I'd stated while slouching in my seat. My voice came out rougher than I intended, but I was not used to speaking with others.

*"How about at least a name?"* she asked, coaxing me like an encouraging schoolteacher. Her smile was warm enough, and it drew my eyes to her lips. Instantly, I wondered what her mouth would feel like against mine. I also had other ideas where she could put those lips on me. She was not my type, though, and I shifted in the cold metal seat to disguise the semi I was sporting, chalking the disturbing reaction up to the fact I hadn't been with someone in seven years. *Yeah, I had that seven-year itch, all right, and I needed to scratch it hard.*

*"Jake."* When I offered nothing more, she glanced down at a clipboard on her lap like that singular name was enough to recognize me. Certain my parole officer had notified the local authorities of my residency along with the local support groups of my requirements, I surmised this woman had heard of me. She smiled sweetly but also with a knowing eye—I was not going to participate. No sob story would be pouring out of me, nor was I sharing my experience with alcohol. I didn't have a problem, which is the first thing an alcoholic would say. The truth is, I really didn't. When I was arrested, I was drunk and fought off the officer, thus adding disorderly conduct, resisting arrest, and intent to harm an officer to my sentence. As I knew Frank Stucco, the charges of belligerence were dropped, but the alcohol consumption increased in jail. I got caught with the contraband. Forget how I got it, it only mattered that I was caught with it. Just like the sentence I served for arson. Forget how it happened. I was the

man caught at the scene of the crime with too many connections and no alibi.

After forty-five minutes of a feisty woman wearing red-rimmed eyeglasses glaring at me, the meeting ended, and Rita confronted me.

*"I know your type."* The bold directness did nothing to dispel the full hard-on I had by the meeting's conclusion. I'd tuned out the sad stories and turned on my own imagination about this vixen and what she could do to me wearing only those eyeglasses. *Naughty schoolteacher? Dirty librarian?* I wasn't going to be particular in my fantasy. Ironically, nothing else about Rita called her *my* type. Sandy brown hair with heavy strips of gray. Wrinkles at the corner of her eyes. The mocking set of her mouth when she falsely smiled. Still, she was instantly under my skin, and again, I attributed it to those eyes, blue and bright behind her glasses and a hefty dose of need-to-get-laid.

*"And what's my type?"* I sassed back.

*"You're not taking this seriously."* Fisted hands came to her hips which had my gaze falling to them. She was petite with a combination of granola hiker and uptight businesswoman in her appearance. The hiking boots did not go with the fitted skirt and silky blouse she wore.

*"Listen, sweetheart, you'll learn real fast that I don't take anything seriously anymore."* I didn't. I couldn't, but nothing I said surprised her more than one word.

*"Sweetheart?"* she snorted. Literally, the most unattractive nasal sound honked between us. *"I am not your sweetheart."*

I shook my head at her disgruntled tone and did the most unnatural thing for me. With my fingertip, I bopped her on the tip of her pert nose.

*"Then if you'd just sign off on this sheet, no one needs to be the wiser, and I can be out of your hair."* It was a risk asking this stranger to place her signature along the ten lines of my required meetings. I could get in big trouble if she tattled, telling my parole officer I tried to cheat the system.

Rita shook her head, adamantly dismissing my request. *"No can do, handsome. Maybe you'll learn something by being here."*

I couldn't imagine what I'd possibly get out of listening to others tell their tales. I'd heard worse. So much worse inside prison. I didn't need some bored housewife telling me how she drank in the middle of the afternoon while she watched soap operas. Or some local business owner sneaking shots behind his cash register.

*"Handsome, huh?"* I mocked, matching her false smile with a teasing smirk of my own. At one time, I knew how to hook a woman. Flirting had landed me my ex-wife, but I didn't waste my time with thoughts of Lisa. And I would never flirt with Rita Kaplan. She will not hold my heart, be sweet on me, or anything other than be a pain in my ass.

To top it all off after that meeting, I find Rita as the supervisor on the job where I've been stationed the following day. It's some restorative justice bullshit where I right the wrongs of the things I've done. I'd believe in it more if I thought I'd done something wrong that needed to be righted.

On that note, I finish my coffee, enjoying the subtle noise of a busy café around me while I sit in solitude. I'll never take for granted being alone again, and while I've longed for decent company, I've grown accustomed to the silence. However, when a dark-haired beauty enters and orders the most complicated drink I've ever heard, I decide she's the company I might like to keep. At least, for an hour or two.

# 3

# RITA

"The couch thief," I snap as Jake Drummond reports for work at Building Buddies, my passion project, the next day. The not-for-profit organization builds homes for those in need in the Vermont-New Hampshire area. It's a program I've been dedicated to for over a decade and remain committed to in memory of my father, who stressed the need to give to others less fortunate. When I was ten, Dad taught me how to wield a hammer and work a power saw as we built my tree fort. As I grew older, I used my skill set to devote time to this worthy cause.

As a part of the Building Buddies commitment to helping others, we take on workers needing re-acclimation into society from hardship, namely the prison system or drug rehabilitation centers. We offer manual labor, which provides tangible completion of a project, allowing our recruits to see what they've done for someone else. The hope is production gives former inmates a sense of accomplishment. In addition, we teach trade skills that can lead to jobs in construction, landscape, design, and utility services. It gives me great pride to be a member of the board and an active participant in the building projects themselves.

I'd heard of Jake Drummond before I met him at the site. We'd been prepped as to who he was. Prison sentence for arson. Prior work as an electrician. We didn't allow prejudice to mar our selection. We also didn't want to form preconceived notions, so we don't inquire further into a person's backstory. If said person wanted to share his history, we listened, but it wasn't a requirement. He was here to do a job in an effort to rebuild himself while constructing a home or facility for others. It was a fresh start at a new future, not a flashback to his tainted past.

Unfortunately, I had a niggling sensation about Jake, and it counteracts the tingling feeling between my thighs when I look at him. The arson conviction alone raised hackles on my neck. However, giving second chances is the cornerstone philosophy of Building Buddies, so I ignored those fine hairs tickling my nape. The lacking warm-fuzzies began after our first introduction, where he dismissed the beliefs of Alcoholics Anonymous while attending the meeting I chaired. The final straw was sitting on my couch at the Busy Bean.

"I've been called worse," he teases in reference to the couch-thief accusation. "Blanket hog. Pillow thief." He gives me that smirk of a grin at the bedding references, and my face heats. Instantly, I imagine him naked under blankets or with his head on a pillow facing me. I do not want to be attracted to him, but I recognize that I am on a physical level. I cannot deny a handsome man being handsome, but I do not like his attitude. He knows he's good-looking. The dimples alone prove it, not that I can fault the dimples, but still, his smile reeks of sex and sinful things. Too bad the scent is overpowered by his attitude that stinks like burnt coffee and poor decisions.

"Huh." I ignore him, glancing over the day's spec sheet although I'm unable to focus enough to read a thing. Jake's nearness distracts me. In reality, he smells good—all spicy male mixed with the scent of fresh sawdust and outdoor springtime—and I shiver. I don't know how I'll make it through the day. Thankfully, the studs are up, and the roof tapped down on this house. Today's order includes window installation and hard-wiring the electricity, which is Jake's assignment as electrical work was listed as part of his skill set. I'm here to supervise. To his credit, Jake is a diligent worker. He jumped in immediately upon his arrival. He's early to work and does additional jobs we don't ask of him, like picking up garbage and scraps at the end of the day.

"Let me make the couch thing up to you. I'll buy you a coffee the next time I'm sitting on it." The implication is clear. If our paths should cross again in the Bean, he'll be taking—and keeping—my seat on the sofa.

"How about if you just move your fine . . . just move the next time you see me?" My traitorous eyes roam his body as I speak, taking in the way his faded jeans dip on his hips, weighted down by a tool belt, and how the fit of his flannel hugs his chest. Jake runs hot, so he'll have that thing off soon enough, giving me a show with the tight T-shirt he wears underneath the outerwear.

"You want to see my moves?" Jake teases. Bending his arms before his chest, he tips his head forward and sways his hips.

*Holy sticky maple syrup.*

Jake starts to dance to some song in his head, and a playlist of music runs through mine, which includes "Afternoon Delight" and "Let's Get It On." Quickly, I turn away from the subtle thrusts of his pelvis, slowly tapping left to right. However, those eyes of mine have their own mind, and my gaze drifts back to him, watching as he lowers his lids and bites his bottom lip. If he moves like that when he . . . and looks like that when he . . . I'd let him steal my pillow, take the blankets, and have the damn couch.

"Okay, Michael Jackson," I snap, more aggressively than necessary.

"Michael Jackson?" His head pops up as he stills his dance. "I'm insulted. That was my best Chase Rice doing 'Ride.' Michael Jackson dates you a bit."

He chuckles, but his humor hits a sore spot for me. I'm newly forty-three. Never been married. Never had children, and I'm sensing a midlife crisis coming on. Not that *the* crisis is like a common cold or anything. It can't be detected by aches, chills, fever, stuffy nose, and the like. It's more a feeling inside me that I need a change in my life. It's time.

"Well, Chase Rice called, and he wants his groove back."

Jake laughs harder. "Rita, you're a hoot."

"Speaking of dating oneself." *Who calls anyone a hoot nowadays?*

"Who's dating?" Sullivan Vance interrupts us, and I'm grateful for the intrusion from our construction manager. Sullivan is a burly guy, complete with bristle brush beard and unruly dark hair under his knit cap. Everything about him is typical Vermont and kind of cute, but nothing that attracts me enough to give in to the constant dates he's asked of me.

"Rita wants to date Michael Jackson," Jake states, and Sullivan glances a little wide-eyed and hurt at me.

"Is he new around here?" His dark eyes show he's seriously questioning me.

Jake snorts before covering his mouth with a fist, pretending to cough.

"Never mind, Sully. We don't have all day to dance. Let's get to work," I state, going into supervisor mode. I have a one o'clock court time, so I need to finish here by noon.

Jake starts humming whatever tune he had in his head, and I make a mental note to find that song and give it a listen. In the meantime, Sullivan leads the way to the house we're building for a family of four who lost theirs this past winter in a fire. Jackie and Bob applied for our assistance after Bob lost his job. They didn't have enough homeowner's insurance for the damage done to their house, and one of their children has extensive medical bills.

By noon, we have a few windows installed. The electrical wiring is still on the docket, and Jake will take the lead while Sully assists.

"I need to head out," I tell Sullivan, and he nods. "But I'll be back after court."

This turns Jake's head in my direction. "What are you going to court for?"

"I'm an attorney by day." Some people consider my law practice fledgling, and I never know if that's a compliment or an insult after all this time. May Shipley is my partner, and I love her energy for the law. Although she started out with the typical real estate contracts and farm disputes when I brought her on, I've handed over more and more of my client list and prospective cases.

I've been a lawyer for almost twenty years, and I've loved it. Taking over Kaplan and Associates—now Kaplan and Shipley— from my father was an honor and a necessity, but I'm lacking luster with the same old thing. I brought May on with the intention that one day she could take over the practice in its entirety although I've never given her a specific start date to my retirement. Forty-three seems too young to retire. Even though I recognize a need for renewed passion in something, I'm not certain what I'll do with the next half of my life.

"Attorney-client confidentiality." I wink at Jake, emphasizing I won't be telling him more about my case although it's nothing other than petty theft. Maybe one day I'll prosecute the couch thief for stealing my seat at the Bean.

# JAKE

Sullivan Vance seems like a decent guy. He's quiet and a little clumsy. He wears your typical oversized jeans, displaying a slight plumber's crack when he bends forward, but he's strong and vested in this project for Building Buddies. I'd honestly never heard of this organization before being assigned here for my parole. I don't need to explain myself to the group. They know why I'm here, at least on a simplistic level. Only those at the top know the severity of my case. What happened. Why I went to prison.

In truth, it's an unsolved mystery. I didn't do it. With the evidence stacked against me, though, and a department-appointed attorney with strong political ties to the State assigned to me, I didn't have a prayer of getting off for a crime I didn't commit. I also had my reasons for *not* fighting the sentence. None of it matters now, though. The bottom line is I don't trust lawyers, which leaves me conflicted about Rita.

"So, what's her story?" I ask Sullivan as we halt for a half-hour lunch break. The job is typically eight to four, and the collaboration of workers rotates with Sully in the lead, Rita as supervisor, and me as a permanent member of the team. I don't mind the work. Every day is one more day closer to freedom, and I keep that in mind every time I hammer, drill, or, in today's case, eventually run wire.

"Who?"

"Rita," I state, hoping not to betray my curiosity.

"She's good people."

Though I wait on Sully to expand his answer, he doesn't, and I swallow a thick bite of my organic peanut butter and raspberry jam on wheat. My brother, Nolan, made me the sandwich like he's my mother or something. If he starts writing me inspirational notes of encouragement, he's fired from lunch-packing duty.

"I know"—although I don't—"but what's her deal? Why does she work for Building Buddies?"

Sullivan shrugs. "Been working here for years. Started with her dad."

Silence falls again, and I see I'll need to pull the string to keep Sully talking.

"And her dad is . . ."

"Judge Kaplan. He died a few years back." Good ole Sully. A man of words.

*A judge?* Jesus, I hate those almost as much as attorneys. Judge Kaplan . . . the name is not familiar.

"And she just kept working here after he passed." It's more of a question, and Sullivan takes the bait.

"Continued on with her fiancé."

"Rita's engaged?" My voice rises. I don't recall a ring on her finger, and I haven't had a hint she's attached to someone. In fact, I swore she was interested by the way she eyed me that first meeting. At least a spark of something flickered as she stared at me that entire session, but then again, it could have been the lighting and how it hit her lenses. She wasn't wearing those stud-hot glasses this morning, giving me a better shot of those baby blues, and the glare she gave said she was on the verge of throat-punching me—or kissing me.

"Nah. He died, too."

*Shit.* I choke on another bite of sandwich I'd taken while waiting on Sullivan's response.

"That's . . . sad." I swallow around the thick chunk of bread in my throat. I've experienced my share of death in my family. My mother died when I was eighteen and a freshman in college. Her death was one of the reasons I was back in the area. Nolan was too young to be on his own, and our father had long since fled the family.

"How long were they engaged?" I ask for some reason, thinking back to my own engagement years ago and the eventual divorce from my wife.

Sullivan shrugs again. "Don't know. She was, and then she wasn't."

My shoulders sag with sympathy. Rita is still a thorn in my side, but this information softens the wound a bit.

"You about done?" Sullivan asks, nodding at the last corner of my sandwich. Shoving the final bite in my mouth, I nod, and we wad up our trash. Nolan's been making my lunch in a brown paper sack because I refused to use a lunchbox like some damn kid. Considering I was once a student in natural resource studies, I should be using an environmentally sound carrier for my meal and need to reconsider the idea of a paper sack. After years of eating off a segmented tray, I need to rethink many things in my life.

Rita returns late in the afternoon, but I've lost track of time. It's been a gloomy day, and the underbelly of the house is dark. I'm in the basement installing the electrical box with a bright halogen work lamp hooked to a generator that highlights the space.

"You can call it quits," Rita says from somewhere behind me.

"I just want to finish this." I hate to leave things left undone, and I have the electrical box hung but no wires installed. Glancing over my shoulder, I notice Rita's leaning on the makeshift railing of the basement stairs. She's wearing some kind of woman power suit, complete with formfitting skirt and a blazer, and those damn hiking boots again. "Quite the fashionista."

Rita glances down at her attire, swiping her hand along the hips of her skirt before gazing up at me with those piercing eyes. The red-rimmed glasses have returned.

"I can't wear heels at a construction site."

It makes sense, but she looks ridiculous, and I turn my back on her. Keeping those hiking boots in mind cancels out the effect of those glasses and dampens any naughty boy fantasies of being punished by Rita as a teacher. I hear her trod back up the stairs and dismiss Sully. This isn't a large house, and without the drywall, it's a hollow shell, so noise travels.

"You don't need to stay," I holler to her, forgetting myself for a second as I concentrate on the work before me. Heavy feet trudge back down the staircase.

"Yeah. I do." The authoritative reminder puts me in my place. *I need to be supervised. I need to be watched.* I hate the distrust.

Around us grows quiet until we hear the voice of Sullivan at the top of the staircase.

"You're sure you're okay?" Sully asks, calling down to Rita, expressing his concern for her safety. "I can stay if you need me."

"I'm not an ax murderer," I mutter under my breath, fingers slipping along the initial wire I'm running through the box.

"I'm good," Rita calls up to him, surprising me. Her confidence speaks volumes. She's trusting me, at least at this moment.

As we hear the stomp of Sully's feet leaving the house, Rita mumbles, "No one thinks you're an ax murderer."

I huff in response and continue working on the box. She's silent, but I can almost hear the gears turning in her head.

"Just ask."

"Ask what?" she snaps, and I twist enough to glance at her at the base of the staircase. She's removed her blazer. Leaning against the bare studs, she's still a juxtaposition in her uptight shirt and those damn boots.

"Whatever's on your mind, sweet." I struggle with another wire leading into the box.

"Whatever you did, you can talk about it, if you'd like."

"Attorney-client privilege," I mock.

"Or if you just need someone to talk to." Her softened voice surprises me, but I ignore the tenderness. I don't have anything to say about what happened seven years ago. It happened. It's over. *Almost.*

"Not much of a talker," I admit, keeping my eyes on the wires before me. I can't concentrate with her watching me, knowing those damn eyes are assessing me behind those red rims.

"You seem like you have plenty to say about my appearance," she mocks, a light chuckle in her tone.

"That's different."

"How is it different to verbally insult my clothes but not talk about what happened?"

She can't be serious. There's a world of difference between her boot-skirt combination and the events of years past. As she's a lawyer, she isn't stupid, so I don't feel the need to clarify the contrast.

Suddenly, there's a sharp crackle, and I turn my head in time to see smoke rising from the halogen light.

"Shit," I hiss, leaning over and pulling the plug, disconnecting the power source. Another spark cracks before quickly burning out. A slow hiss follows the bright snap. These lights run hot, and the slightest bit of construction dust could start a fire. With the lamp suddenly off, we're submerged in darkness.

When I glance up at Rita, enough light filters down the staircase to show me her back is ramrod straight against the stud supports at the base of the staircase. Her hands are behind her, clutching at the narrow strips of wood.

"Shit," I mutter again as I take two steps toward her. "You okay?"

Rita's eyes are still focused over my shoulder at the lamp

where a sliver of white smoke hisses upward from the light source. I shift to block her view.

"Sweet," I whisper, forcing her gaze to my face. "You're safe with me. I swear it."

Her chin dips once to acknowledge what I said, but she doesn't relax. Her hands still cling to the wood at her back as her chest heaves. Slowly, I reach out for her, wrapping my hand cautiously around her nape.

"Rita, focus on me. Take a breath."

She nods again, keeping her eyes on mine as I massage the back of her neck, feeling the tension under her skin. Stepping closer to her, I will her to inhale as I do and then follow my exhale.

"That's it. In. Out."

She exaggerates her breathing, sucking in air before heavily releasing it.

"That's it," I repeat, still rubbing at her nape while her breasts brush against my tee-covered chest. Despite being sweaty from working under the heat of the lamp, I'm not stepping back until whatever frightened her subsides.

"Are you afraid of the dark?" I question, although it's not pitch black. Low light filters down the flight of stairs.

"Fire," she whispers.

I turn to glance over my shoulder, making certain one didn't start, then look back at her.

"No fire," I whisper.

Her eyes close a second, and she swallows hard. My thumb wraps around the front of her neck, slowly stroking up the column of her throat. Her skin is warm while soft under the calloused touch of my hand. I can feel her heart beating through the pulse at her neck. Slowly, her eyes open, and those blues are like fresh flames on a newly lit stove. The heat in them is just as intense.

Leaning forward, I lick my lips, watching where my thumb slides along her neck.

"Please don't be afraid of me." My roughened voice does not match the pleading words; however, I don't want her to fear for her safety. I'd never hurt her. I'd never purposely hurt anyone.

She doesn't respond to my plea, but I can't seem to let her go. My eyes focus on her lips, slightly open and pink. Our breaths mingle. Our noses almost touch. Tipping my head as her nearness is too much, I can see down her loose top and note the swell of her breasts forced together by her bra. The dark purple silk matches the deep violet shade of her blouse.

I lick my lips, wanting to slide my tongue down the column of her throat and between the crease of those swollen globes. Rita has a nice rack on her small frame.

My hand slips from the back of her neck into the collar of her shirt. Slowly, slowly, slowly, I drag my palm to her shoulder, nudging the soft material to the side. Massaging as I move over her skin, I strum my thumb over her clavicle like I'd flick at fiddle strings. I want to play her and hear her sing.

Her chest continues to heave against mine, and my heart hammers in my chest. Leaning forward, I rub my stubbly cheek along hers. My lips almost touch the shell of her ear, and I whisper, "Relax." As if thirsting for blood, my mouth waters, wanting to lower for the pulse thumping at the side of her throat. My thumb continues to stroke at the short cliff of her collarbone. No longer allowing my face to touch hers, I pull back but still feel the warmth of her skin against mine. My fingertip glides the length of her clavicle to the hollow dip at the base of her throat. Tracing along the notch, I lick my lips once more.

I could kiss her.

I want to kiss her.

Then I tell myself this desire is only because I haven't kissed anyone in seven years. And kissing Rita would be a huge mistake. Despite my raging hard-on and racing heart, I cannot make a move on Rita. I'm needy but not desperate enough to fuck my boss.

"I gotta go," I state, my voice gravelly rough. Abruptly, I

release her, hovering my hand over her skin for a mere second as her heat sizzles off my palm. She's a flame, and I'm a moth, and that is just not a game I dare to play.

Taking a large step back, I do a quick scan of the floor, unable to focus on anything I might be searching for, and then I take the stairs two at a time to get myself the hell out of the house and away from the intoxicating draw of Rita.

# RITA

*He almost kissed me.*

Despite the slam of the front door, I remain where I am, holding the studs at my back like I'm nailed to them. I was drowning under him. His scent. His nearness. The touch of his hand on my skin. His fingers massaging my neck before his palm skittered to my shoulder. The calming effect he intended did not work. His hesitant touch made my heart race faster. I was ready to beg for him to lower that thick palm and touch me in other places. Then he stopped.

*I gotta go.*

His touch left my skin scorched.

My gaze drifts to the work lamp, no longer illuminated and evidently cooled from whatever landed on it. I don't know what happened to me. I've never had a panic attack in my life. *Not ever.* One minute, I was watching Jake, heart fluttering, belly twisting, and then the sizzle occurred on the work light. A stream of smoke and the flicker of the bulb set my imagination running.

*Ian.*

I can't say it's been a long time since I've thought of my former fiancé because I think of him nearly every day. But the ache of his loss isn't as strong as it once was or as fierce as when he first passed.

*Fire.*

I wasn't sensitive to flame, but that snap and pop along with the lingering hiss triggered something inside my mind. Forgotten nightmares, I suppose. The ones I used to wash away with alcohol.

While other people might head to a bar after a moment like this to settle their nerves or numb their senses, I typically call my sponsor or go to a meeting to right myself. Tonight, I know where I need to go, as coffee has become my new drug of choice. Sitting on that damn couch might instill more wayward ideas about Jake, but I need my happy place.

*He almost kissed me.*

Those cinnamon-red lips were right here, so close I could almost taste the spicy hotness. Recalling the ruggedness of his cheek against mine sends another shiver down my spine. The toughness of his hand at my throat causes me to swallow, and his phantom caress lingers.

I would have let him take me against these beams if he had wanted me.

Which he clearly does not.

*I gotta go.*

With a shaky hand, I squeeze my forehead dismissing both my momentary panic attack and my overwrought imagination. Pushing off the studs behind me, I take another glance at the darkened lamp. My mind further represses memories of Ian. A refreshing gin and tonic could heal the tremor in my knees, but I know what I need is more than something to numb my thoughts. A dark roast and a baby fix are better than alcohol.

***

My best friend, Scarlett Russell, now Scarlett Eaton, became a momma at forty-two, and I couldn't be happier, especially as I get to reap the benefits of playing Aunt Rita.

"Give him to me," I coo when Scarlett meets me at the Busy Bean. I called her after the incident with Jake. The incident will henceforth be called the *non-kiss incident*. Some baby cuddles and nonsense murmurings will be a good distraction, and Scarlett was more than willing to get out of her house in the late afternoon.

My oldest friend had a rough go of things about a year ago. Her no-good cheating husband had gotten himself in a pickle when he dipped his dill into one of his med students who ended up pregnant. Scarlett left him and came to Vermont for a visit and decided to stay for a bit. Then she stuck permanently when she found herself pregnant from a one-night stand with her hunky cowboy, now husband, Bull. The Eaton clan is one fine man after another, but Bull's younger brothers are just trouble waiting to happen.

The newest Eaton addition, however—baby Harley—he's a heartbreaker like the rest of them with his drooling kisses and sweet giggles.

"Aunt Rita has missed you. Yes, she has," I simper to the babe in my lap while Scarlett chuckles beside me. We've taken up residence on our favorite couch *sans* Jake.

"He's not a dog," she teases at the tone I've taken to speak to the five-month-old.

"But he's as cute as a puppy, and he has eyes just like one, too. He's looking at me like 'give me everything I ask for, Aunt Rita,' and he knows I'll never say no to him."

Scarlett laughs at my ridiculousness. As college roommates, we immediately hit it off upon arriving at Boston University, but our lives took us in separate directions once we graduated. I'd intended to remain in Boston for law school. I was going to fight against true crimes and defend complex cases. Instead, my dad had his first heart attack, and I came home to join Kaplan and

Associates. I was the associate. I worked days as a legal assistant while attending law school at Vermont Law. Once I was a full-fledged attorney, we remained Kaplan and Associates although my father became a judge. For some reason, Dad never promoted me to partner.

"So, what's new?" Scarlett asks, staring at me over the rim of her coffee mug.

"Ugh. Jake Drummond is what's new." I groan while I wiggle Harley on my lap.

"Jake Drummond," Scarlett elongates his name. "Interesting. I didn't know you'd found a stud."

Scarlett was an entertainment news reporter in her life before motherhood, and despite her gossip-loving days being over, she still loves a good story.

"How do you know he's a stud?" I wonder, sticking out my tongue at Harley and making faces at him.

"He must be a stud," Scarlett confidently states.

I laugh, giving away my opinion.

"No man would have you riled if he wasn't."

"All men have me riled. I'm sexually repressed," I mock myself. I might have a pink plastic boyfriend named Bobby, but it's not the same as physical sex. And I can't have nameless, face-less sex. I've already gone that route and crashed. I don't like to recall that moment—and have trouble doing so as I blacked out during it—but I must never forget it as a pinnacle point in deciding to get my shit back together.

"So, he's hot?" Scarlett questions.

"Maybe." I shrug.

"Rita Kaplan, for all the shi-*shitake* . . ." She pauses to glance at the baby, catching herself on the curse word. ". . . you give me about my husband, and you can't give me more than *he's hot*?"

I laugh. "Well, your husband is hunky and handsome. I live through the details of your life because mine is so boring." My gaze remains on little Harley in my hands. I've missed out on many things. Most days, I don't dwell on the loss. *No sense living in the past*, my dad would say, but my future feels uncertain. I'm going to be forty-five in a few years, and if I live double that, what will I plan to accomplish with the remainder of my life? As I hold Harley, a zigzag of regret travels through my chest. I think I've missed out on something big by never having a child, but that ship sailed when I lost Ian. There just hasn't been another man for me since his passing.

"Your life isn't boring. You're a successful lawyer with your own practice, and you dedicate your extra time and talents to Building Buddies. Plus, you're an advocate for AA and supportive of that community."

"Yeah," I whisper, noting those are achievements, but many of them are service to others. What have I done for only me? What do I have that's only mine?

"Tell me more about this stud," Scarlett softly demands, sounding like she's ready to break into her rendition of the *Grease* classic "You're the One That I Want."

As I speak, I focus on Harley. "He's part of our restorative program at Building Buddies. I shouldn't be attracted to him, but I just am. There's something about him." His scruffy jaw. His heated eyes. His rough hands on my skin. My chest clenches like I'm being pulled forward by simply thinking of him.

"Why shouldn't you be attracted to him?"

I shrug, unable to answer.

"What do you know about him?" Scarlett's voice softens even more as being a recruit in our program means he's had an addiction in the past or trouble with the law.

"He's been in jail. He's on parole." Silence follows my statements. "That's it. That's all you know." I shrug again. "I don't research those who come to us, respecting their privacy."

"You aren't even a little bit curious. Just a little social media digging . . . er, research."

"No, Scarlett." I'm not a sleuth like her in that manner. I don't scroll social media for evidence. I deal in fact, and the facts were given to our director to review before being presented to the board for approval. I could use my connections with the DMV to run a background check on Jake, but I trust Alfred Jennings' judgment on who might benefit from our Building Buddies philosophy. Most of our candidates did not commit a crime directly against another person, but more a misdemeanor of sorts. Curiosity has gotten to me, and I've wondered why Alfred thought Jake would be a good match with us, but I still have not looked into Jake's history.

"I'll look him up," Scarlett says, reaching for a pocket in her diaper bag.

"No. Don't." In the grand scheme of things, it doesn't matter what she finds. He committed a crime. He served his time. He works with Building Buddies. That's it. That's as far as I need to know because Jake and I will not be more to each other. We should not be more. Jake is not for me.

However, if I search deep down inside myself, I don't want Scarlett playing investigative reporter because I don't want to learn he dates around or, worse, has a family with a wife and children. So, there will be no diving into his present life or his past.

He almost kissed me. *He wouldn't do that if he had a family, right?*

The plea in his voice, asking me not to be afraid of him, echoes through my head, mixing with his quiet reassurance he wouldn't hurt me. Does a man who has a woman in his life touch someone else so intimately?

Shaking my head, I erase my questions. I'm being silly over nothing. So he stroked my neck. So he caressed my shoulder. He was only trying to distract me from that momentary surge of panic.

"I thought of Ian today," I say, diverting Scarlett from her phone as I bounce Harley on my knees.

Her head lifts. "You never talk about him," Scarlett states, opening the door for discussion. Scarlett flew in and out during Ian's funeral, but we often spoke after his death until I couldn't talk about him anymore. It was just too painful to keep bringing him up. Of all the people who offered sympathy and pity, Scarlett was the first to let me drop the subject and discuss anything other than what I'd lost.

"What's there to say? He was a good man, and then he died."

"Rita," Scarlett whispers, understanding passing through my name. Scarlett knows me better and doesn't accept my flippant answer. I'm not upset, though. Not in a manner of hysterics and rants, like I once was when I cursed God for taking Ian from me and then threw myself at men and alcohol in hopes to sew up the hole in my heart. Alcohol became a patch instead of a stitch, and one night with the wrong man ripped through my attempts to hide how I felt.

Scarlett is one of few who understood my spiral. I didn't even see the downward spin into alcohol dependency happening. A drink—or two—to help me through the quiet, lonely evenings in the house we shared before his death. A glass of wine—or the entire bottle—to help me sleep in an empty bed we'd bought to make babies in after we married.

"You're a survivor, Rita. Don't ever forget that."

I huff but agree with her, which is why my reaction in the basement earlier has me baffled. Was it a warning? I'm not superstitious like that. Was it the universe forcing Jake and me together? Even that seems farfetched. It was a fluke, plain and simple.

"Okay, enough of the maudlin. How about dinner, chickie? I could go for a burger the size of my head at the Goat, but Tuxbury is the opposite direction for me. How about a bite at Speakeasy?"

Speakeasy is a brewpub located on the old gin mill property along with the Busy Bean Café, where we sit, and the Gin Mill, another bar specializing in Vermont beers.

"Are you sure?"

Given my history with alcohol, people are cautious about asking me to visit establishments that serve the damning liquor. Still, as long as there is good food and I leave before the rowdy crowd starts, I'm okay in a place that pours my past poison. I know my limits. While I appreciate Scarlett's concern, I don't want my friend to be squeamish about us eating at the brewhouse.

"Are you willing to take your baby to a bar?" I tease, recalling a similar line in one of our favorite movies, *Sweet Home Alabama*.

"Well . . ." Scarlett chews her lip.

"Want to call that hunky husband of yours and ask him to join us?"

"What I'd really love is a night off mommy duty. I promised to help you find a stud, and we haven't done that yet. That is if Jake isn't already the one that you want."

I laugh at the reminder that I once told Scarlett I needed a stud because she hooked up with a man named Bull.

"Let me just check in with Bull. We can keep it just us girls tonight."

"Us girls and Harley as our man," I tease of the baby, bouncing him on my lap. Scarlett excuses herself a second, and I'm grateful. Sometimes, it's difficult to listen to the sappy happiness that drips from her to Bull. I'm thrilled my friend has found a happily ever after, but I'm also slightly envious. The sweetheart and honey endearments, plus the way they look at one another like no one else is in the room . . . *gag me with a spoon.*

"Your mommy and daddy are so in love, Harley man," I coo at him with a sickening tone, but in my head, I add, *And they are so lucky.*

---

We are just finishing up our dinner as Speakeasy begins to fill up. Tomorrow will be another long day of splitting my time between the law practice and Building Buddies, so I need to put an end to my evening.

"Oh my God," Scarlett whispers, reaching over for my wrist as we're settling the bill.

"What?" I glance up, curious at her lowered voice.

"Louisa Miller has found herself a new man."

Craning my neck, I stare across the room at the youthful, raven-haired woman who had a thing for Bull Eaton when Scarlett arrived on the scene.

"Stud alert," I mutter, and Scarlett turns her attention back to me.

"What?" She chuckles.

"That's Stud. The man behind her." Standing at Louisa's back is a man all too familiar to me. The same man who hours ago had his hand on my neck and his face next to mine, whispering calming words into my ear as I thought of Ian. "That's Jake."

"That's Jake? *Your* Jake?"

"Well, he isn't mine—"

"Rita, he isn't hot." Her incredulous tone has my gaze remaining on Jake as he escorts Louisa to a table in one of the most possessive moves ever—his hand on her lower back. It's a sign of "we go together," and now I have a *Grease* classic playing in my head. I hate that hand on Louisa's back.

"Well, I—"

"He's *frick*ing hot." Her grasp on my wrist tightens. "He's flaming hot. He's sex on a stick hot. He's—"

"I get your point, lady. He's hot." I chuckle as the simple word does not do him justice, but Scarlett has to take it over the top.

"We need to get him away from Louisa."

"We need not do any such thing." My voice rises with the real fear that Scarlett will cross this restaurant and make a scene.

"But he can't be with her."

"Yet it looks like he is." The two of them take a seat, and Louisa drags her chair closer to Jake. Maybe she just wants to hear him better. It's loud in here with the high ceilings and the wood accents. Of course, I'm only making excuses. If I was on a date with Jake, I'd want to sit closer to him, too. Alas, I am *not* on a date with him. I haven't been on a real date in seven years. "Time to go."

I hastily stand, sending my chair scraping across the wood floor, adding to the symphony of noise in the place. Keeping my head lowered, I lift Harley's diaper bag as Scarlett already holds the baby. As I glance up, I notice Jake across the space looking at me. Our eyes lock as they did at that first AA meeting, in the Busy Bean, and on occasion at the building project. Then he leans toward Louisa and whispers something in her ear.

*Relax*, he said to me earlier, like a lover's voice before he slips inside. Deep down low, my belly flips with the thought, and I swipe fingers over my brow, pinching at the tight skin of my forehead. Jake stands, and I watch him cross the bar for the restrooms.

"On second thought, I think I need to use the bathroom before we leave."

Scarlett tips up a brow. "Should I wait for you?"

"No . . . I just need a minute." I clutch at my belly, implying a clearly embarrassing stomach issue, but she's my friend, and us women share a lot of shit with each other. No pun intended.

"Go get 'em," She growls like a tiger, and I burst into laughter.

"It's not like that," I say. *Then again, what am I thinking?*

"Love you, Rita," she says.

"Love you too, chickie. And you too, little man." I lean forward and press a kiss to Harley's head before swiping my hand along his pudgy cheek.

Heading toward the bathroom area, I smooth my hands down my hips and nearly run into Jake as he exits the men's room.

"Rita."

"Jake."

We stare at one another for a second, neither person moving. Everything rumbles inside me like a furnace ready to burst. I fight the words, desperate to escape, wrestling all accusations. I even roll my lips inward, hoping to keep myself quiet, but I cannot stop myself.

"Louisa Miller? Really Jake?"

He tips his head, roaming his gaze down my body. "Gonna tell me she's not my type?" His question recalls what I said to him at that first AA meeting.

"She's . . . she's not." It isn't fair of me to pass judgment. I have no idea if Louisa is or isn't his kind of catnip. She's beautiful and young. *Maybe that's it.* "She's something like ten years younger than you."

His brows lift at my outburst, and then his eyes narrow. "Age is only a number."

I snort. An uncontrollable, unattractive honk. Jake steps closer to me.

"And what should be my type, Rita?" His gaze scans down my body once more, and the scent of cinnamon wafts off his breath. "A woman wearing power suits and hiking boots that clash with her outfit."

My mouth falls open.

"Or maybe it's a woman with red-rimmed eyeglasses, gray streaks in her hair, and a know-it-all attitude."

Immediately, my hand lifts for my mousy brown hair with silver striping, heavier in some areas than others. While I'm slow to register what he's implying, I'm quick to note the tone of his voice and the insinuation that I'm unattractive to him.

"Or is it someone who thinks she knows *me* when she doesn't."

"I—" My mouth falls open, but I don't have a response for him, and I'm quickly cut off from all thoughts.

"Want to join us for a drink?" His voice is full of disdain.

My eyes narrow. My glare is flames. "You did not just ask me that." He knows I'm a recovering alcoholic. He's been to a meeting which I chaired, and he's due at the next one.

As he glares back at me, it takes a moment for him to comprehend what he's just asked, but I don't care. I don't care if he doesn't like my comfortable boots, or my snarky red glasses, or the changing of my hair. I don't care if he wants a younger woman or to drink his night away. I don't care about him, and I don't know why I followed him to this hallway.

Turning on my booted heels, I give him my back and stalk away, cursing myself. I was so close to giving in to him earlier. He almost kissed me, and I would have kissed him back. It would have been my first kiss in years.

And one of the biggest mistakes, as well.

## 6

## JAKE

*Fuck.* I don't know why I said what I said to her. I don't know what I was thinking other than she'd gotten under my skin earlier, and I had to push her back. Rita was getting too close. She muddled my thoughts and stirred shit that didn't need stirring, not from the likes of her.

Still, what I'd just said was a total dick move.

"Rita, wait," I call out to her, but she's quick in those hiking boots, easily exiting the restroom area, and although I reach for her, I'm too late. She slips back into the main area of Speakeasy and hastens for her table. I don't want to make a scene, but I quickly follow her.

Other than to the Busy Bean and Building Buddies, I haven't been out since I've been released. Meeting Louisa the other day at the coffeehouse was a fluke. I thought I'd get lost in her, finally dipping my wick and relieving the tension inside me, but before I knew it, I was asking her out to dinner.

Then Rita had to be here, and my thoughts have gone to hell, reminding me I almost kissed her earlier. *Fuck.*

"Rita," I call out one more time as I near her table where she's grabbing her coat. Whoever her friend was, she left with her baby.

Rita doesn't respond to her name but moves forward as if not hearing me. She's ignoring me.

My eyes drift to Louisa, awaiting my return to the table. Despite my eagerness to fuck someone and rid my thoughts of Rita, Louisa's slow smile does nothing to quell all thoughts of Rita. I turn my attention toward the front door. My head tells me to forget her. My body warns me this is a mistake. I cannot be interested in Rita Kaplan. She's the supervisor where I work. Where I work because I'm on parole from prison.

She's also an attorney, which means she's smart, and she wouldn't want to be mixed up with a dumbass criminal like me. She's also so freaking cute, and regardless of what I said, I'm attracted to her. I love that her hair shows her age, and her smile says she doesn't care about such a thing. I love those quirky, bright glasses although I can't always see her eyes, which are bright and kind behind her glares. I love her sass while I hate her know-it-all attitude.

Her reaction to that small spark earlier tells me there's a story behind her power suit and hiking boot veneer. She's afraid of fire, and that detail adds to the list of she *shouldn't* be my type. She isn't going to want an arsonist, even if the accusation is false.

Still, I'm drawn to Rita, and I can't pull my gaze from the door she's disappeared behind. Glancing back at Louisa, I hold up my finger, indicating I need a minute. Then I stalk off after Rita.

"Rita!" I holler as I enter the dark parking lot. Her petite legs work fast, so I break into a jog to catch up to her. "Rita, wait."

Drawing near, I reach forward to cup her elbow and tug. She's forced to turn and face me, but her eyes avoid mine.

"What?" While her hip juts to the side, she gives me the side of her face, staring off into the distance.

"I'm sorry. That was . . . that was uncalled for." She's a recovering alcoholic, and it was insensitive of me to imply she should join me *and my date* for a drink.

*Fuck.* I am so fucking this up with both women, yet the only woman I want to make this right with is the one before me.

I don't like how Rita isn't looking at me. She isn't giving me that glare she gives through those glasses. She isn't huffing in my face. Her mouth isn't close like it was earlier. Her cheek isn't gently rubbing against mine. Her entire demeanor dismisses me. *Isn't that how I knew she'd be?* Yeah, I know her type, too, and it isn't me.

Removing my hand from her elbow, I hold it up high, surrendering to her. "Fine."

"Fine." Her neck quickly twists so she looks at me. "That's all you have to say?"

"I just apologized. What more do you want?"

Her chest heaves like it did earlier today. Those damn glasses are reflecting the lamplight in the lot, and I can't see her eyes. I want to see her eyes.

"Nothing," she replies, shaking her head. "Absolutely nothing." Her gaze lowers to her feet, and she kicks at the gravel surface.

"Your boots are okay, Rita. They look good with your outfit," I lie. "You rock the *Working Women* vibe, all power savage and determined to take on the world."

"Now, you're just being cruel." Her head pops back up, and I just know she's giving me that glare. I can feel it, just like I felt her watching me during that first AA meeting, wondering who I am. *If only I had that answer.* The glare is a flame lighting something inside me I don't recognize, can't seem to control, and don't know if I want to.

*Dammit, Rita.*

"No, sweet. This would be cruel." I cup her cheeks and drag her to me, meeting her in the middle of the space between us. Then I crush her mouth with mine, sucking at those pouty lips. This is cruelty because I want this woman when I shouldn't. Her sass. Her attitude. Her trust. I want it.

The second she responds, meeting my lip's lead with her own, my tongue joins the torture, sweeping into her mouth and tangling with hers. I haven't kissed someone in seven years—seven long fucking years—and she tastes so good, like freedom, and futures, and faith. This feeling is more than an irritating itch that needs a good scratch. This is Rita. I don't know what it is about her, but I want her nails to dig in and her heart to open.

Then reality hits me. *What am I doing?* Just as quickly as I started down the slippery slope of desire, I pull back. Rita follows me, leaning into the space I put between us, chasing that kiss. Her eyes remain closed for a second as her lips seek mine, and I've crossed a line again.

"Fuck. I'm sorry, Rita." Her lids flip open, and she stares at me. I should not have kissed her. Every part of my being screams, *I should not have kissed her!*

"I'm so sorry," I repeat in a whisper, releasing her face like she's scorched my skin and turning away from her once again.

---

"Rough night?" my brother asks. Nolan has no idea. Then again, as I glance over at him in his wheelchair, I imagine he does.

"Fuck, man. I fucked up." I toss my head back on the couch in the house we share. It's the same home where we grew up and inherited at our mother's passing. The small house had a mortgage on it when my father left, and we were still little kids. My mother worked night and day to pay what she could, so we'd have a safe place to live, as she called it. I'd worked construction jobs as young as I could to help out, and we eventually paid it off. She died one night on a snowy mountain road.

"How was your date?" Nolan's voice matches the wiggle of his brow. My brother is a horny bastard. It's how he got in trouble when he was sixteen and ended up a father too young. Now, he doesn't date. Losing sensation in the lower half of his body from a back injury has curtailed his extracurricular activities. Still, he's a horndog.

"It went to hell." Louisa deserved an explanation after I chased Rita, but I didn't tell her that I'd kissed my supervisor, the woman who could make or break my probation assignment. Louisa didn't know that my employment is actually a restorative program from prison. Instead, I explained that Rita was my boss and I'd forgotten to tell her something at work. The thing I actually had not forgotten, though, was my desire to kiss Rita.

*I don't know why I did it.*

"I'm a dumbass," I say, swiping a hand into my hair and holding it at the top of my head.

"Sounds like a story," Nolan teases, and I hear his chair shift. When Nolan left the hospital, modifications had to be made to the house, and I wasn't here to help accommodate his new condition. I was arrested while he was still heavily sedated. Arrangements were made for him as best I could from inside a cage. Thank goodness most of the volunteer firemen he worked with were good men and handy. They pulled together and did what needed to be done to make this house wheelchair accessible.

For some reason, I don't want to tell Nolan exactly what I did tonight. Instead, I tell him what I didn't.

"I don't think I'll be seeing Louisa again."

"Why not? She wouldn't put out on the first date."

My head snaps up, irritated at the remark, although that's exactly why I asked her out in the first place. I wanted in her pants without really knowing her.

"No, asshole. She didn't. But I also didn't ask her to."

Nolan shakes his head. "You know that's a waste of a perfectly good dick." He nods at my lap, and I instinctively cover myself with a pillow from the couch. Guilt riddles me. Nolan's condition isn't my fault. I didn't do what I'd been accused of doing, so there's no way I was to blame for his injury. Still, I felt responsible. I'd always been responsible for my younger brother. Three years younger than me, he was only a kid himself when he got his girlfriend pregnant, and Rory came along. We'd lost our mother, and he took comfort in his girl. *Idiot.* We'd talked a hundred times about keeping himself wrapped up to prevent such a thing. I had played the role of father most of his life. When our mother died, I took her place as well.

"Don't be looking at my junk. It might shrivel up and fall off."

"Gonna fall off from disuse," he mocks.

"Yeah, well, ain't that the truth." *Whose fault is that?* I almost state the sarcastic question, but I bite my tongue. Nolan surely isn't at fault either that I got caught at the wrong place, at the wrong time, and accused of a crime I didn't commit. *Falsely accused.* I had my suspicions about who did start the fire, but it never made sense. It didn't seem logistically possible, so the accusation never crossed my lips. I'll take it to the grave. Either way, I took the punishment, and I did what I did to protect someone not entirely innocent but still not guilty enough to go to jail.

It was an accident. I had to believe it was an accident.

"How was work today?" Nolan asks, interrupting my thoughts.

"It's fine." It's going to get worse, though, as I kissed my boss. Leaning forward, I place my elbows on my knees and swipe both hands over my face.

"You okay?" Nolan's concern feels like a role reversal. I'm the one constantly worrying about him, not the other way around.

"Yeah, just a lot on my mind."

"You think too much." He used to tell me I worked too hard. *All work and no play.* I was always serious, he joked, but someone had to be the adult, and it wasn't him. I'd always taken care of him, and that was an issue. As I look at him, shame washes over me because I want my freedom. I want to rid myself of the memories and the past, and that means separating from my brother, who is another reminder of what happened. When I met my ex-wife, a small part of me was relieved. She was my excuse to put some much-needed space between my brother and me. He was a man then and could stand on his own. Now, he can't stand without support.

"I'm not thinking," I mutter in response. I certainly wasn't thinking tonight when I followed Rita to apologize and then kissed the crap out of her. Her mouth against mine lingers on my lips, and I chew the lower one as if I can still taste her. Her taste was unfamiliar, but like a hit of good coffee, I want another sip. "And speaking of work, I need a recyclable lunch bag. Something environmentally safe."

"Yes, dear," Nolan teases, and I scowl at him.

"Your peanut butter and jam sandwiches could use some improvement, too," I mock, although I'm grateful he wants to do something for me. He feels just as bad as I do that I went to prison, serving time for a crime I didn't commit. Add in his injury, and I know he wishes I'd been here with him. At seventeen, his son had to grow up too quickly, just like Nolan did.

"What does it look like I'm working with, a gourmet kitchen?" he jests. Our kitchen had some improvements after Nolan's accident. Compact and tight, shorter cabinets and lowered counters were installed, allowing better access for Nolan's reach. In general, the house I'm building for Building Buddies is going to be nicer than this place, though.

"Yeah, yeah." I laugh. "I'll get right on it, along with the fifty other things this place needs."

Nolan sobers a bit. "We don't need anything, Jake." His dropped tone has me looking up at him.

"I didn't mean—"

Holding up a hand, he stops me. "I didn't mean anything either. I'm only teasing. I can work with that kitchen. I'm just grateful you're home."

Twisting my lips side to side, I glance down at the hardwood floor and nod to agree.

"Yeah," I say. "Me too." I am glad to be home. I'm happy to be outside the four walls that confined me for seven years. I'm happy to be free to kiss a woman, even if I did take the liberty with someone I shouldn't. But Rita kissed me back, accepting what I gave to her. She responded to me, chased that kiss even, and I have little doubt if I wanted to take things further, I could have.

And thoughts like that warn me I need to keep my distance from Rita Kaplan.

Lots of distance.

# 7

# RITA

For several days in a row, I arrive early at Building Buddies, check in with Sullivan, and then disappear as quickly as I can. I haven't lingered at the building site for more than a few minutes each day, which means I have successfully avoided Jake for three days.

However, this morning, I'm not quite so fortunate. Jake is already present and digging through a toolbox at Sullivan's feet as I hobble into the yard. *Damn heels.*

Jake is crouched down, his body low to the ground, and I force my gaze away from him. Almost as soon as I've arrived, Alfred Jennings pulls up to the project. The director of Building Buddies exits his car, and I note his paunchy belly looks even paunchier, stretching his button-down enough to strain the buttons over his middle.

"Alfred," I call out as the older man nears where I stand.

"Rita, I was hoping you would be here. I wanted to speak with you a moment." The roughness in his voice gives away the years he has spent smoking cigarettes. After my father's second heart attack and subsequent death, I have more concern for the health of his older friends, especially Alfred. Still, there's a sharpness to his tone that unsettles me, and for some reason, my gaze shifts sideways, noticing Jake slowly standing from his lowered position. With his body aimed toward mine, I avert my eyes from Jake and return my attention to Alfred.

"What can I do for you?" I ask, sensing something urgent and serious in his voice. My eyes shift once more to Jake's unnerving presence. Feet from me, he's stone-still, watching our interaction. I take a step toward Alfred and wobble again in my heels. *Heels have no place at a building site.* Cursing under my breath, I reach out for Alfred's arm as if he can anchor me before I topple over. Once steady, Alfred shifts my hand to the crook of his arm and leads us to the front door of the house. We've had heavy rains this week and more predicted for the weekend. We need to get the siding on this place.

"Is everything okay?" Hesitating, I clutch at Alfred's elbow as walking in heels on muddy earth isn't ideal.

"Everything is fine. I just wanted to let you know that I'm thinking of stepping down from the director position."

"What? No, Alfred. This is your program." Alfred started Building Buddies back in the 90s with a few of his business colleagues, my father being one of them. The original crew of men rotated the responsibility of the directorship amongst themselves. Alfred is the only one who remains connected to the organization.

"It's time. I'm overdue to retire, actually, and Regina wants to move south. She also wants the liberty to spend more time with our grandkids." Alfred and Regina have several children scattered around the United States. A small pang of regret hits my chest as my own parents never had more children, thus no grandchildren. My father died before Ian and I were engaged. My mother wanted to remain in Vermont until I married. When that didn't happen, she went south herself.

"I wanted you to know I'm going to recommend you take over the program."

"Me?" I stare up at Alfred. "I don't know anything about running a not-for-profit organization."

"Yes, you do." Alfred pats my hand. "You've been working with us forever."

"Yes, working. I build, construct, design, supervise, but only when I can. I have a full-time job."

Alfred chuckles. "We all did at one point," he states, speaking of his status as still working. "The directorship is outside the scope of a job. It pays a stipend, but it's not comparable to what you make as an attorney. Still, I think you can handle this. In fact, I'd hate to turn the directorship over to anyone else, so I'm recommending the board consider you as the new, permanent director."

"Permanent director?" I question.

"We need someone with longevity, and as you aren't going anywhere, I wouldn't want Building Buddies to go to anyone else." The comment should sting, implying I have nothing else in my life, so why not run the organization. Then again, I'm honored Alfred has this kind of faith in me. Still, I'm not certain I'm the right fit. While I've been splitting my time between the office and here—handing over more cases and contracts to May—is this what I want to do next?

"I'd need to think about it," I say, and Alfred turns his attention away from admiring the single-story home to level me with a liquid gaze.

"What is there to think about?" Once again, his question suggests an unspoken assumption that I have nothing else to do in my life. Alfred takes a deep breath. "You know, when I started this group along with your father and some friends from the church, we wanted to give back *and* beef up our resumes." He softly laughs.

"Nonprofit organizations look good on resumes. It says you're involved in your community, care about others, and take on leadership roles, but over time, this work became a passion for many of us. We loved handing over the keys to a family in need. We appreciated what we had a little more, even if we wrestled with loss." He pats my hand still tucked into his elbow.

"You've always been a go-getter, Rita. Leadership is within your blood. There's no doubt you care for others, defending what's been wronged, dealing with what's right."

I snort, not certain livestock disputes or housing contracts right wrongs.

"You need this," he states, smiling back at the house, and now, he's lost me. I glance up at it myself. I take great pride in working for Building Buddies. This is my third official project as a supervisor, and I've been honored to handle each build in the area. We span two states, so I'm not involved in every construction site. That falls to the directorship position.

"At our next board meeting, I'm going to recommend you. The board will need to vote, but I have no doubt they'll lean in my favor."

The next board meeting is a month away.

"As I said, I'd like to think about it, but I'm honored you consider me worthy."

Alfred pats my hand once more, but this time I feel that pat as patronizing. It implies I have nothing else going for me, so I might as well take on the position.

Alfred leans forward, and air kisses my cheek, pressing his clammy skin to the side of my face. Releasing my hand, I watch him turn back for his car and notice Jake following the movements of Alfred's retreat. As soon as the director enters his sedan and backs out of the yard, Jake approaches me.

"Everything okay?" His hesitant tone has my brows pinching.

"Why wouldn't it be?"

He holds a screwdriver in one hand and taps it against his other palm. "No reason, just wondering." He peers back to the space Alfred's car vacated and then returns his attention to me. "Did something happen?"

I shift entirely and cross my arms. My ankle wobbles again in my cursed shoes.

"What is your concern, Jake?"

"I don't want to get you in trouble."

My brows pinch again. "Why would I get in trouble?"

Looking directly at me, he waves the screwdriver between us. "Because you and me . . ."

"We what?" I give my head a little shake, suggesting I don't understand and ignoring the discomfort between us.

"We . . . you know."

*The kiss.* The incredible kiss that sliced me down the middle and zipped me back together in one swift movement. Kissing has been off-limits for me, but that kiss shattered all limitations. However, Jake's cautious eyes have the fine hairs on my arms sticking upward.

"You aren't worried about me. You're worried about you." I step toward him as I speak. Wobbling once more in my heels, I fight the urge to reach for him for stability. It's hard to be tough when your shoes don't support you. "You're worried I told on you."

"Told on me? What? Are we in second grade?"

"You know if I wanted to report that kiss, you might lose this position."

Jake's brows lift. His forehead furrows. "Would you do that? It was only a kiss, Rita."

My mouth falls open, but I quickly shut it. Only a kiss? *Only a kiss!* I can't even respond to that comment. However, I could do what he said. I could file a complaint and put Jake at risk of losing this parole situation, but I'd never do such a thing.

"You're right. It's just as you said," I state through clenched teeth. Lowering my hands, I fist them at my sides. "It was only a kiss. I've had lots of kisses in my life. It wasn't even a particularly good kiss. It was just . . . a kiss."

*Good heavens, what am I saying?* However, Jake does not need to know it's the only kiss I've had in seven years. He doesn't even need to know it might be the best kiss I've ever had. I've never had someone just grab me and kiss the stuffing out of me. He kissed me like I was his first kiss and last breath all in one. And he most definitely does not need to know I went home and gave my pink pleasure toy extra time from *only a kiss*.

"Well, I wouldn't say it was awful," Jake defends, stepping closer to me. We're only inches apart, and the screwdriver in his hand stops tapping.

"I didn't say it was awful. I said it wasn't particularly good. I'm certain I've had better."

"Oh, you have, have you?" My gaze falls to his lips, and he drops the screwdriver to the ground. His breath mixes with mine. He smells of dark roast, cinnamon, and construction sites, and my mouth waters for another not-so-great kiss from him. His hands lift, and he leans forward.

"Rita, everything okay?" Sullivan's voice breaks my trance. As I turn to our construction manager, Jake takes an exaggerated step backward. He bends at the waist for the screwdriver he dropped, and I meet Sully's questioning glare.

"I'm good. Everything's good. Not awful. Not great. Just good." I huff out a nervous laugh. *What am I saying?* "I can't stay again today. Office work." It's a lie. I've been purposely avoiding the site, and I hate that it has to do with Jake because Alfred was right. These projects are my passion.

"Okay. Well, see you later then." A question lingers in Sully's statement, along with his large mass suddenly stationary as Jake remains close to me.

"Yeah, I'll be back later to check on the day's progress."

Sullivan nods but doesn't move. Taking my first step in the ruts of the mud, my feet fumble, and I automatically reach out to balance myself.

"Nice heels," Jake mutters, catching my forearm to steady me. As that smirky smirk of his slowly curls his lips, I glare at him. "They go well with your outfit."

I'd like to show him where these heels can go, but instead, I tug my arm free of his support and stalk off. Only, it's difficult to make a grand exit when your ankles wobble, and a heel collapses.

*Damn these shoes and Jake Drummond.*

Later that night is an AA meeting. I'm not chairing this one, and if Jake appears, he'll have to beg someone else to sign off on his card. *Good luck with that, handsome.* Quickly, I rid my thoughts of Jake. I'm dressed in comfortable clothes of jeans and my hiking boots, telling myself I need a long hike this weekend to right myself. Taking a deep breath, I close my eyes, bringing myself into the mindset of the meeting.

The meeting begins with a reading of the AA Preamble, a prayer of the chair's choice, and then the serenity prayer. I blindly follow along, keeping my eyes closed, until the chair mentions new members and introductions.

As I slowly open my lids, I see Jake directly across the circle from me. Our group is small in this community, so we're often led by what the group needs. A chairperson could offer AA literature or discuss the 12-Step Traditions. If a new member joins and wishes to speak, we allow them to take the floor, guiding where we will go for the evening by their needs. Other than Jake's intro-duction a few weeks ago, he remains quiet again tonight.

"Is there anything anyone wants to share this evening?"

I swallow as it's always difficult to know where to start, but I have something to say, and I can't shirk the sensation even if Jake watches me.

"I had something happen this week," I begin. "I haven't thought of Ian in a while." I swallow around his name and shift in my seat, lowering my focus to the floor because the intensity of Jake's eyes hurts my already aching heart.

"I don't know if it was a panic attack or what actually happened. One minute I was fine, and the next, my thoughts were all muddled." I lift a hand for my head, waving it around the side. "My heart raced. My chest constricted. I thought of Ian," I say again. "And I wanted a drink."

Some people nod around me. A few hum in sympathy with me.

"But then again, I didn't want that drink. I knew I shouldn't have it, but this . . . moment . . . it freaked me out." Like Ian was sending me a sign. Like he was pushing me toward something or maybe warning me against it. It was all very hocus-pocus, but I couldn't shake the feeling. The universe was speaking, but what was it saying to me. Maybe it was just my thoughts of wanting something different in my life colliding with—and confusing the issue of—Jake's sudden presence. A person cannot be a replacement for what I need. I learned that lesson the hard way, and it's why I'm sitting in this chair.

Alcoholics Anonymous isn't therapy, so I don't expect anyone to offer any advice or words of wisdom, just encouragement. A pause allows me time to collect my thoughts and continue or signal that I'm finished.

"Anyway, I wanted to share how I know the struggle can be real, continuous, and strike at any time. Sometimes, it's at the most unsuspected moments, but I didn't take that drink. I didn't need it."

I look up at the chairperson. "Did you do something else?" Often alcoholics are encouraged to find another means of distraction—prayer or physical exercise—but nothing that could lead to a secondary addiction.

"I had coffee with a friend." I slowly smile, recalling how thankful I am Scarlett has moved to Vermont. My eyes drift up to Jake for only a second as he knows where I drink that coffee. "I went to my happy place."

The chairperson smiles back at me, and I nod to signify I'm done. Another person begins his tale, and I fall into the story, sympathizing with mental support and offering up a prayer for his continued recovery.

*You can't help those who won't help themselves.* It's a basic principle in life, but also something my father used to say often. It's also a major philosophy of Alcoholics Anonymous. If Jake doesn't think he has an issue, there's nothing we can do for him other than hope honesty happens one day.

When the meeting closes, Jake stands for the chairperson, and I make quick good-byes. Mentioning Ian to the group has me shaken again, and I hastily take the stairs to exit the church when I hear a familiar voice call my name.

# JAKE

I call out to her the second I clear the exit door. Rita disappeared as soon as the meeting was finished, and I needed a second to get my card signed.

Calling her name one more time, she halts on the sidewalk and spins around. "What?"

"I . . ." Now that she faces me, I'm stumped. *Why am I chasing her?* Blurting out the next thought, I ask, "Who's Ian?"

Rita crosses her arms and turns her head to the side, contemplating an answer. "Look, we don't need to do this."

"Do what?" I ask, scratching the back of my neck.

"Share our sob stories."

*Sob stories?* Shit. Was he her fiancé? The one Sullivan said passed away?

"Okay, but—"

Rita has already turned her back on me and begins walking away.

"Wait." I reach for her elbow, causing her to spin around once more.

"What happens in the meetings stays in the meetings, Jake." Her eyes blink from behind her glasses.

"Okay, I—" *I what?* Want to know more about you? Want to

understand you? What the hell am I doing? "How about that coffee I owe you for taking your spot at the Busy Bean?"

Rita sighs. "The Bean is closed this late at night." It's almost eight, and she's right, but I still don't want her to walk away for some reason.

"What about the diner?" I don't live in Colebury, so I'm not familiar with all their haunts. The pubs and the coffeehouse are on the old gin mill property and the diner is in town. Those are the only spots I know that would have coffee.

Rita eyes me a second and then gives in. "Fine." Giving me her back once more, I smile with a small sense of victory.

The church is near enough to walk to the diner, but Rita drove, so I follow her. In the short jaunt, I realize I have no idea where Rita lives.

The diner is nothing special—just your typical diner in a small Vermont town—but it's cozy enough despite the bright fluorescent lights.

"Two coffees," I state to the waitress behind the counter as we walk toward a booth in the corner. As we sit, I address Rita. "Want anything else?"

"Coffee's good." We could have enjoyed a cup outside the meeting, as a percolator pot offers the brew to those who need something to drink or just something to hold in their hands.

The waitress quickly arrives at our table with her pot and fills mugs before dismissing herself when I tell her this is all for now.

"So, what's your story?" Rita asks as soon as we are alone.

"I thought you said no sob stories," I tease, lifting my mug for my lips. This coffee could rival the Bean's. "But it's not like you don't know."

Rita peers at me across the table. "I don't."

Setting my mug down, I meet her puzzled gaze. "*Ri*-ight."

"No, really. We're only told who is joining us. The board has to agree on placements, but only Alfred reads a person's background. He vets the information, mainly assuring there isn't a concern of physical harm or threat to our team. That's the truth of it."

I stare at her in disbelief. "And you haven't looked me up?" I'm floored that she actually doesn't know anything else about me. With a quick internet search, I'm certain the once newsworthy story is present somewhere.

"Good people make bad decisions all the time." She shrugs. "I believe in second chances and don't want to make a preconceived notion. So nope."

I take a second to absorb what she said. *Good people make bad decisions all the time.* Don't I know it.

"Not even a little social media sleuthing?" I tease, although she wouldn't find anything. I'm not on any social media sites, having deleted my accounts years ago. Rita shakes her head, and I'm surprised again.

"How about you? Tell me how you got started in Building Buddies."

Rita slowly smiles. It's a pleasant smile as though she's about to share a secret, but a secret she can't wait to share. I find myself watching her lips move as she speaks.

"My dad was involved in the program. He started it with a group of men looking to do service for others. Construction service specifically." She shrugs. "My father's father was a builder of sorts, but my dad became a lawyer. I think a small part of him always felt guilty he didn't use his hands more than his brain, so he began the program with Alfred and a few business friends."

That explains her ease with Alfred. Even though I know the answer to what I ask next, I still ask. "And what happened to your dad?"

"He passed almost eight years ago." Her smile softens with fondness but sorrow. "Second heart attack. We were close, and I worked in his office after his first heart attack. When I finished my law degree at Vermont Law, I became a full-time associate in Kaplan and Associates." She sits straighter, speaking as if making a proud proclamation.

"My nephew goes to Vermont Law," I state with as much pride, and her smile deepens.

"My associate went there, too."

"Impressive."

"So, you have a nephew. Who else makes up your family?" The shy grin accompanying her question hints at wanting more information—like do I have a wife or a girlfriend.

"It's my brother Nolan and myself. That's it. Nolan had my nephew Rory when he was too young to be a dad, and coincidentally, I've been acting as Nolan's father most of his life as ours left when we were little kids."

"I'm so sorry," she interjects, and I see she means it, especially as she just told me how close she was to her own father.

"My mother died in an auto accident when I was eighteen. I'd been at Burlington U then, but Nolan was too young to live alone, and then he thought with his dick instead of his head." I make a face at the crude reference. "Sorry about that."

Rita shrugs. "It happens. The dick-thinking, that is."

Softly, I chuckle. "Anyway, so here I am."

"Wife? Children?" She cuts to the chase.

"I was married once," I state, lowering my eyes for the mug in my hands on the table. "But we divorced right before I went to prison."

Silence falls between us a second before Rita quietly responds, "I'm sorry to hear that."

I nod. I'm over it. At the time, I was angry. I thought Lisa was my everything, but I was wrong. Your *everything* loves you through thick and thin—good times and bad.

"And you?" I eye Rita, lifting my mug once more for another sip.

"No wife. No children," she teases. I cock a brow at her, wondering if I've misread her tastes. "Ian was my fiancé."

Slowly, I nod again, having made the connection. When Rita doesn't offer more, I tip my head to catch her lowered gaze. "No sob stories necessary," I remind her. She dips her chin to agree. "And your mother?"

"My mom stuck around after my dad passed. She was waiting on me to get married. When that didn't happen, she moved to South Carolina. It's the place my parents always intended to retire together."

"Is she on the ocean?" I ask, hoping to keep things light and not backtrack to why she didn't marry her fiancé.

"She's not, but she's close. I visit her twice a year. She doesn't like to come up here anymore. Too cold in the winter."

I laugh as I get that about our Northern weather, but I'm also looking forward to winter, when I can go outside and actually move around in the snow without some barbed wire and metal fencing caging me in.

"No siblings?" I inquire, feeling like we're playing twenty questions.

"Only child syndrome." She laughs. "It's why I always want my way."

"Oldest child here," I tease. "I never get my way."

Rita tips her head, giving me a sideways glance. "Why's that? What would be your way? What would you be doing if you weren't working for Building Buddies?"

Here comes the tricky part. "Initially, I went to school for environmental studies, think natural resources, but I'd been doing construction work most of my teenage years to help my mom out and save for college. When I returned home to make sure Nolan graduated high school, I took up an electrician apprenticeship but also worked as a volunteer fireman."

Rita sits up again in her seat. Her eyes focus more intently on me.

"I eventually worked my way into an arson investigator position, doing small electrical jobs on the side." There should be pride in my voice for what I eventually accomplished and the years it took to get where I was, but none of who I was or what I'd done mattered in the end. I was found guilty of a crime I did not commit because of what *others* thought.

"That's how you have the skill to work for Building Buddies." It's not so much a question, but a clarification as Rita puts things together.

"It is."

"And if you could do anything, what would it be?"

As much as I wish I had a solid answer, I don't. I hadn't thought much beyond serving the remainder of my time and my desire to leave Vermont. "I want to leave this state and forget all that's happened here." The statement comes out harsh, and Rita blinks at my directness.

"Not a fan of Vermont?"

"Not anymore," I admit because it's the State's fault for making budget cuts to our fire safety programs that placed me in the position I'm in. Serving time. On parole. "But my brother has a complicated injury, and I'm not certain I can leave him behind."

"More sob story?" Rita purses her lips, twisting them a bit as she considers what I've said. The truth is, Nolan's been on his own for a while, and he doesn't actually need me like he once did. It's a bit of a relief, but I still feel guilty. I softly chuckle to dismiss explaining Nolan's condition, and Rita shifts gears. "Do you knit?"

My laugh blurts loud and sharp. "Um, no. Sorry. Why?"

"How about hiking?"

"Uh, sure. I mean, I haven't been on one in a while." Hiking reminds me of my past studies in natural resources. I thought I might be a forest ranger or an environmental scientist of some type. At eighteen, I wasn't certain what path I'd take. Then my life was decided for me with my mother's death.

Hiking also makes me think of asking Rita if she'd like to take one with me sometime. She's always wearing those damn boots, so I'm assuming she knows how to use them. But a date would be out of the question. This was only coffee.

Rita doesn't say any more, taking final sips of her now-cool brew, and I feel like I've run out of things to say. I double-tap the table, and Rita startles at the motion. Then I lift my hand for the waitress, signaling I'm ready to pay our bill.

"I should probably get going." The transition is awkward, but if I sit here any longer, I just might share that sob story Rita doesn't want to hear, and it's been nice to chat with someone who doesn't know of my sordid past.

"Oh. *Oh*," Rita says, looking over her shoulder as the waitress approaches. Twisting back to the table, she fumbles in her pocket.

"I got this," I offer. I'd never let a woman pay. Rita's face pinkens for some reason, and I hand over a twenty. Sliding out of the booth, I wait for Rita to stand and then escort her to the parking lot.

"You okay to drive home?" It's dark out, and I glance up at the sky, noting the ink black color and the brilliant display of stars. The freedom to enjoy the night is something I won't ever take for granted again.

"It's not far. I'm good, handsome."

"Handsome, again?" I laugh, noting she didn't give me more information as to where 'far' is. She dismisses me with a wave of her hand as we stand beside her SUV. Stepping closer to her, I ask, "You think I'm handsome?"

"As if you don't already know it. Your good looks have already gone to your head, or I'd warn you against letting it get there."

"Ri-*ta*." I drag out her name. Everything in me wants to kiss this pretty woman under a starlit sky right now, but I've already taken advantage of her once before. This night was my apology.

"I gotta go," she says, while her blue eyes say otherwise, and her body leans against her driver door. I want to pin her against the metal and have my way with her sassy mouth. She's so close I could stroke her cheek and marvel at the softness of her skin. Or better yet, clutch the back of her neck and drag her to me, closing the distance, and crushing my mouth to hers.

But I'm not looking to cross any more lines with Rita Kaplan, so I take a step back, and Rita rolls against the door, quickly flicking the handle and opening it. I wait as she climbs inside and watches as she backs out of the parking spot, wondering if I'll ever feel free enough to kiss a pretty woman under a star-bright sky again.

## JAKE

It's a few days before I see Rita again. The weekend interfered with work, and although the project continues, I'm not obligated to be there, allowing for volunteers to take over and push things ahead. On Monday, we're just finishing up when Rita arrives.

"What's this?" Rita questions. She does a check-in at the end of the day, but I don't understand why Sullivan can't just call her with updates on our progress. Then again, I'm not disappointed she's here. I've strangely missed her the past few days, and I can't help the smile on my face when I see her.

"It's a couch," I state, noting the piece of furniture that arrived in the middle of a construction site.

Her head pops up, glaring at me as I've stated the obvious. "Yes, but what's it doing here? Furniture doesn't arrive until the end of the project."

I shrug, having no idea, and Sullivan interjects. "Some mistake at the warehouse. The date said May, not July, so here it is."

We don't have a garage yet that we can store it in, and it's too large to lug to the basement. We'll just have to work around it. The item is wrapped in plastic, so it should be safe enough.

Rita sighs, rubbing at her forehead like I've seen her do from time to time.

"Better get a move on," Sullivan warns. "Storm's coming." We've had tons of rain lately, making the yard a soggy mess of streams and mini mudslides. I notice Rita is not wearing her heels but returned to her hiking boots along with dress pants, but she's still wearing a fancy, feminine blouse.

"Okay," Rita says to him. "I'll be right after you. I'm just going to cover this." She turns around looking for something to give the couch an extra layer of protection.

"I can wait," Sullivan offers, glancing at me before back at Rita. I see the longing in his eyes, and I feel for the guy as Rita doesn't look at him the same way. She sees him as an asset to Building Buddies and a hard worker, but nothing more.

"No, you go. You put in another long day." Rita's encouraging words hit me wrong. Sullivan is the construction manager, and it's his job to be here. Strangely, I want praise from her myself, but I bite my tongue. Sullivan eyes me once more.

"There are drop cloths in the back room. I'll go get one." While I turn away from Rita and Sullivan, I don't miss him grumbling to Rita. Reminding myself I don't need Sullivan's approval, I retrieve the heavy cloth, and when I return to the front room, Sullivan is gone. We have electricity in the house now, no longer using the generator from before, but we only have temporary outlets until the drywall is complete. Within seconds, the weather seems like a faucet from heaven turned on, and the rain intensifies, coating the front window in a sheet of water.

"Think it might be best to wait this out a few minutes," I suggest as Rita doesn't have a raincoat or an umbrella. She glances at the window but doesn't respond to my warning.

"Help me cover this thing." An early arrival couch doesn't seem like it should irritate her as much as it does, but I don't question her mood. We cover the thing, and just as we stand back to inspect our work, the light nearest us goes off.

"What the hell?" I mutter, stalking over to the outlet and pulling the cord from an industrial work lamp. Plugging it back in, I see the electricity is out. The room is pretty dark due to the gloom of the late afternoon and the enclosed space. The sheet of rain coating the window isn't helping either.

"Now what?" Rita grumbles.

"Bad day at the office, dear?" I jest, and Rita snorts that honking sound she makes. I have to admit the noise is growing on me.

"It's nothing," she mutters, and I toss myself down on the newly covered couch. "Aren't you leaving?"

"I'm not running out in that rain. I'd be drenched before I shut the front door," I state. Rita glances back at the three-panel window, streaming with a deluge of water. It's beautiful and alarming.

"We can't stay here," Rita snaps.

"Why not?" I question, pulling my phone from my pocket and wondering if I can get cell service. I send a quick text to Nolan, hoping it goes through to him.

"We just can't," Rita says, placing her hands on her hips, but her sight drifts to the window once more.

"You go right ahead and leave."

"I can't leave you here alone," she reminds me.

"Afraid I might burn the place down?" I ask, an edge to my voice.

"That isn't funny," she remarks, and I have to agree.

"I guess you're stuck, then. And if you think you're not, your SUV will be if you try to peel out in this downpour."

"Ugh." Rita tosses herself on the opposite end of the couch, which crinkles under her slight weight and the plastic underneath us. I scroll on my phone, finding it won't power up to data, but I have another idea.

"How about some music?" I don't wait for her reply before I find my downloads and click a song. Music reminiscent of the 1980s fills the dark living room, and I spring upward.

"What are you doing?" Rita's voice still holds an edge, but I'm not letting her sour my mood. I start moving to the beat with a little hop left and hop right, kicking out my feet to match. The lyrics begin, and I start to sing along, ignoring Rita as I dance around the room.

"You're acting like a nut," Rita says over the music, but her voice holds more humor.

"You wanted to see my moves, so I'm showing you." Continuing to dance, I turn to her. "Dance with me."

Rita crosses her arms from her position on the couch. "I don't dance."

"Everybody dances," I tell her, singing with the lyrics and then changing them when the chorus hits. "Rain on me," I belt out, and Rita laughs.

"Those aren't the words," she teases, but I continue singing off-key and ad-libbing the refrain to match our current situation. The song is actually "Take On Me" by A-ha. It's got a bouncy beat, and my feet match the rhythm.

"Rain on me," I draw out again, holding out both my hands and wiggling my fingers at Rita, implying she should stand. She waves a hand at me and turns her head, but she can't fight a grin. I do a spin and slide side to side, holding my hand at my waistline. I love to dance, and I haven't done it in years. I also want to make Rita smile and wipe away whatever has her in a bad mood. My show carries on until the end of the song, and then I bow. Rita laughs harder and gives me a slow clap.

"Alright." Reaching out for her hand, I catch one before she claps again and pull her upward. She stumbles into my chest, and I grab her other hand.

"I can't dance," she states, holding out her ankle to show me her hiking boot, but I kick out my foot to show her mine. Rita huffs, closing her eyes while I remain holding her hand in mine. "No, really. I can't dance, as in I don't know how."

I stare, disbelieving her. "Rita. That can't be true. Everyone can dance. It's like sex. You just know how to do it, and you use your body in almost the same way."

Her mouth falls open as I glance down at myself and sway my hips, lifting an arm for the back of my head.

"First off, handsome. If that's how you have sex, you're gonna hurt yourself." She laughs. "And second, I don't do that either, so I wouldn't know."

I stop moving and stare at her. "You don't do what?" I ask, swallowing around the fear of what she'll say next.

"I don't have sex."

*Mother of all things holy.* My eyes widen, and Rita's mood sobers again. "I mean, I know how, but I haven't . . . and the last time just wasn't . . ." Rita pulls at her hands and slips free of mine, but I capture one of her wrists to keep us connected.

"Relax," I say quietly, stroking my thumb over the veins at her wrist. "We'll take it slow."

"I am not having sex with you," Rita blurts, and I'm the one to let out a snort.

"As if," I state. "I meant we'll take the dancing slowly." Not releasing her wrist, I lift my phone again and scroll through my music. Finding something I think she'll like, I smile slowly. Adele's "Set Fire to the Rain" fills the room. The song is all Rita. She's fire, and I'm rain, and I'm burning for her. I turn the volume down a bit, then toss the phone to the couch and place my hands at Rita's hips.

"Just follow my lead."

"This is stupid," she mutters.

"Good thing it's only me then," I jest, glancing down at where my hands are placed. "It might help if you touch me."

Her head pops up, and our eyes meet. "I mean, place your hands on my shoulders." Rita does, but she's stiff. As the song begins, I move her by guiding her hips.

"Side to side," I state, leading her with a subtle double bounce with each sway. As Adele carries on, I slip an arm around Rita's lower back and clasp her hand in mine, holding her in a typical dance stance. As the tempo builds, I swing Rita around and dip her to the singer's rising voice. Our eyes meet as I right her before we dance faster, our hips coming closer to match the rhythm.

"You're doing it," I mutter, pride in my voice as Rita follows my lead, and I hum the lyrics about fire and rain, and all things burning between them. Rita slowly begins to relax in my arms, following the sway of my hips and the gentle thrust of my pelvis near hers. The song is energizing while seductive, and it might have been a poor selection, but I'm not letting Rita go now that I have her in my arms. Let her fire burn my rain. I'll take the torture.

As the song ends, I bend for my phone on the couch but don't release my hand at Rita's hip. I quickly find another song I enjoy although it's more somber. John Hiatt's "Feels Like Rain" is a sultry song about rain and love, and keeping my voice low, I sing. Rita watches my lips as I murmur, and the anxiety she had over dancing slips into me with my singing.

"I don't have much of a voice," I whisper.

"I like it," Rita quietly says, but her eyes say more. Heat flames in those blue orbs. Our bodies are responding to each other as my lower half presses against hers. Her breasts rest on my chest, but she doesn't dip her head. She watches me.

When that song ends, I pick one more, knowing I need a break from holding Rita in my arms. She's too close, and I want to kiss her again. Like the rain, I'm thirsting for something more with this woman.

The next song begins, and I step back from Rita, belting out the opening rap. "Come on, Rita. Give me your best *Flashdance* moves."

"You cannot be serious," she teases.

"Totally serious," I state, moving to the beat and holding out my fisted hand like it's a microphone. Rita slowly follows my lead, exaggerating her leaning hips, swinging her arms back and forth.

"Come on, sweet. Everyone knows this song." Rita joins in singing "It's Raining Men" by The Weather Girls. She's awful, but she's so dang cute in her red glasses and her work pants while swinging her arms. Her head gets into it as she repeats the words. Her hair starts flying around her face. Her hips join next, and she's really moving—hands in the air, double clapping. I wrap an arm around her, thrusting my hips at her, matching the repetition in the song, until Rita stumbles against the couch and takes me with her. We fall to the covered cushions.

My phone drops, and the plastic under the drop cloth crinkles. Rita breaks into laughter, and I join her, taking a second to catch our breaths before Rita checks the window. It's still raining just as hard as it was before.

Slowly, she clears her throat. "Maybe I should check the basement for water." She quickly stands, and I follow her retreat.

"Sweet," I quietly say, stopping her by catching her wrist again. She turns to face me.

"Why do you call me that?" I shrug, not wanting to tell her the real reason. Then a surprise lands on my lips. Her mouth has crashed onto mine. Unprepared for the sudden rush, I remain still like a dufus. My brain is slow to catch up, but my body takes over. My lips respond to hers. The rain is our new soundtrack as we stand in the dark living room and kiss.

And Rita can kiss.

This isn't like that first attempt I made on her. This is a woman who wants something from me. Slowly, I guide her backward until I have us returning to the couch once more with the crinkling plastic and musty drop cloth underneath us.

"This okay?" I whisper to her lips, lingering against mine. Rita doesn't answer, just continues to kiss me. What I notice as we lay horizontal is how the kiss slows. It's still heated, still demanding, but something more is happening here as we settle into the tender nips and soft suction of lips on lips. The kiss stays sweet but never-ending, and as far as I'm concerned, it can rain all night.

# RITA

I'd blame it on the rain, but I can't. This was all Jake. Jake washing away my bad mood when I can't even remember why I was out of sorts. Jake making me dance and not making me feel silly about it. Jake kissing me.

I'm pinned to the inside of the couch, my back along the back while Jake cushions me against his chest. Our mouths move as one, but his hands aren't roaming, and I want him to roam. I want him to travel the topography of my body, so I have an excuse to explore his.

Slowly, he pulls back, brushing at my hair, curling it around my ear. "You okay?" His voice is quiet. I don't know why he's asking, but I appreciate it all the same.

"We don't have to do anything you don't want to do," he says, and it's even sweeter than checking in with me.

His mouth returns to mine, and finally, his hands move. Sliding down the front of me, he cups the swell of one breast, and I arch into his touch. He's hesitant at first, like a schoolboy on his first feel. Quickly, the pressure increases. He squeezes. He kneads. He pinches my nipple, sharp and ripe under my bra.

Jake breaks the kiss to glance at his movements. His hand slips back to the center, and he gently tugs my blouse upward.

Slipping his callused palm underneath the silky material, he touches my skin. I'm still dressed in my work clothes from the day—a pantsuit minus the jacket and my hiking boots. I should feel clumsy, but the care he's taking to skate up my belly and cover my breast once more makes me feel sexy. He makes me feel alive.

I reach down and unbutton my own shirt, not wanting him to stop what he's doing. Once the buttons are free, Jake pushes the material back, exposing me to him.

"Purple again?"

"Again?" I question, wondering when he saw me in a purple bra the first time. He doesn't answer but removes my shirt completely. His fingertips tease over the swell exposed above the silky fabric. He traces along the lacy edge before dipping his fingers into the cup and pinching my nipple hard. His mouth returns to mine, swallowing my shocked gasp as I arch into him once more. It's been so long since I've been touched by another, so long since a touch has been this intimate, yet this is nothing like what I remember.

Too soon, his hand leaves my breast and travels down my middle, leading to the catch at my waist. He pops the clasp on my pants and then pulls back from kissing me.

"Maybe we should stop." He's leaning away from me, but I fist his T-shirt just above his heart.

"Please," I whisper. "Don't stop."

Jake works at the zipper next, watching his fingers maneuver the closure before dipping his hand lower. He dives fast and deep, right into my underwear to cup me where no one has touched me in too long.

As I moan at the tenderness, his fingertips stroke over sensitive folds, damp and desperate for more.

"How long's it been, sweet?"

Licking my lips, I meet his eyes in the darkness. "Six years." Raspy and rough, my answer chokes a little as I fight the past and focus on the present. The year after Ian's death, I was a mess, but

Jake doesn't need to know those details. His thick fingers quickly divert my thoughts.

"You're wet," he tells me as if I'm not aware of how soaked I am. "And that's for me."

I nod to agree. *He's* turning me on. He's the one touching me. He's the one present. His fingers continue their magic, slipping easily over the swollen nub and entering me first with one finger and then another. Relishing the full sensation, my hips rock, drawing him deeper. I don't want the feeling to end, but he pulls back quickly, pressing at my trigger spot. My eyes close in bliss as he rubs in circles, teasing me, toying with me, and bringing me to the brink so quickly, I break within seconds.

"Oh. My God." I purr, curling into his hand between my legs, and groaning at the rush. I've never come so fast, and I need a moment to catch my breath. I don't allow myself too long, though, as I don't want my head catching up to what we're doing.

Once I settle, Jake withdraws his fingers and shifts so he's over me. He removes his shirt, pulling it over his head with one tug from the back of his neck, a sexy move mastered by men. Balancing over me, I admire the full effect of his chest before he lowers to place his warm skin against mine. He kisses me, and I'm lost again.

His kisses travel down my jaw and above my bra, where he sets his tongue in the valley exposed between my breasts. Then he moves down to my belly, sucking at my skin as he lowers. At my waist, he pauses.

"Still okay?" he asks, with his hands on the waistband of my pants. My eyes prickle for some reason, but I nod. Blinking several times, I wish away the telltale warning of tears. He's being so . . . understanding? Considerate? Tender? I can't think. He's moving so slowly, taking his time to touch me. Every motion is deliberate, cautious even, and it's so unexpected.

I don't want to think about the past, so I fight it as my pants are removed to my boots, and then Jake makes quick work of tugging my feet free of the footwear. He stands next to the couch for a second, peering down at me in my purple bra and underwear.

"You're so pretty, sweet." It's not something I often hear and definitely haven't heard in seven years, so those damn threatening tears blur my vision. Jake hastily kicks off his boots and removes his work pants. He pulls out his wallet and fumbles within it for a second. Then he's back over me, and I open my thighs, allowing him between them.

"Rita?" he questions, noting my water-filled eyes.

"Please," I whisper again, my voice hoarse and low. "Don't stop." This isn't about him. This is about me. I need him to continue. I need us to connect. I want to feel complete with him.

Pressing kisses to my belly again, he works my underwear down to my knees, where I wiggle them off my shins. He removes his own boxer briefs and then reaches over my thigh for the floor. Holding up a square packet, I can see what it is.

"It's new. After Nolan's oops in high school, we kept stock, but it's been a while. I want to assure you this is new." I watch the concentration of his face more than his motions to cover himself. He's such a handsome man. Those cheekbones. Those dancing eyes. Those puffy lips. When he settles between me once more, he notices a tear trickles free.

Jake reaches for the wet drop with his thumb, wiping it clean but doesn't mention it. His hand lowers, stroking down my side, taking his time to outline my body, which is nothing spectacular. I'm not curvy or straight; I'm just me. Jake travels back up my side to my armpit, then presses his open palm down the underside of my arm. He pushes my elbow upward, forcing my arm over my head as he coasts his hand along my forearm to my wrist. Eventually, he clasps my hand, linking our fingers together.

I feel strangely treasured by his touch and this final detail. Holding me, he balances up on a knee and positions himself at my entrance.

"Are you sure, sweet?"

I nod and feel the slow pressure of him enter me. He leans forward and licks at a second tear rolling to my hairline.

"Relax," he whispers as he enters me, filling me in a way I haven't been filled in a long, *long* time. Sliding inward, he's so gentle, I swear I feel every ridge and ripple until he's to the hilt. Pausing when he's buried within me, he clutches my fingers tight and returns his mouth to mine, kissing me tenderly once more. My heart races as his tongue strokes over mine, savoring the seconds before I can't take it anymore.

"You can move," I mutter under his lips, softly chuckling.

"It's been a long time for me, too, and I'm almost afraid to." His eyes glance from one to the other of mine, taking in my face and brushing back my hair. "This could be over embarrassingly fast."

"How long has it been for you?" It's an awkward time to ask, but I'm curious as he went out with Louisa. I don't dare ask if he slept with her specifically. I don't even want to know if he kissed her.

"Seven years," he admits, his voice low and quiet. We've gone from rousing dance partners to whisper-soft lovers. Seven years is a long time. In his case, I suppose he hasn't had much of a choice. Jake kisses me again and mutters directly to my lips. "I feel as if I've been waiting for this exact moment for seven long years."

His hips shift, and he pulls back, teasing me at my entrance before sliding forward with deliberately slow movements once more. We both moan as he continues to hold my hand like he's holding on for dear life, but the dam has broken, and at any second, we're both about to lose control.

"Gotta move," he strains as he balances on an elbow while continuing to grip my hand. His hips jut back, and then he rushes forward. A few more thrusts matched by my reaction, and he moves his free hand to the back of the couch, pressing himself upward. He slips a leg off the cushions, placing one foot on the floor. The position forces my leg up over his hip, causing me to open wider to him. He's got a Spiderman appearance happening, as his limbs spread in all directions while pinning me in place. And then he really moves. He moves like he dances. Hips thrusting. Legs flexing. With his dick thick and long, he's tapping me in a way I've never been tapped, and he lowers his gaze, watching himself disappear inside me.

"You're so . . . it's so . . . Oh God, sweet. *Oh God.*"

He hammers harder, rocking faster. When he pistons into me, the entire couch quakes, and the plastic underneath us somewhere below the drop cloth crinkles. It isn't exactly how or where or who I thought I'd have sex with after all this time, but I wouldn't change one second of this experience.

Because Jake Drummond is an experience.

The way he moves. The way he squeezes my hand. The way he falls apart, slamming into me a final time, giving me every pulse, every pump, all the pressure of seven years. *I've been waiting for this exact moment.* Stilled in this sprawled position, he lowers only his head and kisses me hard. Lips meld together. Tongues crash and twirl. If I didn't know better, I'd think Jake was claiming me for the next seven years.

He releases my hand and moves it between us. Instantly, he's stroking me, circling my clit, and brushing the slickness while he's still inside me.

"What are you doing?" My voice chokes as the tension builds. He might be only semi-hard, but he's quickly recovering.

"I want to feel you, sweet. Come alive on me."

*Come alive.* It's exactly how I feel. It's not that I've been dead inside or even numb, but I haven't felt this electrified in years. Maybe not ever, if I'm honest. Jake works at my tender nub and rocks into me, restoring his hard-on. The sound of us coming together, along with the intense friction he places on *that* spot, sets me off. My toes curl as everything rushes to my center and bursts. With my back arched and my head tipped back, Jake follows once more and then collapses over me.

As he breathes heavily into my neck, I wrap my arms around him.

"I thought I'd be too old for that to happen, but I couldn't help myself."

I softly chuckle. I'm not sure if there's a compliment in that confession, but then Jake pops up on his elbows, his face only an inch from mine. He drags his nose along mine and closes his eyes.

"Thank you for giving that to me." His whisper is just as tender as all his touches. The words are a kiss against my lips. I feel the same way. I'm grateful for what he's given me—at least for a few precious minutes.

# JAKE

The slam of a truck door has me jolting awake, and it takes me a second to register where I am. I'm covered by a drop cloth on a couch, naked as the day I was born underneath it, and alone. My thoughts catch up to me.

*Rain. Rita. Sex.*

My head twists, and the bright sunlight blinds me. It's morning, and the rain is finished for the moment.

Another slam sounds like the release of a tailgate, and everything flips in my head.

*Naked. Work. Sunshine.*

Quickly, I roll out from under the covering, scrambling for my clothing piled beside the couch. Keeping low to the ground, I slip into my underwear and pants. My fingers shake as I rush to redress, needing more time and a stiff cup of coffee. My shirt comes next, and I tug it over my head, smoothing down the smelly, wrinkled front of a day-old tee. I skip the flannel and pop up to the couch, forcing my feet into my boots as Sullivan walks in the front door. The entrance opens directly into the living room, and I'm the first thing Sullivan sees.

"Um."

"Hey," I croak, my voice rough. Where the fuck is Rita? Panic sets in. Did she leave me? Is she still here somewhere? I reach for my phone on the floor. There's a blow-up of text messages. I ignore the ones from my brother and note the final message from my probation supervisor.

Shit. *Shit!* I had a meeting this morning, and I missed it.

Quickly, I stand and follow Sullivan's eyes to something on the floor. My wallet lays open on the ground, along with a condom wrapper and the spent rubber.

"Sully, I—"

He holds up a hand. His mouth falls open, and then his lids shut tight. I know what he's thinking, or perhaps *who* he's thinking of. I choke on my tongue, wanting to defend myself but not expose Rita. I'm thinking she wouldn't be pleased if I shared what happened. What we did isn't anyone's business. She might not even be pleased it happened with me. Fighting off images of last night, I lower for the garbage and tuck it into my pocket.

Sullivan shakes his head before his lids open and turns his gaze out the open front door. Sunlight streams into the room, and I wonder again when the rain stopped. I was lost in Rita last night. In her laughter. In her kiss. Inside her. Swiping a hand over my face, I find her scent lingers on my fingers. *Shit.*

As Sullivan stares out the door, Rita's SUV appears in the soaked front yard. She exits her vehicle looking fresh as a spring morning and smiling just as brightly. Coming up to the house, she's wearing her boots with jeans today.

"Hiya, handsome," she greets Sullivan, and a sledgehammer hits my chest. Apparently, calling me handsome isn't something special. Not that it should matter. It doesn't matter. What Rita and I had was only one night, right?

"Hey. We have a problem," Sullivan mutters as Rita enters the house to see me standing like a dumbass next to the couch. Her expression falls. She had to know I was still here. My truck is still parked in the same position as last night.

"What's wrong?" Her gaze stays on me, and she works at keeping her face still.

*What's wrong?* What's wrong is I woke on this couch without her? "I missed my probation meeting this morning," I blurt. Not that it explains why I'm really suddenly upset. She walked out on me, left me to potentially be caught, and now I'm scrambling to wrap my head around what happened last night.

"Jake spent the night here with a woman," Sully adds, pouring salt into the wound, or maybe he's fishing for Rita to admit it was her and not just some random woman.

Rita's head turns from me to Sullivan, and I twist my neck just once—a crack snaps to adjust the kink in my neck. Her expression remains stoic, not giving away a hint. Not a blush that it was her spread under me. Not a twitch that she was the one to warm this couch with me.

"We should call your probations supervisor," Rita states, facing me once more. "Explain the situation."

Is she turning me in? This wasn't a one-way street. She slept with me, too. My heart hammers in my chest. It's too early in the morning to think straight. I'm missing out on a serious caffeine fix, and my dick has a damn mind of its own seeing Rita standing there in fitted jeans and those darn hiking boots.

Sullivan doesn't respond, and Rita hesitates. She looks like she wants to step toward me but doesn't—or won't.

"I can call the officer on your behalf." Rita's statement is a reminder she's my boss of sorts. She's equally important to the completion of my parole. One slipup with her, and I'm done. Back to prison. *Do not pass Go. Do not collect two-hundred dollars.*

I lick my lip and bite the edge of it, wondering what Rita might say to my probation supervisor. She turns to Sullivan again and asks him to give us a minute. His head snaps up, and he glares at me once more, and if I could read his thoughts, they'd include nothing short of physical torture. He grunts before stepping around her and exiting the house. At his disappearance, I rush to Rita.

"Where did you go?"

"What are you still doing here?" Her eyes roam my body,

noting my day-old clothes. She meets me halfway to her, and we're hidden from the outside of the house by the wall between window and door.

"I fell asleep."

"I couldn't wake you."

I swipe a hand through my hair.

"You sleep like the dead," she adds, crossing her arms. The corner of her lip slowly curls before she straightens her mouth and her posture. Her arms fall to her sides. "What were you thinking?"

"Last night?"

"This morning."

I stare at her, caught between wanting to throttle her for this conversation and kiss that sassy mouth.

"What was wrong with last night?" she asks, her voice lowering.

"Why weren't you here this morning?" My tone softens as well. I didn't like waking without her. "You could have left a note."

"And what would it say?"

For some reason, that hurts. That hurts hard, like a slap to the face or a punch to the sternum. My lips twist in confusion. I've misread everything, I guess.

"I've never done this before," Rita quietly adds, and I don't know what she means, but I can't keep going back and forth with her. I have larger issues at the moment by the label of probation officer.

"Would you really call my parole supervisor?" What will she say?

"I think we should and explain what happened."

"You're going to tell him you slept with me?" Rita's head snaps back like I've slapped her, and I see I've misread something all over again. Her shoulders fall, and her fisted hands raise to her hips.

"No, I was thinking I'd explain the rain. Say you had truck

trouble, and we approved for you to spend the night. Then I'd apologize for not informing him. Or maybe you could take some credit and say your phone was dead."

She's certainly good at the alibi. All plausible issues in a rainstorm and much better than admitting I lost myself in her for a night. My head turns to the rumpled drop cloth draped over the couch, and I take a minute to consider what happened last night.

We had sex on a dusty covered couch in a partially built house. Not exactly how I imagined my first time after so many years. Not exactly who I imagined I'd sleep with after all that time. I turn back to Rita, taking in her appearance. The curve of her hip in her jeans. The fit of her T-shirt against breasts I touched last night. The tension in her lip as she stares at me.

"Thanks for covering for me," I admit, hating how wrong that sounds. Rita's expression holds firm, but there's the hint I've been looking for. She's hurt, and it's all my fault. I'm handling this wrong. I'm not handling it at all. She's taking the lead to cover for me. "I'm sorry."

"For last night?" Her brows lift as her eyes widen. Her voice rises with a squeak.

"For right now. It's morning. I'm foggy and I—"

"We ready to get started yet? I've got things to be done today," Sully interrupts us, poking his head around the opening of the front door. Rita takes another moment to look me right in the eye before twisting her neck and then turning her entire body, giving me her back.

"Yeah. I'm going to step outside and call Jake's parole officer. Then I need to get to the office."

She isn't dressed for her office. She looks like she was ready to spend the day working around here, but she's already walking toward the door, not giving me a second glance.

Everything in me wants to reach for her, tugging her back to me, and explain. Last night meant a lot to me. Being like that with her, entering her, it felt honest and real. For the first time in years, I didn't have to think. It was only thoughts of her.

But this is the morning after, and I should know better. I'm always in the wrong place at the wrong time, and Rita confirms what I've already thought of myself. I'm not the right man for her.

---

The rest of the day was shit, and it only got worse when I finally arrived home.

"Where the hell have you been?" Nolan asks, both concern and a chuckle fill his voice, hoping I've caused mischief which I'm not allowed to do.

"It's a long story."

"I hope there's a woman involved."

"Nolan, not now." I sigh, heading to the staircase. I need a shower and a beer. My room is on the second floor, having traded places with Nolan. When our mother died, I took her room on the first floor, and Nolan gave Rory mine, so they shared the upper space. When Nolan was injured, he had to move to the lower level, and my things were put into his old room, stacked in a corner, awaiting my return.

"Rory's coming home tonight for dinner."

I freeze partway up the staircase. I haven't seen my nephew in years. Seven to be exact. Everything happened so fast. Nolan's injury. My arrest. Rory was simply left alone at seventeen. Nolan and I only had communication via telephone for the longest time, and when he finally did come to see me, he came alone. He didn't want Rory seeing me in that place.

*Good people make bad decisions all the time.*

I shake my head at the notion of seeing Rory after all this time. Turning around on the stairs, I gaze down at my brother in his chair. He loves his son. He'd do anything for him, and so would I.

And I did.

"I can't wait to see him," I say, trying to keep my voice steady as my brother smiles with fatherly pride. Rory might have grown up fast, but he also kept his shit together. He eventually went to Burlington U on scholarship and currently attends Vermont Law, graduating this summer. It's almost ironic Rory wants to be a lawyer, putting away the bad guys, fighting for the good ones. I don't want to be bitter, but between Rita's dismissal, the issue with my probation officer, and now Rory's visit, I'm worked up.

"I want to hear about this woman," Nolan says, pointing a finger up at me. "I need all the details."

"After I shower," I say, suddenly wanting to collapse in bed and skip dinner.

A half hour later, I'm on my third beer when Rory arrives.

"Uncle Jake." I stand on shaky legs and hold out a hand to greet Rory. He's a man in every way and the spitting image of his father. Same dark brown hair. Same dark eyes. Only he's skittish with good reason. He knows I know. Over seven years ago, my nephew and his friends might have caused a fire that spiraled out of control, and I took the fall for it.

It's difficult to look Rory in the eye, and he's suffering the same. Still, we put on a good show for Nolan. Everything for Nolan, especially now. My brother has become quite the cook in our kitchen at a wheelchair-accessible height, despite the peanut butter and jam sandwiches. He'd been a volunteer fireman like me, and his favorite thing was making dinner for the men and women in service. Typical Nolan, he loved to gather people and make them laugh, stirring in a little innocent trouble.

"How is school?" I ask as Rory takes a seat in the living room.

Rory rubs his hands against his thighs. "Yeah, good. Things are good." Awkwardly, we pause in a position of sit and stare without actually staring at one another. With a tight smile, Nolan glances between Rory and me. My brother's brows pinch as his eyes flit between us.

"So. Dinner?" I turn to Nolan, who nods, and Rory and I stand again, following my brother into the kitchen. The space is already tight with his wheelchair and the addition of me. Putting three of us in the room, it's cramped. Still, we sit and eat in staggered silence and single-word answers to questions Nolan prompts, trying to pull his son into the conversation.

"How's Brynne?" Nolan asks his son.

"Brynne?" I ask. "You got a girl?" A smile fills my voice, but Rory's gaze drifts to his plate. He pushes around his food. Brynne. For a unique name, it sounds familiar.

"I'm getting married."

My fork pauses midair as I turn my head to Nolan. "What? When?"

"This fall," Nolan says, offering a weak smile.

"Why haven't you told me?" Rory will be graduating this summer. *Is the wedding a secret?*

"I'm marrying Brynne Dunhill."

I take a moment, but then the name registers. "Lisa's niece?" My head twists from Nolan to Rory and back.

"Lisa came around a bit when I first got home, and she'd bring her niece. Rory met her then, but they didn't start seeing each other again until he entered law school."

"Brynne. Lisa's niece?" My ex-wife's niece will be joining our family, and no one told me. Hell, no one even told me Rory was getting married. "Why didn't you say something?"

"I didn't want you to be upset," Nolan states. "I know it was hard when you and Lisa separated."

"When she divorced me," I remind Nolan.

"We didn't want to make things difficult for you."

"Difficult? How?" My heart begins to race, and the most awful thoughts about my younger brother enter my head. "Did you fuck my ex-wife?" I see it all playing out like some damn romantic drama. Younger brother loses older brother who takes care of fucking everything for him, and the ex-wife arrives having her heart broken, even if she did the breaking, and they find consolation in one another.

"Hey," Rory defends.

"You know I couldn't fuck someone at first," Nolan states.

"Why is this even a discussion?" Rory interjects.

"You aren't answering my question," I demand of my brother.

"No. No, I didn't fuck her. I wouldn't do that to you," Nolan states, staring back at me, and the implication becomes clear. Lisa wanted it. Maybe Nolan wanted it, too, but he didn't act on it. I press my chair back, causing the feet to screech across the tile.

"I need some air," I state. I toss my fork to my plate and stalk to the front door, pulling it open with more force than necessary. I don't bother closing it. Racing down the ramp we now have installed before the house, I head for the street and walk.

Immediately, my thoughts fill with my ex-wife. She wanted the divorce. I didn't. Can't make a screwdriver fit a nail. We were in the middle of our separation when the arrest happened. Our future became one more part of my history. We were over. Still, I can't get over the shock of Rory getting engaged and to a Dunhill of all people.

Continuing down the street, I inhale the fresh mountain air deeply, dismissing memories of my ex-wife. Our house is in an area of smaller homes a few blocks from downtown Ashbury. It's a community where homes outside the town are growing larger and larger while the historic district grows more decrepit looking. The closest high school services five municipalities, making it a community unit school, and my thoughts drift to it. While it's been over twenty-five years since I've attended high school, my nightmares return to the building often.

Most haunting in those nightmares is Rory and his friends standing outside the school on a dark night. I was driving home after another fire investigation. Assigned to the entire county— one man for almost twenty firehouses and a slew of volunteer fire people—I'd been stumped for the first time ever in my career. A rash of blazes had occurred over the past three months in vacant warehouses throughout the county. Nothing was making sense other than their vacancy.

*Suddenly, nothing mattered as I neared the high school, finding another blaze roaring at one end of the building and a group of teens standing around watching it.*

*I pulled into the parking lot, jumped from my truck, and called out to the boys.*

*"Hey," I yelled as the air filled with the strong scent of smoke. "Hey, what the hell is going on?" A few heads turned. Others didn't. At the sight of me, the boys began to scatter, but I recognized one. Rory.*

*Chasing him across the empty lot, I was quick to catch him, tugging him by the collar to stop his retreat.*

*"What are you doing here?" I snapped, holding him by the neck.*

*"We didn't mean to do it," Rory said. His gaze returned to the school, telling me something was amiss. The scent coming off my seventeen-year-old nephew was a mix of sweet weed and explosives.*

*"Rory, tell me the truth." Fear rose inside me.* What had they done?

*"We were smoking behind the maintenance shed and setting off fireworks. The fireworks were more boom than sparks, but . . . I don't know. One must have gone astray."*

Idiots.

*"Don't move," I warned Rory. "Call 911." I remember wondering why the fire department hadn't already arrived. The fire alarm should have gone off, but I didn't hear it. Releasing my nephew, I decided to investigate on my own. I headed toward the building, rounding the side, hoping any late-night cleaning staff might have already left. As it was summer, the school would be vacant, and at the late hour, I didn't fear anyone would be present in the school.*

*Checking a side door entrance, I found the doors locked. Heading around the back of the building, I was eyeing the maintenance shed near the football field when an explosion occurred. Windows busted. Flames flared into the night air. I raced back around the front of the building to find I was the only person in the lot other than the first sheriff to arrive on the scene.*

*Instantly, I knew how it looked. I was running around a burning building. The boys were gone. When I was brought in for questioning a few days later, I was caught on the schoolyard cameras on both the side of the building and the back. There was no sight of the boys near the football field.*

"Uncle Jake." My name rings out in the quiet darkness of the lone street, and I turn to find Rory racing after me.

"Jake, I—" Out of breath, he stops running and bends at the knees. "I-just. Give me a minute." He lifts a finger to signify a pause.

"Need to work on your stamina if you're getting married, kid," I bitterly tease.

Rory stands to his full height, which matches mine. He's broader than me, huskier like my brother once was, but it's evident we are related. We all share the same dark brown hair, the same cut to how we stand with our shoulders hunched forward, same tilt to our heads when we speak.

"About that." He exhales. "Nothing was held back to hurt your feelings. We just thought it would be better to let you settle into one thing at a time." His voice even sounds like my brother, rough and low, with a hint of ease underneath it. I'd like to accuse him of having an easy life, but after I went to prison, I know he didn't. He was suddenly raising his father, and my bitterness falls back to Nolan. He's always being taken care of.

Turning away from Rory, I continue forward on my path, needing the fresh nighttime air. Rory falls into step beside me. He isn't wearing a jacket, and his hands slip into his jean pockets. We walk in silence for the rest of the block and turn toward town.

"Should we talk about it?" Rory questions. "I know what you did."

I stop, but Rory takes another step forward before turning to face me. "You went to jail for me, didn't you?"

"Rory." I sigh. *What can I say?*

"We didn't mean for it to happen." He pauses to exhale. "We were stupid kids."

"I know you didn't mean it." *A stray firework?* The fire didn't make sense. It didn't add up. However, I wasn't allowed to investigate the scene because I was accused of the crime. "And I'm not even convinced you did anything to that building."

"I'm still so sorry, Uncle Jake."

When I'd been arrested, I wasn't in a good state of mind. My brother was in the hospital with a major injury, still in a medically induced coma to ease his pain. Rory was full of guilt, but I told him not to mention anything to anyone until I could learn more. Then I was arrested.

"And I'm sorry for Mr. Sanders," I say. Someone *had* been in the building after all.

"I know." Rory exhales. "I liked Mr. Sanders." Liking him won't bring him back to life, though, and the man lost his life that night. The principal was in the high school for some reason. The best summation was he smelled smoke and investigated on his own. I didn't understand why the fire alarm didn't trip until deeper investigation showed the alarm system had been tampered with. It didn't make sense. The principal's body was found in the wreckage.

"I still don't understand how a single firework could have set the building on fire. We didn't even hear a window break."

The investigation claimed the fire began in the chemistry lab. Chemicals within the lab ignited. A firework was never mentioned, but something sparked the blaze.

"I never thought it was a firework," I admit. I wasn't able to prove otherwise, but a stray firework still didn't make sense to me. Deep down, I'd always wondered if my conviction had all been part of some bigger plan. The state was mandating cuts in civil services, including fire prevention. They didn't believe an arson investigator was necessary. *Let a regular fireman handle the cases* as if it were that simple. The number of full-time firepersons was on the chopping block, cutting back chiefs which were the only paid position in the department. The state believed volunteers would be enough for our smaller community firehouses, suggesting they could run themselves and solve their own mysteries.

Taking a deep breath, I look at my nephew. He has an innocent face with a permanent expression of curiosity. Nolan and I always knew he'd amount to more than us. We wanted him to be more.

At seventeen, almost eighteen, he would begin his senior year that fall. If he had started that blaze, he'd be tried as an adult, and his future would have been ruined. I couldn't do that to Rory, and I couldn't do that to Nolan.

Upon my arrest, Nolan needed Rory more than anything, and I couldn't strip my brother of his son.

My nephew was more than a nephew. He was like an extra little brother, closer to a son himself to me, which I'll never have. I didn't want to resent him, and I'd had seven years to forgive the doubts that crept in from time to time. I didn't know what to believe, but I couldn't imagine Rory and his friends set off a blaze that ignited a school and killed a man.

"In many ways, it no longer matters how it happened or who did it. I've already served the time. I've already lost seven years of my life. I can't get any of that back."

"I could turn myself in." Rory sheepishly offers, but his suggestion is not genuine or necessary. His admission would be based on guilt, not a confession.

"You'd never be tried for something the court already considers solved. There's no evidence a firework began that blaze, and you wouldn't be able to handle prison." Rory wasn't weak, but he was soft enough that prison would not be the place for him. He was better trying to right wrongs on the outside of jails than be placed inside one.

"Tell me more about Brynne." I take a step to restart our walk and dismiss a discussion I've circled over in my head too many times in the past seven years. Rory's face shifts. His expression lessens from contrition to something else. His cheeks brighten.

"She's amazing." His voice lifts. The lilt is one of love, and I'm so damn envious. I remember that feeling, even if it didn't last.

"Yeah, what's so great about her?" I listen as we cross into town and walk along a quiet, decrepit main street. Rory tells me about the assets of his girl. How pretty she is. How kind she is.

"She's a teacher. She loves kids." Without asking if he wants his own, I know the answer. Rory will be a great dad. He's learned humility from his own and devotion from me. Or at least, I hope that's how he's seen it. His father's injury certainly was a lesson for Rory.

"You know Dad would never have done that to you," he states, breaking into my thoughts.

"Done what?"

"Slept with Aunt Lisa."

I huff. "Yeah, I don't really think he would either, but you never know what attracts people. Sometimes things happen, or we just choose someone for a night without explanation." My thoughts leap back to Rita and images of her underneath me. We took it slow, and that made all the difference. I didn't want to rush through my first encounter after seven years, even if I knew it wouldn't last more than a few seconds. What surprised me most was my ability to immediately recover and start again without even leaving the warmth of her body. Rita was a wonder. I couldn't explain why I was so attracted to her. I just was.

Like Rory, I could gush about how pretty I thought she was or how kind, but those were only on the surface. What I saw the other night was a vulnerable woman, and that attracted me even more to her. I wanted to know her secrets. I wanted her sob stories.

"I guess I wouldn't know for certain, but I don't think Dad's been with anyone since the accident."

I snort, uncertain myself as my brother never mentions anyone, even though he's always talking about sex. Then again, men who brag or fixate the most on sex are usually not the ones getting it.

I don't have a response to my nephew's comment. If Nolan slept with Lisa, I'd have no way of knowing, and I honestly didn't care. Not any longer. Lisa was out of my life by her choice, not mine. My choices had all been stripped from me.

"We're good, aren't we Uncle Jake?" Rory pauses, bringing us full circle. "I don't want you to hate me."

I stop in my tracks and face my nephew. "I could never hate

you, kid." Reaching out for him, I awkwardly pull him into me, finding his larger frame and taller stature less manageable to embrace than when he was a skinny teenage kid. Still, I hold on to him, patting his back as tears prickle my eyes. It'd be easy to blame a bunch of kids for the fire, but my heart felt it wasn't their fault. Even though I had no proof, I just didn't believe they had caused that blaze, accident or not.

"I love you, little man," I say to him, finding the words strange as I haven't said that phrase in years to anyone, and calling him the endearment from his childhood felt wrong. He certainly wasn't little anymore.

"Love you, too, Uncle Jake. And I'm so glad you're home."

Rory pulls back from my embrace and offers me a slight smile, matching his father once again.

"Me, too, kid," I state, wishing I could mean it a little more.

# RITA

I felt sick about leaving Jake the other morning, but I could not rouse him in the early hours. He was wrapped around me so tightly I'm surprised I was able to climb out from under him. When I could not disturb him enough to wake him, I covered him and left. Not only am I riddled by how things went the morning after, but I can't seem to stop thinking about what we did the night before that morning. Staring into the abyss over scattered papers and my open laptop, I sit at my desk with my feet on the corner and my head in the fog.

"Rita, I've been calling your name for five minutes."

Blinking up at my law partner, I slowly sit straighter in my seat, kicking my hiking boot-covered feet off my desk. "Oh, sorry. What do you need, chickie?" I like May Shipley. With dark hair, a tall stature, and long legs, she could have been a model, but I'm happy she uses her brains over her beauty. From the moment we met, I knew she'd be a good fit for me. She went to my alma mater for both undergrad and law school. She was a recovering alcoholic, and she understood my sense of humor.

"I have some questions about this case, but you seem distracted today. Is everything okay?"

Tipping back in my seat, I allow it to bounce on the springs.

"I'm just all over the place lately." I glance up at my laptop, open to a case report I've never had the heart to read. I didn't need the details.

Ian was gone. That's all I needed to know.

"Is there something I can help you with?" May asks from across our shared office. As a recovering alcoholic, May knows the slightest deed or subtle hint can trigger old desires. I like to think I have my shit under control, but there's no doubt Jake Drummond could drive me to drink if I so desired to return to that road, which I do not.

"Man trouble."

May's mouth falls open while her eyelids rapidly blink. She doesn't speak for an entire minute.

"I didn't know you were dating someone."

"I'm not." I don't know what I'm doing with Jake. I certainly understand the particulars of what we did the other night, but I still had questions. Was it a one-night stand? Did what we did mean something to him? And why now? Why him? After all this time of skirting dates and turning away interested parties, why was Jake the one under my skin and over my body?

A rush of warmth travels down my spine and settles uncomfortably between my thighs. I cannot stop thinking of him. How he took his time. How he watched every move he made. How he kissed me afterward.

"You didn't knit him a sweater, did you?" May teases me, reminding me of when she gave a hand-knit sweater to her beau Alec Rossi before he was officially hers. I told her about the sweater curse.

*If you knit a man a sweater, you'll break up or something like that.*

"No, ma'am. I certainly did not." I gave Jake Drummond something else. I'm not a virgin—*heavens no*—but I have not had sex since that disastrous night six years ago when I thought I was ready after losing Ian. When I drank too much and woke alone on my hallway floor, certain I'd been with a man who came home with me but had disappeared during the night. That poor decision scared the drink right out of me. *How could I do that to myself?* That morning, I accepted I wasn't ready to move on from Ian and I needed other coping mechanisms rather than those gin and tonics that filled my nights. I sought grief counseling and Alcoholics Anonymous. I had trouble accepting my weakness, but I'd nearly lost my business because of it. I definitely had lost faith in myself and my judgment.

"So what's the problem?" May questions.

"I slept with him instead."

"And that's a problem, how?" May slowly gives me a mischievous grin.

"Don't give me that look, lady," I sternly warn her, but my lips lose the battle and match her smile.

"I have two questions for you. Did you enjoy yourself, and were you safe?" May dropped her voice as she spoke in a poor imitation of me, recanting our conversation when she considered Alec only a rebound hookup. Then she laughs.

"Yes, Mom," I tease back at her, although I'm over a decade older than her.

"I do remember a certain someone once telling me as long there was no alcohol involved a little rebound loving never hurt anyone," May reminds me. "But this wasn't a rebound, was it?"

Ian and I hadn't broken up. He'd died. My first bounce into sex was a wake-up call to my deeper issues, which May knows about as I first sponsored her in AA. I glance back at the case report pulled up on my computer and touch a key to close the file.

"Maybe I should have just knitted a sweater," I state, dismissing my slip with Jake. If I knit him one, will he go away now? Do I really want him to?

"Nah. I'd always go with sex," May says, winking at me, stealing all my lines. I'm paying for teasing her about Alec, but there's nothing to joke about. Her beau is a hot, hunky man who does right by my girl.

Suddenly, I'm considering that sweater and decide some retail therapy in the yarn store in Montpelier is a better use of my time than staring at a report I don't want to read.

---

Two days later, I'm still ruminating over what Jake and I did. I went to an AA meeting for professional women only in Montpelier intent on avoiding the meeting Jake attends in Colebury. I'd also been avoiding the building site, although Alfred called me, wondering if I've made a decision about the directorship. I hadn't yet.

In addition to all that, I'd been thinking about what Jake told me about being a former arson investigator. Curiosity had me wondering if he worked on Ian's case. I hadn't followed the story in the news or anywhere else for that matter. I had a funeral to plan and a wedding to dismantle. Some say I should have gone to the trial, for closure or retribution or something, but I disagreed. What would facing the person who killed Ian prove? It was ruled involuntary manslaughter—a fancy label for an accident. Whoever committed the crime wasn't aware Ian was in the building.

Still, I wondered if I should ask Jake about the case. So many emotions were conflicting lately as I'd done what I'd done with him, and memories of Ian had returned with a vengeance.

Finding myself aimlessly driving toward my home east of Montpelier, I see Jake as if thoughts of him conjured him up in my small town. He's standing outside the old firehouse, and I slow to a stop before the ancient brick structure and roll down my window.

"Jake?" I call out in question although it's definitely him. Slowly, he turns away from looking up at the two-story building.

"Hey," he says as if shaking himself from deep thought. He steps over to my SUV and angles an arm against the roof.

"What are you doing in my neighborhood?" I tease, noticing my heart fluttering just from seeing him again up close.

"You live around here." He lifts his head to glance up the street.

"Hampshire is my hometown."

"Huh." His sound leaves me stumped.

"Why are you looking at the old firehouse?"

Jake turns back toward the building before responding. "I'm curious about the place. I'd love to see inside." The building is vacant as the county merged fire departments, building a newer community department outside of town a few years back.

"Hang on." He steps away from my SUV, and I pull over to park along the curb. Searching for a phone number on my dash, I find who I'm looking for and make a quick call. When I exit my crossover, Jake is still standing in front of the old brick building. Two large bay doors flank the front to accommodate fire trucks, and a bell tower stands on the left side of the structure. It's charming and a little enchanting.

"Come on," I say, leading Jake to the front door.

"What are you doing?"

"This place is for sale. I know the realtor and gave her a call." Once we stand before the main entrance, I lift the security lockbox and enter the code my realtor friend gave me.

As we enter the old lobby, a staircase leads to the second floor. I stand still, watching Jake spin in a slow circle around the entry. Eventually, I follow him up the narrow stairwell to the second floor, where rooms are sectioned off, and an old fireman's pole leads below.

"Want to ride the pole?" he asks, wiggling his brows. I'm wearing heels with a skirt and a blouse today.

"Not certain how that would work in my present attire."

"Just wrap your legs around the pole and glide." He chuckles softly, glancing down at my bare legs exposed beneath the hem of my skirt. "Although, I can't promise it won't burn."

"You just let me worry about where it will burn," I remark, smirking at him.

Jake goes first, sliding down the old metal cylinder like an expert but the pole wobbles as he descends. When he reaches the bottom, he jiggles it back and forth.

"I don't know how safe this is," he hollers up to me. "But I'm liking the view."

He can't really see up my skirt from his angle, so I know he's teasing until he says, "Purple again? It's my new favorite color."

Stepping back from the hole for the pole, I take my time to descend the narrow stairs and meet Jake in the large, open garage space. He's twirling in a circle again, and I'm wondering what he's thinking.

"What's going on in that head of yours?"

"Someone asked me what I'd want to go my way in my life." He narrows his eyes at me and gives me a teasing smirk. "And I've been thinking about an answer."

"A firehouse?" *This is what he wants?*

Jake paces around the pole. "A place to call mine. For the longest time, I thought I wanted out of Vermont. I wanted distance from here. From what happened. From what didn't." He bitterly chuckles. "But now that I'm out, I see once more I can't leave my brother." His brows pinch, and he shakes his head like he isn't pleased with what he's saying.

"There's just something fun about this old building, but it needs work."

I gaze up at the ceiling and around at the walls. "A lot of work, handsome."

"I didn't like when you called Sullivan handsome," he admits, and my gaze falls back to him. Slowly, I approach where he's leaning against the fireman's pole.

"I'm sorry," I state, uncertain why I'm apologizing.

"You know, I've been to the Bean every day."

I stare at him. "I haven't visited the Bean this week."

"I know." He chortles.

"Why were you there?"

"Because I was hoping you'd show up. You've been avoiding me."

Guilt riddles me as he's right. He steps away from the pole and circles me. I turn to face him as he watches me and end up bumping into the pole with my back.

"What are you afraid of, sweet?" The endearment alone does something to my insides. Butterflies flutter in my lower belly, and my mouth dries. "If you want me to apologize for what we did, I can't."

He reaches out for my hair and brushes it behind one ear.

"You don't need to apologize. I practically begged you," I admit, recalling that tears and pleas were part of our night.

"You don't need to beg me," Jake says, watching his fingers stroke over my ear and coast along my neck. He's so close I can smell him—cinnamon and sawdust and all man. His voice drops even lower. "I want to fuck you again."

That should not be sexy. It was not even romantic, but there's a tenderness in his voice along with a question that has my hormones bumping into themselves.

"When?" I whisper. His eyes widen for only a second, and then he leans closer to me, bringing that scruff-covered jaw to mine. He exhales near my ear.

"Right now." He turns his head at the same time I do, and our mouths crash. This is not the sweet approach he took the other night, but fire and flames ready to burn this old department down. My mouth surrenders to his, following his hungry lead to claim my lips and my tongue. He leans forward, and my back presses into the pole behind me. As our mouths move, he slides a hand down my arm and lifts it above my head.

"Hold on," he mutters as he takes my other hand and matches it to the first. Holding the pole over my head, Jake lowers his lips for my jaw, my neck, my throat. He's sucking at my skin, and a blaze of need rips through me.

"Jake," I groan as he unties the bow of my blouse and loosens a few buttons to get at my breasts. He didn't touch me the other night but nuzzled me over the silky fabric. Today, nothing is held back. He tugs one cup to expose a full breast, and his mouth latches on hard. He sucks me until my nipple is so sharp it aches. When he pulls back with a pop, he recovers me and moves to the other breast, swirling his tongue over the hard nub before sucking it just as hard. I squeak as he pulls free.

"I know you're wet," he tells me, as his hand slides down the curve of my hip and slowly tugs my skirt upward. Still holding the pole over my head, my heart races, and my chest heaves as he tortures me with the drag of my skirt against my thigh. Once it's high enough, his hand cups my center, and he moans. "I knew it."

Drenched from his attention, he tugs at the center of my panties, forcing the material down my legs until I can wiggle my underwear to my ankles.

"Step out of them." He uses his foot to hold the material to the floor, and I remove one leg, allowing my thighs to spread. Two fingers explore me under my hiked-up skirt, and his mouth returns to mine, kissing me like I might be that thing he wants most in life. That thing he wants to go his way.

As his fingers delve into me, I moan into his mouth. My knees give a little at the rushed intrusion, spurring my hips to match the thrusts of his fingers.

"Jake," I break away from his mouth, gasping for air, clenching for release. When his thumb starts to stroke over the trigger spot, I'm sliding down the pole at my back a little bit. I curl into him, desperate for the rumble in my body to release.

"God, you're beautiful," he says, glancing from my bra-covered breasts, heaving through my opened shirt, to his hand disappearing underneath my skirt. As my hips move faster, Jake begins to work his belt, releasing his pants' clasp and lowering his zipper. He one-handedly shoves his pants just below his hips.

Not once does he break stride in touching me.

"Need to be inside you again," he mutters, catching himself in his fist while his fingers work at me.

"Oh God, Jake. I'm so close," I warn, watching him touch himself and touch me. Sensory overload caused me to tip my head back to the pole, clutching it harder with my sweaty hands. My legs quake.

"There you go," he whispers as if he already knows my body, and I crash. The wave is lava over a volcano, pouring down the sides with heat and fire and red-hot lust. I lean forward for his mouth, taking it with mine as I ride his fingers and hold the fire pole. It's the craziest position I've ever been in, and I love it. I love everything about Jake because it's different. He's different.

Pulling back from his mouth when I come down from the high, Jake removes his fingers and lowers his jeans even farther. He reaches into his back pocket, pulling forth his wallet once more and dropping it to the floor once he has what he needs.

"I'm as clean as clean can be, but I'm using this to respect you."

I nod. I haven't been with anyone in so long I'm just as clean and certain I'm too old to get pregnant. Then I think of Scarlett, who became a momma at forty-two, and I agree with Jake's decision.

"Thank you."

With the condom on, he guides himself to my center. My skirt at my hips, but Jake forces my legs to spread wider. With one thrust, he's within me, and I squeak. He grunts in satisfaction, reaching around me for the pole, clutching it with one hand while the other comes to a breast. He moves like he dances, rhythmic and seductive. Sliding in and out of me like a man on a mission, he tugs one breast free again and lowers to suck the swell. I release a hand to touch his hair, but he pops off my breast.

"Hang on," he warns, moving faster, rocking harder. Pressed into the pole, Jake's hand remains behind me on it. His other hand comes to my hip, holding me in place as he bumps and grinds. His pelvis thrusts, and I squeeze around every surge of him inside me.

"God, Rita," he curses like he can't believe how incredible this feels. This energy between us. This connection we have. With the sensation of him driving into me, I'm ready to combust again, and I warn him with a slight cry.

He looks up at me, giving me that knowing smirk of his. His eyes twinkle with devilish delight. "That's it, sweet. Alive. On me." He smiles with pride, knowing what he's doing to me, knowing my body cannot deny what's happening. He shifts the slightest bit and taps me in a spot I didn't know needed tapping.

"Jake," I cry out. His name echoes in the empty space around us as my body caves a second time. My back arches while my head taps the pole behind me. My sweaty hands struggle for grip against the metal, but I hang on for dear life.

Jake uses the pole for leverage and surges forward, flattening himself to my body and pressing my back to the thick tube. A hitch to his breath is the only warning before he stills. Every pulse and pump prolongs my own lingering release. His forehead lowers for mine, and his hips tip forward once more with a final jolt. We remain like this until my arms collapse and circle around his shoulders. His forehead slides along mine until his face falls to the crook between my neck and shoulder.

"Don't disappear on me again," he whispers to me, and I hold him tighter.

How do I let him know I'm worried he'll do the same to me?

# JAKE

After our firehouse tryst, I ask Rita on a hike. I know the perfect place to take her. On Saturday morning, I meet her at her home. It's a classic two-story, L-shaped house with a long front porch. It looks newly painted in a mustard yellow color, and flowers in pots grace the wood decking of the light gray porch.

"Hey. Do I need anything?" Rita asks as I stand outside her front door.

"Just you." I smile, feeling both nervous and excited. I haven't been on a date in over seven years—there was Louisa, but I didn't count that—so, as much as I told myself this isn't one, I don't know what else an organized hike with a woman could be called. We've certainly put the cart before the horse by having sex first, and I'm looking forward to getting to know more about the woman behind the lusty eyes and sensual body. I can't stop thinking about her against that fire pole, and I warn my own pole to simmer down. Today is about discovery, not getting dirty with Rita. If that happens, I won't complain, but it isn't my intention.

I drive us in my truck until I find a spot to park near the river. I haven't been to this area for a while, and I had to look up places with walking trails for our day together. As we start out, we casually chat about the area.

"I grew up in Hampshire and never thought I'd be back here when I left for Boston."

"Wanted the big city and brighter lights?" I tease.

"I just wanted to make a difference in the world." Her voice softens.

"You do, with Building Buddies."

Rita snorts. "It's funny you should mention them as Alfred wants me to take over the directorship."

"Really?" I ask, watching my step as we follow the trail.

"He offered it to me almost two weeks ago, but I haven't decided."

"Why not?" I ask.

"I don't know. I guess I've been an attorney for so long I can't envision myself doing something else. The irony is, I've been feeling like I want to do something else with my life. Real estate contracts and farm disputes are fine, but I just want something . . . different."

"And Building Buddies isn't different?" I chuckle, noting it's quite the opposite of pushing papers and arguing cases.

"It is, it's just . . . I think I'm afraid of change."

My head pops up, and I glance over at her. Rita comes across as one of the strongest women I've ever known. I can't imagine her afraid of anything, least of all running something as great as Building Buddies.

"Who says you have to change anything? Maybe cut back on the law practice and increase the interest in Building Buddies. Or not. It's your life, Rita. Find something else that claims your passion."

Rita chuckles. "Is that what you're going to do with the firehouse?"

I laugh. "I'm not certain the firehouse is a reality. I looked into the cost of the place, not to mention all the work it would need. I don't think I can afford it." I'd been saving up for a house before Lisa pulled the plug on our marriage. I still had the money in savings, but I wasn't certain it would be enough to purchase an old fire station. Not to mention, I didn't really know what I'd do with the place. I just wanted it. It was something . . . different.

"You mentioned your brother when we were at the firehouse. What happened to him that makes you think you can't leave him?"

"Nolan was a volunteer fireman like I'd been, and he went into a burning building that collapsed. It clipped his lower back, essentially making him a paraplegic."

"I'm so sorry," Rita says, and I squint at the trail ahead of us.

"He's been struggling for years to regain his legs. His injury is considered incomplete. I don't understand all the details, but I'm told he was fortunate. It could have been worse." Nolan could have lost his life, and that would have been worse than anything else. "It's going to sound insensitive, but the injury really changed Nolan for the better. He was so reliant on me to take care of him, he didn't do much for himself other than follow in my footsteps. When he was on his own, with only his son to aid his recovery, he really grew up. He didn't let the chair bring him down."

"Was he also an electrician like you?"

"He was." I laugh, recalling how very similar our paths have been, but then I consider Rory and remember Nolan had a curveball thrown into his life. "I've always felt responsible for him. Our father left when we were still little. I became the man of the house at a mere eight years old, and I've been taking care of him ever since."

"That's a lot of pressure," Rita states, glancing up at me.

"I've put it on myself." I weakly smile, knowing the truth. No one other than myself made me feel that I had to care for Nolan or help my mother. "It's in my nature to take care of things." Of course, I messed up when it came to going to jail.

"Maybe it's time to take care of only you," Rita says, reaching forward for my arm.

"Maybe," I state, although I'm not certain how that would work. I've done a bang-up job of handling myself over the last seven years.

"I told you before I believe in second chances. This is yours." Rita gives me an encouraging smile. "Apply for a loan. Get a restoration grant. There are options if that firehouse is what you really want. Would you live there or use it as a business?"

Sheepishly, I look away from her, taking a step forward to suggest I'd like to keep walking. "I'm undecided." Although, I'm not actually. I'm just not ready to share my thoughts with Rita.

"You'll figure it out," she says, her voice full of encouragement as well. "You've already figured out everything else in your life. Why not this?"

I huff and nod, taking in her words. I'm not certain I believe her, but the confidence she has in me is refreshing. It would be nice to have a woman like Rita have faith in me.

Eventually, we come across a covered bridge crossing a narrow portion of the river.

"Don't you love a covered bridge? They're so romantic." Rita sighs. It's the first time I've heard her sound so wistful. I've also not given covered bridges much thought.

"Fan of romance, are you?"

Rita chuckles. "Once upon a time, but then happily ever after didn't happen." Her voice lowers. "I guess I believe in it for other people but not myself."

I want to ask her what happened to him. *What happened to her Ian?* But I also don't want to know. I don't want to bring her sob story into this date, even if her thoughts skip to him at the moment.

Stepping up to Rita, I grab her hand and tug her forward.

"What the heck?" she hollers as I pull her along, forcing her to run with me up the short incline and under the covering of the bridge. Once the shadow of the wooden structure covers us, I spin to face her.

"Holy cow, handsome. You nearly pulled my arm from its socket." Rita laughs, but her laughter is quickly captured by my mouth on hers. Our lips connect as I cup her nape and tug her to me, swallowing down the last dregs of her chuckle. She molds against me, and I walk her backward until her back connects with the inside of the bridge wall. Continuing to kiss her, I angle her head just so. So I can deepen the kiss. So I can invade her mouth with my tongue. So I can give her the romance she deserves under a covered bridge.

We kiss with heavy groans and hitching moans. My body grinds against hers. With one leg between her thighs, I rock my hip, pressing my hard length against her soft center. My hand reaches for a breast, kneading the firm swell, pinching the nipple peaked through her shirt. We're frantic for each other, making out like two kids stealing a moment. Only, I want all her moments.

I need to touch her skin and wonder briefly if I'll ever take Rita in a bed. My hand tucks under her shirt, finding her side warm from our exertion and the afternoon sunshine. Traveling north on her body, I almost connect my fingers with the silky fabric of her bra when a truck horn interrupts us. We break apart, and I look up as a pickup enters the bridge.

"Go get her, son," the driver calls out. If we don't get out from under the narrow confines of the bridge, he isn't going to be able to pass us.

With laughter on our lips, I drag Rita back out from under the bridge and down the slope again. The truck honks once more after exiting the wood structure, and Rita tucks her head into my shoulder.

"That was embarrassing." She rolls her forehead on my collarbone.

"Damn, I was hoping for romantic."

Her head pops, and blue eyes meet mine. "Oh. Oh, it was that, too." A slow smile curls her swollen lips, and I take them once more before deciding we better cool down or I'll do something even more embarrassing like take her along this path. Although I'm not thoroughly opposed to the idea, I don't want any passersby to see Rita in all her glory. I'm reserving that for only me.

"How do you feel about fishing?" I finally ask, pulling back with a final tug of her bottom lip before ending the kiss.

"Is that a euphemism for playing with your pole?"

"If it is, I like your thoughts, but I was thinking of actually fishing."

Rita is still tucked against my chest, and her eyes sparkle up at me. "I'm in," she states.

Slipping my arm over her shoulders, I lead us back in the direction of where I parked the truck, feeling for the first time in a long time like kissing a pretty girl under the afternoon sun might be proof of second chances.

After an afternoon of fishing, Rita invites me to dinner, and I'm grateful as I'm not ready to leave her yet. It's nice to be outside the house I share with my brother and away from the building project. It feels like it could be any other day, although it's not. I have Rita to share the time with me.

We end up working together in her kitchen to make a simple meal of roasted chicken and potatoes as well as steamed green beans and carrots.

"I don't typically cook like this for myself," she admits. "It's too much effort for one."

The comment reminds me Rita's been alone for a while.

"I'd like to ask about Ian, but if you don't want to talk about him, I understand."

"What do you want to know?" Her eyes remain on the carrot she's chopping.

"You were engaged, and something happened."

"He died." She says it so fast and sharp, the thrust of the knife through the carrot to the cutting board matches her tone.

"I'm sorry."

Rita shrugs, not glancing up from chopping, and I slowly

round the kitchen island. There have been updates to this large home which is too big for a single person. Coming up behind her, I cover her wrist with my hand.

"Stop." Rita stills her rapid slicing, and I press my nose into the crook of her neck. "You don't have to share if you'd rather not."

"It's just difficult to talk about, but I've actually been meaning to ask you something. I just didn't know how to bring it up. I don't even know if I want to discuss it."

The ominous tone raises the hairs on the back of my neck. "Ask me anything."

"Ian died in a fire. I was wondering if you worked on his case."

Suddenly, the air around me fills with heaviness. "I don't know. I don't recall every case, but if you give me more details, I can try to remember."

"He was—" Her phone vibrates on the counter, and Rita glances over at it. With my arms still around her waist, she reaches for the device and answers. "Hey, Scarlett."

A feminine voice filters through the phone, and I shift to release Rita from my hold, but she catches my forearm around her middle, and I still.

"I'm with Jake." Her voice softens as she says my name, and I'm assuming her friend knows a bit about me. I'm curious what she's told her, and I smile into the curve of her neck again. Tenderly, I pepper her skin with kisses before reaching the shell of her ear and nipping at it. Rita tips her head against mine, and a smile fills her voice.

"Yes," she says at first.

*Pause.*

"Not yet." She giggles.

*Pause.*

"Okay, next weekend." She laughs again and then hangs up after saying, "Bye."

"Scarlett?" I murmur into Rita's neck, working my way to her shoulder and tugging her shirt to the side to suck a trail along her skin.

"She's my best friend and wanted to know if I wanted to go to the farmers' market next weekend."

"That was a short conversation. Why were you giggling?"

"I don't giggle," she retorts, and I spread my hands over her belly, digging in my fingertips. Rita lets out a squeal and then that heavy snort she has on occasion.

"That sounded like a giggle."

"I sound like a piglet," she says, spinning in my arms and imitating the snort that escapes her on occasion.

"Here, piggy, piggy," I tease to her face, rubbing my nose against hers before pressing my lips to hers. Her arms wrap around my shoulders. "Tell me what she said that made you blush."

"She asked me if you were the same Jake I might have mentioned once or twice."

"Ah. Did you tell her I was handsome?"

"I might have called you a stud."

My lips curl as a brow hitches. "A stud, huh? Gonna ride me?"

"That was the *not yet* part."

I stare down at her before rubbing my nose along hers again. "Are you hoping to get something from me?"

"Whatever you're offering," she says, her voice dropping with an edge of seriousness. What am I offering her? I'm an ex-con without a job, living with my brother. I don't know what she could see in me.

"Should we finish talking about what we were discussing before the phone rang?" I ask, not wanting to return to a conversation about her ex but also not wanting her to think I'm blowing it off.

Rita's eyes focus on my mouth, and she shakes her head.

"Good," I state. "Because you have a riding lesson. Right

now." With that, I scoop her up, and she squeals again. Reaching awkwardly over at the oven, I turn it off and carry Rita to her room on the upper level.

# RITA

It should have felt strange to have Jake in my bed. I'd lived in my parents' home until I moved out in my thirties to live with Ian. Their house was large, and we didn't get in each other's way much. My parents moved their room to the first floor when my father had his first heart attack, and I moved home to help them out. Ian never spent the night here, never slept in my bed with me, so this was a new experience—just like everything else with Jake.

I hadn't ever had sex at a project site, and I certainly never had sex against a fire pole. I didn't make out under a covered bridge or kiss between fishing casts. Jake didn't keep his hands or his lips off me, and it was a new sensation. Ian and I weren't reserved, but PDA wasn't something he often did. He had a reputation to uphold, and I respected his position.

*Impressionable young minds are watching,* he'd say if I went to a school function with him.

Jake was everything opposite Ian. For one, the way he moved over my body, especially in my bed, made me feel cherished. It was a reminder he'd been locked up for seven years, but was his solitude any different than the prison I'd put my own heart in? I didn't want to feel things for him like I felt. I didn't want him to be that rebound May mentioned, but there was no denying I wanted him.

His mouth moved over my body, sucking at my jaw, down my throat, and along my collarbone. Commenting about the purple color of my undergarments, he quickly undressed me, and now I lay naked and sprawled out on my bed. His mouth moves to a breast. My legs spread to accommodate his body between them as he traveled down my middle, licking and nipping at me as he goes. Eventually, his teeth scrape at my inner thighs, and he spreads them wider.

"God, sweet," he groans, rubbing his nose over coarse hair before dipping lower with the tip of his tongue. I almost sprang from the bed at the first lap. He outlines slick folds before his lips clamp over my clit and a finger joins the ministrations. He retreats to delve deep with his tongue and then returns to that nub with his lips while two fingers thrust into me. My hips buck, and my head tips back. I don't remember the sensation of oral sex. The wetness. The slurping. The licking. It is too much and not enough, and I rock into his face as he lavishes me with that wicked tongue of his.

When I finally break, Jake redoubles his efforts, sucking me harder, working those two fingers faster through my soaked entrance.

"Another one," he demands against my lower lips, and I nearly scream as my body bows, and I release just as powerfully as the first time. Silver speckles dance before my eyes, and I'm not convinced I didn't pass out for a second. Jake tenderly bites the inside of my thigh before he brushes his scruffy jaw against the opposite one and crawls up my body. His mouth covers mine, forcing me to taste myself on him, something I'd never done before. It's dirty and delicious, and I realize my previous sex life had been slightly refined compared to Jake.

He pulls back, and I fear he's read my thoughts. Scooping his arm under my lower back, he flips our position and drops his voice. "Riding lesson." My legs straddle him on instinct. My drenched core meets the hard length of him, bare and thick. Coasting over him, the heavy moisture he created between my thighs dampens him. The movement drags my already swollen, ripe center in a striking manner against him. Like a flint to rock, I'm ready to spark again.

"Need inside you, sweet."

"Condom?" I question, and Jake twists his head on the pillow.

"My pants." We'd stripped out of our clothes as we stood at the end of my bed, and his pants are somewhere in that pile.

"Do we need one?" My voice hesitates. It was a risk. Even on the pill and with a condom, my best friend had gotten pregnant. "I have an IUD." I had one inserted a while back for feminine issues.

"Are you sure?" His question answers mine, and I slide to his tip, catching on the thick bulge before lowering my hand to guide him inside me. Gliding over his stiff length, bringing him into my body, he tips his head back as mine does when he's entered me in the past. A vein strains along his throat, and I lower to drag my tongue against the roughness of his jaw.

"Sweet, you're going to be the end of me."

I have no idea what that means, but my body knows what it needs to begin. I rock up his length, drawing myself to his tip as if I might release him. Then I lower to draw him deep inside. I repeat the movements, the rhythm building. Walking my hands down his chest until I sit upright over him, I use my knees to lift and lower me. Jake glances down to where he disappears inside me.

"Might be the prettiest sight I've ever seen." His eyes flick up to my face. My hair is all over the place as I roll my hips over him, moving faster with short, sharp thrusts. My fingertips dig into his belly while his hands pinch my hips, forcing me to rock harder. "So deep like this."

His stuttering tone tells me he's getting close, and I want him to give in to me. I want to feel the power of breaking this man. I want to be the end of him, as he said.

"I'll pull out," he warns around a shaky breath, returning his gaze to where I ride him.

"No," I hiss, afraid to lose the edge I'm experiencing, the crest that's climbing. Jake glances up at me.

"Sweet?" he questions, but I'm lost in my head, riding him for all he's worth, giving in to the all-consuming sensation of us joined together. I don't want to end the connection.

"Jake." His name catches in my throat, but I repeat it three more times before I still, clenching at him buried to the hilt inside me. His fingertips dig into my hips as he follows my lead and bucks upward, drilling himself deeper before coming alive within me.

Heavily breathing, Jake jackknives upward and grips the back of my neck. His mouth takes mine, fierce but tender.

"That probably wasn't smart," he mutters to my lips.

"For once, I wanted to use something other than my brain." My heart made me do it.

Jake seems to understand, and he returns to kissing me, tugging me down to my side on the bed. We stay just as we were, joined as long as we can before thoughts get in the way.

The week passes in a whirlwind of Jake and sex, and sex and Jake. I can't seem to stay away from the worksite, and Jake pulls me into a corner or empty space every second he can to kiss me silly. I'm drunk on this man who is dangerous for a recovering alcoholic. We're warned in AA about replacing one addiction for another, and I am heavily addicted to him.

The following Saturday, I give into some separation and attend the Norwich farmers' market with Scarlett as I promised. I meet her here as we came from different directions, and she has baby Harley with her. The market is in full swing as we saunter, and I babble on and on about Jake. How he invited me to his nephew's graduation from my alma mater. How we'd spent time together on a hike, cooking dinner, and hanging out. How the sex with him is incredible.

"You're quiet, lady," I tease as Scarlett has hardly said a word. "Bull stampede over you last night?"

Scarlett stops walking and turns to me. "Rita, we need to talk." The directness of her tone startles me. My comments can be over the top at times, but Scarlett knows this about me. Still, I quickly apologize, concerned by the tenor of her voice. My best friend waves it off as she leads us out of the mayhem of the crowd.

"I don't know how else to tell you this other than being straight with you." She reaches for my wrist and holds on tight once we stand off to the side of the vendors.

"Whatever it is, I can handle it," I assure her, but genuine fear creeps into my veins.

"I know you said not to look into him, but I couldn't help myself."

"Scarlett," I hiss, tilting my head.

"You're my best friend. You've been through a lot, and I just don't want to see you hurt."

"What did you do?" I ground out. The fine hairs on my arms rise.

"I did a little research."

My heart races faster. My belly feels ill. I should scold Scarlett for playing sleuth. I want to remind her that snooping into people's lives could lead to misinterpretation and misrepresentation, which is exactly what she did to Bull before she knew him. A reprimand would be justified, but I don't do it. Curiosity has the better of me.

"And?" I pause, trying to laugh off the anticipation but sickly sweat breaks on the back of my neck.

"Rita, he went to jail."

My shoulders fall, and relief washes over me. "Duh, chickie. I know this." So does she, as I've told her how he is a worker in the restorative program of Building Buddies.

"He went to jail for setting a fire."

My brows pinch. "He was an arson investigator," I state to defend him. He was a fireman. Firemen don't set fires. They put them out. Still, my heart hammers faster.

"He set the fire at Waterson Community High School."

"No," I whisper, my body breaking into feverish perspiration.

"I'm sorry, honey," Scarlett whispers to me, still clutching my wrist.

"I don't believe you," I say too quickly, too emphatically. My nostrils flare. My chest heaves. This cannot be true. Scarlett has been wrong in the past. She's skewed information. It's what she did as a gossip reporter. She lied.

"I don't believe you," I repeat, louder while my tongue grows thick, and my throat burns. Bile churns in my stomach.

Scarlett stares at me, pinning me with those large dark eyes of hers. "Remember it was an accident. I'm certain there's an explanation." The weak hope in her voice does nothing to dispel the anger rising inside me. There could be no excuse, accident or not. There can be no justification for killing an innocent man.

A man inside a high school, working late one night as the conscientious principal he was, double-checking something during his summer vacation when the building caught on fire. When the high school burst into flames, and a portion exploded, taking with it the life of the man I intended to marry.

*Ian.*

---

*Incredulous.* I do not want to believe any of it, but I break away from Scarlett, racing away from the farmers' market. I don't want to think anything until I speak to Jake. I'm a woman of facts and principles, and the best solution for answers is to go to the source.

I didn't know Jake's exact address other than he lives in Ashbury, a small town on Montpelier's west side. Calling Albert, I make up some excuse for needing Jake's address. Seconds after hanging up the phone, I don't even remember what I said, certain the excuse was not feasible but necessary.

Pulling up in front of the small, run-down home, the ramp before the house hardly stalls my ire. I stomp up the slight incline and harshly knock on the front door. When a man in a wheelchair opens it, I'm still not deterred although my breath catches at the similarity between brothers. Fuller in shoulders and rounded in face, he's still a twin to his older brother minus the salt-and-pepper scruff.

"Well, hello beautiful," he says, immediately flirting with me and giving me the charming smirk of a Drummond.

"Don't *hello beautiful* me, cookie. Where's your brother?" My body vibrates as I speak through the screen door. I'd like to open the barrier and let myself inside but refrain.

"Rita?" The questioning sound of my name and the smile I hear within his voice quickly fades when he sees me standing on his porch. "Rita, what's wrong?"

Jake steps outside, and I step back, putting much-needed distance between us. My body hums while the sickening sensation coils through my veins. I let this man enter my body. He's crawled into my heart. He stole my soul.

"Tell me why you went to prison, Jake."

"Rita," he whispers, taking a step toward me, hands lifting to touch me, but I stalk backward down the ramp, keeping space between us.

"Tell me," I demand, fisting my hands at my sides.

"I was accused of setting a fire."

I shake my head at the simplistic answer. "Not enough, handsome." The endearment is bitter, and Jake flinches at the term.

"What did you hear?" he questions, but I'm not here to speak. I'm here to listen.

"Talk," I command.

"There was a fire at a local high school."

"Which one?" I snap, not wanting anything left out and briefly closing my eyes as I brace myself for the truth.

"Waterson Community. It was a misunderstanding. I'd seen the blaze and stopped to investigate. As I was around the back of the building, an explosion happened."

My imagination runs wild. Visions of Ian I don't wish to see haunt my thoughts like ash floating in the air.

"Because you started the fire," I clarify, shaking so badly I'm surprised words even form in my mouth.

Jake sighs and tilts his head for the ground, shaking it side to side. "I was seen on the school surveillance cameras. It looked like I was exiting a side door and then wandering behind the building when the blast occurred, but I had not been inside. I'd been driving home after an arson investigation—"

"How ironic the arson investigator committed arson," I interrupt, not happy with his quiet tone or the sketchy holes in what he's telling me.

"It is ironic," he snaps back at me, his head lifting. "I didn't do it. And I wasn't allowed to investigate a crime I *hadn't* committed because it was determined before I was even tried that I *had* done it. There were holes all over the reports. It was completely inconclusive to catch me on camera at a door without proof I ever entered or exited the building that night, which I did not."

"There was someone in that building," I say through clenched teeth. "He could have let you inside."

"He didn't. I didn't know anyone was inside until after . . ."

"Until after the building burned and he died in those flames." My voice carries as my too-calm voice recounts what happened. Tears stream down my face at the truth.

"You set the fire that killed the love of my life."

15

# JAKE

"What?" I step toward her, hands primed to grasp her arms, but she backs up again, putting even more distance between us. "Rita, no."

Tears stream down her face, and my heart clenches from the hurt written in her expression. The hurt she thinks I caused her.

"Rita, I didn't do it," I say, pleading with her to believe me. Reaching for her once more, she trudges to the end of the ramp to keep space between us, and I stop halfway down the slanted structure.

"Then who did?" She turns back to me, her eyes question everything.

"I don't know." *Please don't doubt me.* It was difficult enough that I was going through a divorce when the fire happened but the added doubt from my ex-wife, a woman I'd loved, drove nails deeper under my skin. I couldn't handle that level of distrust when I'd been nothing but loyal my entire life. Loyal to my brother, to the department, to my wife.

"The arson investigator doesn't know who started the fire." Rita scoffs.

"I just told you I wasn't allowed to investigate the scene once I was a suspect." I couldn't defend myself. The department heads were afraid I'd tamper with what little evidence they had, and I wasn't allowed to examine the ruined building even though I'd been the best investigator the State ever had.

"Rita, you have to believe me. I didn't do it."

"Well, I don't." The finality in her tone tells me I have no hope of convincing her otherwise. After all we've shared, after all we've done, she didn't want to give me the benefit of the doubt. So much for second chances and fresh starts.

"I sure as shit didn't know anyone was inside."

"Stating that makes you sound guilty. It makes you sound like you set the fire where someone *was* inside."

"I didn't start that fire. I had been a volunteer fireman. I was the arson investigator. Why would I ever do such a thing? Why the hell would I start a blaze?" It was a question answered by the judge. He'd seen it before where cuts were made, and fire personnel took matters into their own hands. A fire was set to make a statement about the need for the fire department.

"Why not?"

"I didn't do it!" I holler louder. *Is she kidding me?*

"The county was trying to take away your job."

"So you think I set a fire to save myself?"

Rita huffs, assessing me for no more than a second. "Why the hell do people do anything?" she mocks. Her eyes roam the length of my body, but it's not the look of desire she's given me every time I've seen her in the past week. "Good people make bad decisions all the time."

"Am I the good person or a bad decision?"

Rita's eyes narrow behind her glasses. Unbelievable. I don't need this shit, and I don't need her.

"I didn't do it," I repeat through gritted teeth. This was the day of my arrest all over again, where I pleaded with the sheriff and arresting officers. People I'd known for years, who worked side by side with me to investigate crime scenes, only to have them not believe in me. My own anger rises.

"My brother could have died in that fire."

"And my fiancé did," Rita states again. The man inside was the high school principal, working during his summer vacation for some reason. There was no hint anyone was in the building. No car in the lot. No lights on in the school. For all I knew at first, the principal could have started the fire himself, but there hadn't been a motive or evidence for such a thing. It was assumed he hadn't desired his own demise, either.

In addition, my own brother was hurt in that fire as a first responder to the blaze. He could have died under the weight of a fallen support.

"I don't believe this," I mutter under my breath, swiping a hand into my hair before slipping to the back of my neck. I cannot catch a break in life. I have no idea where I'd gone wrong. My brother. My wife. My department. And now Rita.

Suddenly, I'm so angry. Angry with everything.

I don't need her acceptance. I didn't need her to believe in me, but I still thought she understood. Rita seemed like someone who would take me as I am. She'd already trusted me with her body. We'd spent time together, learning about each other. For all her talk of second chances, *she* felt like a second chance.

Hope is almost as bad as karma.

"I don't want to see you again," Rita states, and I cannot bite my tongue.

"Gonna be hard to do, sweet, as I work for you."

"We'll find you another placement."

Shit. *Shit.* This is bad. This is really bad. I could return to prison if Rita wants to take this to task. She could tell my parole supervisor what happened between us, or how the placement was a bad decision. She could tell the system she doesn't trust me. I could be investigated all over again. Insubordination for sleeping with the supervisor or something ridiculous like that would land me behind bars once more.

"Please, Rita," I beg, thundering down the remainder of the ramp. "I cannot go back to prison." Rita glances over my shoulder toward the front door, and her eyes soften for the breath of a second before her arms fall to her sides.

"Well, too bad."

Stopping in my tracks, I stare at her as she stares back.

"You don't mean that," I whisper, swallowing around the lump in my throat. "I'm sorry for your loss. I'm so very sorry, but I didn't set that fire. Do not send an innocent man back to that hellhole." My voice chokes around the possibility. It's been roughly a month. I have five more to serve.

Rita shakes her head, tears now dry as her eyes are ice cold.

"I can't do this," she says, turning away from me.

"Rita, wait." I catch her by the elbow, but she yanks her arm free, glaring at me. "Please."

"No, Jake." She looks up at me. "Your charm will not work on me this time." With that, I watch her cross my lawn and climb into her SUV, driving off with my heart and my destiny.

---

"Boy, that was rough," Nolan states as I re-enter the house, passing his chair and heading for the stairs. I need to get out of here. I need my keys for my truck and some escape.

"Fuck off, Nolan," I holler over my shoulder as I take the stairs two at a time.

"Yeah, that's what she said." Humor fills his voice.

Spinning on the stairs, I lean forward, gripping the railings as I glare down at my brother from my height on the staircase. "What did you say?"

"She kind of told you off, but who needs her?" Nolan scoffs, dismissing Rita, whom he's met for all of two seconds.

"Nolan, you don't know what you're talking about." I twist for the remainder of the stairs, but Nolan won't let it go.

"You don't need her making you feel guilty for something you didn't do," he states. His comment is like a knife to my back because Nolan doesn't get it. He wasn't in love with his high school sweetheart, who became the mother of his child. He never had a wife like I did. He's been reckless and loose his entire life, never giving his heart to another. Turning back for him, I brace my hands on the railing once more.

"You know what, Nolan? Just shut the fuck up."

"Dude," he mutters, chuckling under his breath.

"Dude, nothing. I like that woman. And she liked me. When she didn't know anything, she thought I was the shit. Do you know what that's like?" I glare at him, driving in my own knife of regret. Nolan isn't a bad man, but he makes poor choices.

"That's a low blow," Nolan hisses, squinting at me.

"No, it's not. All you do is think with your dick. It's how you ended up with Rory. It's how you ended up like this." I wave out at him in his wheelchair.

"This has nothing to do with my dick," he snaps, shifting his chair so he can face me head-on, but I'm half a flight above him.

"All you cared about in life was getting laid and having a good time. You had no concept of responsibility. You had no idea what it was like."

"What *what* is like?" He fights back. "Having my teenage years taken from me?"

"You did that to yourself, Nolan. You fucked a girl and had a baby. You took away your teenage years and spent the rest of your life still acting like a teen."

"Yeah, and you fucked some pretty pussy, and now you're just pissed because she doesn't believe in you. That's on her, Jake. You don't need that."

"No, it's on me because I went to jail for a fire I can't prove I didn't set, and that fire killed a man. A man I never met and loved that woman." I wave out toward the front door behind him at the base of the stairs. "He was her fiancé, did you know that? She loved him. Love, Nolan," I emphasize because it's an emotion I don't think he comprehends. "And now, she'll never look at me again."

"Love?" Nolan scoffs again. "Now who's thinking with his dick?"

I make it down the stairs so fast, I'm not certain I've touched them. Gripping my hands on the armrests of his chair, I lean over my brother, getting right in his face.

"Have you ever been in love, Nolan? Were you the one married? Oh wait, that was me, your brother. Whose wife came onto you and wanted to sleep with you while I was in prison for a crime I didn't commit. So don't preach to me about thinking with my dick."

"Fuck you, man," Nolan yells at me. I should feel sorry for him and his condition. I should apologize for my outburst, but I don't have it in me. I've coddled my brother for too long.

"No, fuck you, little brother." I turn for the stairs once more, making a show of using my legs to hike up them two at a time. When I return down them, Nolan is no longer in sight, and I don't care.

I don't care about anything but getting out of here.

I couldn't say I cried myself to sleep because that would imply I actually slept. For over twenty-four hours, I sat and stared, fighting the pull to close my swollen eyes. The nightmares behind my lids threatened to return with a vengeance. The betrayal I felt ran deep within my veins. I hadn't felt this lethargic in seven years.

Thoughts of Ian filled every crevice I worked hard to seal over that time. Machlian—*Ian*—Sanders had been the love of my life. I was a late bloomer in respect to love. I'd had sex, but that deep-rooted desire to be with one man had not settled in my heart until him. I wouldn't say I was a loose cannon before him; I just enjoyed having a good time. I blew off steam where I could, but I didn't have one-night stands, and I didn't date long term until Ian. I worked with my father in his law practice, and I had Building Buddies to fill the gaps.

We met through the program. As Waterson Community's principal, Ian ran a summer service retreat for his students. Instantly, I loved his demeanor with the teenagers. He understood them on an elemental level that offered them respect while enforcing his authority over them. In my early thirties, my ovaries were calling, and his interaction with the older kids was endearing.

Eventually, he asked me out for a drink. One date turned into two years of dating before Ian popped the question. My father died in that time, and perhaps that prompted Ian to finally ask me to be his wife. Prior to that, we'd fallen into a routine as two working adults in no rush for the next step, but still, my ovaries were knocking.

Our wedding was scheduled to be a late summer affair so it didn't conflict with the high school calendar. As principal, Ian didn't have summer hours like his teacher colleagues. He only had a few weeks off in July, but it hardly stopped him from entering his building. He always had something else to work on. As a school with high graduation rates and rising test scores, he prided himself on the accomplishments he'd achieved. He certainly made me feel like he'd done more in his few years as a principal than I'd done in ten years as a lawyer at that time.

The night of Ian's death was a week before our wedding. He wanted to check on something before we met for dinner to discuss some final wedding arrangement that no longer seemed relevant to remember. The only memory I have now is a phone call I received informing me of a fire at the high school. An explosion had occurred. My future husband was dead days before our marriage began.

I never understood why Ian didn't get out of the building. Standard fire drill procedures teach children starting at the age of four to exit a school building when the alarm rings. The investigation into the explosion found fault with the alarm system. I didn't know all the particulars. I never wanted to read the report.

The sudden sound of feet on my front porch turns my head from my perch in my great-grandmother's rocking chair. I'm sitting in my parents' old bedroom on the first floor, feeling their loss more than ever. At forty-three, I want my father. I could call my mother, but I don't really want to talk. After several calls from Scarlett, I turned off my phone, finally sending her a text to say I'd call her later, leaving *later* open-ended.

Slowly, I stand from the old wooden chair and walk to the

curtain-covered window looking out at the porch. Only a finger's length presses back the sheer material, but I quickly pull back when I see Jake standing on the porch, a Busy Bean Café to-go cup in his hand, and some other object under his arm. I press myself flat to the wall beside the window and close my eyes as if that will hide him from my mind.

As much as I've been recalling Ian, I've been struggling with thoughts of Jake. When I first returned from his house, I showered. I couldn't get the water hot enough to scrub myself clean of what I'd been doing with him. With trembling hands, I next called my AA sponsor who I hadn't reached out to in a while. I didn't need a drink as much as I needed someone to talk to, someone unbiased, unlike Scarlett, who might have been tainted by what she'd learned. As much as I wanted to curse my friend, the rational side of me said she was only looking out for me. The irrational side felt like my heart had been ripped out once again.

Because, like it or not, I had fallen for Jake, the hunky, swanky charmer. I'd been hooked like the fish we caught only a week ago. Now, I was released. Tossed back into the cool water to flounder with my emotions as I struggled to regroup.

Eventually, I hear the tender footsteps of his retreat and the gentle hop down the front steps. A truck engine roars to life, and I glance at the digital red numbers on my parents' old alarm clock. Jake is on his way to Building Buddies, where he'll continue his parole. A probationary period he has because he went to prison for starting a fire that destroyed a school and took a life.

*Rita, you have to believe me. I didn't do it.*

Isn't that what all criminals say? I'd never defended a case for a crime like arson, but I imagine anyone accused would plead innocence.

My body sags against the wall as innocence before proven guilty is always presumed in my line of work. Jake must have been found guilty despite his confession to me. A collection of his peers or perhaps even a single judge found him responsible for a crime. The proof was in the decision.

Still, my head taps against the wall at my back because I want to believe him. I want to believe he couldn't possibly start that fire. The Jake I'd learned more about in the past few weeks wasn't vicious or vengeful or even unkind. He was funny. He was charming. He loved to dance, and he had glorious sex just like he moved in sync with the music. He kissed me under a covered bridge when I said I wanted romance. He fucked me against a pole when he wanted to be reckless. He made me feel alive, like I haven't felt in years.

Most of all, I had to accept that Jake never intended to kill Ian. My former fiancé's death was ruled involuntary manslaughter. Essentially, he was an unplanned circumstance of the initial crime. *An accident.* It was difficult to wrap my head around the concept. It also didn't explain the fire and Jake's role in a blaze that destroyed half a building.

My eyes close again, but I've had enough of my cycling thoughts. Pressing off the wall, I decide to head to the office in hopes of losing myself in work as I'd done since the day Ian died. I press back the curtain just enough to check again that Jake is gone. Then I make my way to the front door to retrieve the coffee and the object he left behind next to it.

---

Sitting at my desk, I vacillate my eyes between the object Jake left for me and my laptop. Once I arrived at the office, I felt like a sick joke had been played on me. I've turned so many contracts and cases over to May, I don't have anything pressing to busy myself. Instead, I went through a stack of mail in hopes of avoiding the object on my desk and found an invitation to Vermont Law's summer graduation ceremony. Alumni are always invited to support the future bar members. Flipping the card stock in my hands, I stare blankly at the lettering and recall how Jake invited me to attend his nephew's commencement.

*"My brother and I are so proud of him. We always knew he'd be something more than either of us."*

I hadn't liked how Jake put himself down at the time he mentioned the future accomplishment of his nephew. Jake's life hasn't been a failure. At least, not from what he's told me. He'd been a success in his own right, working his way through an apprenticeship to become a master electrician while volunteering as a fireman and raising his brother, and eventually, helping raise his nephew. He'd given up a lot to see that his brother turned out to be more than a teenage dad and his nephew leveled up. The recall puzzles me as it's a reminder that Jake has been loyal to his family and hardworking at that. However, he could also be an excellent liar, and everything he's told me could be total bullshit.

Then I look over at the unique sculpture sitting on my desk. It's made of industrial pieces—plumber pipes, copper conduit, and electrical wiring—positioned in a manner it looks like an abstract person fishing. I'm assuming it's a woman with flowing hair in strips of copper material mixed with electric wire wrapped in gray casings. She holds a pole made of another copper pipe with a thin wire dangling off it. A miniature light bulb hangs from the wire, representing a fish. An engraving on the bottom of the lamp reads: *Hook, link, and sinker, you've captured me.* I don't understand the significance of the lamp other than the fishing metaphor, and the fact Jake and I spent a day doing such a thing.

"Rita?" My name draws my attention to May standing before my desk. Her eyes fall to the to-go coffee cup and then drift to the artistic piece. "What's this?"

Her fingers reach forward but don't actually touch the artwork. There's really no other way to describe the fixture before me.

"I don't know. It was on my porch along with the coffee this morning."

She's still smiling, but tears blur my vision once again. I should have tossed the coffee, but that's a waste of perfectly good liquid gold.

As I reach for a tissue, May clears her throat and lowers for the chair opposite my desk.

"I'm assuming the tears are heartbreak and not excellent nookie," she assesses of the sudden swipe to my eyes. "What happened?"

May's soft voice opens the fountain, and I explain the events of the past forty-eight hours. I tell her what Scarlett did and how Jake responded when I confronted him.

"First, let me ask if you are okay? Did you drink?" Moments like these could certainly push someone off the proverbial wagon.

"I'd considered it for all of three seconds. Then I called Meredith." Meredith had been my sponsor from the start. As a fellow lawyer, she took me on when I decided I needed help and wanted a professional women-only AA group. Talking amongst peers felt like the right course of action in attempts to keep my law practice afloat while I tried to navigate my emotions.

"But you didn't drink?" May confirms, and I nod. "Okay. Next, he didn't hurt you, right?"

My head pops up, and I stare at my young friend. "Jake isn't violent."

"Right," she states. "Broken heart, not broken body." May pauses again. Her mouth opens and shuts as her hands clasp together on her lap.

"Just speak your thoughts, cookie," I weakly demand.

"Is it possible he's telling the truth?"

"He was found guilty," I state, reminding May of Jake's circumstance.

"Yes, but . . ." She waves, her eyes drifting to the unusual lamp on my desk. "We both know there is fault in the system sometimes. Who was his lawyer? Maybe we can contact him or find the old case report."

"I have it," I mutter, lowering my eyes to the law school invite on my desk.

"You have the report? Have you read it?"

My lids close, and I shake my head. "I can't bring myself to do it." The declaration makes me sound like a coward. I feel like a coward, but I just cannot read the document and remain impartial to the details. This isn't a case study with random persons but my former fiancé in the file.

"Let me read it," May states. "I'll pull out questions if I find any."

"May, it won't matter. What's done is done. He went to jail for setting a fire. He's served the time for the crime."

May sighs. "You remember my friend, Jude, right?"

"The silent, broody one?" I've met the entire Shipley clan and their friends on a few occasions.

"Yes, the one who came to live at the farm for a while. He's also in recovery for narcotics." I stare at May, waiting on her point. "He was convicted of a crime and served time for it as well, but it was later proven he didn't do it. He was exonerated."

I recall the details of the crooked police chief and his son's untimely death.

"That's a wonderful story, cookie, but what does it have to do with Jake?" My tongue swells on his name, and my hand lowers for my chest, where I ache inside like I've only ever hurt one time before.

"I just think you need to do your own investigation into the case. Find out why he set the fire, if he set the fire."

May's right. I shouldn't accept the hearsay of Scarlett's research, and I hadn't listened long enough to Jake to allow him an explanation other than the basics.

"I don't know if I can," I admit, hating once again the defeat in my tone and lack of will in my drive. Then I admit my greater concern. "I don't know if I can be with a man who burned down a building. It was a crime, the very thing I defend against. For a moment, forget Ian in the equation. I've been so wrapped up in lust with Jake that I've ignored the fact he committed a crime," I reiterate. "Holding people accountable for their actions is important to me. It's the essence of our restorative program in Building

Buddies, yet I've been blindsided by a sexy smirk and pretty eyes."

May weakly grins. "We've all been duped by lust at one time or another. You're raw today, Rita, but for your own peace of mind, you need answers. Maybe not today, tomorrow, or even next month, but soon you'll want to know the truth. Your curiosity will best you, my friend."

She's absolutely right. My desire for facts and details, and justice to be served, will prevail.

I'll want to know more.

Just not today.

Probably not tomorrow either.

Maybe not even next month.

But soon, I'll want the truth.

# JAKE

For a week, Rita avoids the building site, and every day I wait on her at the Bean in hopes she'll show somewhere neutral so we can talk. It's torture, and by Friday, I've decided I'm waiting on false hope. I'm ready to leave the Busy Bean, taking the last dregs of a second cup of coffee I shouldn't have so late in the day when Rita enters. She does a double-take at me as I sit on the plush peach couch where my attraction to her started. Where she cussed me out for taking her spot, and lust filled my thoughts about taking her on this sofa. Now, my emotions are so much more than lust. *Was I in love with her?* I'd almost said as much to Nolan, but that might have been a rash declaration after such a short time. However, I'm old enough to recognize how I feel, and what I felt was honest and real.

I watch as Rita places her order, waits on her mug, and then crosses the distance to stand before the couch. She glances at the emptiness beside me.

"Is this seat taken?" The vulnerability in her voice is everything opposite what I know of her.

"Only by you," I admit, giving her a weak smile that falls short when she doesn't smile back. I clear my throat as Rita lowers for the velvety cushion but doesn't relax into the couch. Watching her lift the mug for her lips—lips I've missed kissing—I stare as she sips and swallows the warm brew. I miss her tongue wrestling with mine. I miss her arms around me. I miss her body against me.

"Did you like my gift?" I ask, finding it difficult to know where to start.

"It was very interesting," she states. "A lamp is . . . different." Uncertain how to read her impression of the piece, I don't press. Rita remains quiet.

"I didn't do it," I start, but when Rita's eyes close, I realize I need to start at the beginning. "I was driving home that night from an investigation. There had been a series of unexplained fires in the area. Vacant warehouses. Three in total. I was completely baffled by them. There was no connection between the warehouses, only their vacancy. Normally, a string of fires has a link. A disgruntled employee, perhaps. Even faulty wiring could have been linked back to a similar manufacturer or a poor electrician, but it wasn't that either. I prided myself on assessing situations easily and efficiently. I understand fire—its pathways and how it moves—but these blazes made no sense to me."

Fire to me was like a dance. It thrived on oxygen and followed a pattern of movement. It was almost sensual how it could lick and lap along on an object before bursting to life. I'd been very good at my job, decoding fire's motive and movement.

Rubbing my hands against my thighs, I glance around us. We're rather secluded where we sit, and other than a woman at a table typing away at her laptop, the Bean is empty. Still, I keep my voice low as I continue.

"I was almost home. I'd been living with my brother again as my ex-wife and I were separated. Passing the school was on my way. I noticed the blaze immediately upon rounding the corner and pulled into the parking lot. My nephew and a group of his friends were present, just watching the building burn."

I pause, swallowing around the lump in my throat as Rita closes her eyes again.

"When I confronted the boys, they took off, but I chased Rory." I follow with his explanation about the fireworks and the boys smoking behind a maintenance shed. There's no reason to keep the details from Rita. She deserves to know the truth, and I never believed my nephew was guilty.

"I decided to investigate, rounding the building, looking for open doors. It was stupid, actually. Everyone knows you don't enter a burning building." Licking my lips, I decide to skip the next details about the blast. Glass shattering. Windows exploding. The heat of flames pouring from the school. "Video surveillance of the schoolyard caught me walking away from a side door I checked for entrance and around the back of the building, but I swear on my life I never entered that building that night."

Rita continues to hold her coffee mug with both hands, eyes forward as I speak to the side of her face. Her red-framed glasses hide her eyes, and I desperately want her to look at me.

"Rory thought he and his friends set the fire." Rita finally faces me. "He thought a firework gone wrong might have broken through a window, but it just didn't add up. And when the investigation discovered the fire alarm had been dismantled—"

"The fire alarm was dismantled," Rita repeats, her voice quiet and low, processing what I've said, before adding, "I don't recall hearing about fireworks."

"I told the boys not to mention it."

Rita stares at me. "Why would you do such a thing?"

"Because Rory was only seventeen. I didn't need him admitting to something out of fear or guilt. He was almost eighteen and would have been tried as an adult, even if it was an accident. His chances of pre-law would be ruined."

"Ruined," Rita echoes under her breath.

"It didn't make sense that a stray firework started the blaze." I pause for a moment, recalling my own doubts about the possibility of a firework setting the building on fire. It wasn't an impossibility.

We'd heard of it in the department, but it was rare unless the explosive was already within the building. Rory admitted a few of the explosives the kids used were self-made, which was all kinds of dangerous in its own right, but it still didn't explain if one fired into the school. He was adamant they had aimed all the fireworks away from the structure. Still, a loose cannon is a loose cannon.

"When Nolan was injured in the fire—"

"Nolan?" Rita questions, shifting slightly on the cushion to face me better.

"My brother was one of the first responders. The second floor collapsed and narrowly missed killing him. Remember I told you he injured his back."

"Yes, but you said he was injured in a building . . ." Rita lets the rest of her statement drift. The building was a school. I guess I hadn't specified.

"While my brother was still in a medically induced coma because of severe burns and his injuries, I was arrested. I never believed Rory and his friends did it, but I also couldn't even hint at the suggestion. The prosecutor was looking for a fall guy, and I couldn't risk Rory being taken from Nolan on a possibility rather than fact. My brother needed his son." I couldn't risk separating them on suspicion. Nolan had already lived without a father. Rory would not suffer the same.

Rita's eyes widen. Her brows lift. "You withheld information."

"A firework didn't start that blaze," I repeat.

"You don't know that."

"I do." It was my job to understand fire, and a firework did not do the damage caused by that blaze. "The investigation said faulty wiring started the fire, but was it an accident or tampering? The blaze started in the chemistry lab where chemicals aided in the explosion."

"I don't understand how you were *accused*, then," Rita emphasizes a word I don't mistake, and her eyes narrow at me.

"The evidence was circumstantial. My appearance on camera,

along with my presence as the first on the scene, perpetuated potential. Plus, my knowledge of fire, all the way down to my skill with electrical wiring, caused probability. I could have done it, had I entered the building, had I had intent, which I didn't on both counts."

"Your nephew could have been an alibi. Maybe he saw something or someone else."

"He didn't." The boys were too busy getting high behind the maintenance shed and reveling in their fireworks to notice someone sneaking in or out of the building. Plus, I didn't want Rory linked in any way to that fire. "The judge concluded that the circumstances of the fire department at the time warranted additional motivation."

"What circumstances?"

"The State didn't think an arson investigator was necessary. Some departments were being shut down. Others were being consolidated. Cutbacks in paid positions occurred, which included job loss for chiefs and increased the need for volunteers."

Nolan had been up for a chief position. He was just as upset as I was when the State's discussions dwindled to us. I'd be losing my job. He'd be losing a chance at a promotion. "I still don't understand."

"The judge felt I had intent. He'd seen it before where firemen started fires to save jobs."

"That's absurd. This isn't . . . *Backdraft*." She snorts in that manner she does as she mentions an old movie where this same action occurred in fictional terms.

"It's the same thing you accused of me," I remind her, recalling how she seemed to agree with the judgment that I had a reason to start a fire, causing potential harm to fellow firepersons, destroying any possibility to retain my job. Rita has the wherewithal to look chagrined for a moment.

"None of it mattered. I couldn't prove my own innocence

because the investigation wouldn't allow me to investigate my case. My career was ruined."

"Ruined," Rita repeats, the word choking her as it did the first time she repeated it.

"I'm sorry again for your loss, Rita. I'm truly sorry. I didn't know . . . your fiancé . . . but Rory did, and he said he had the highest respect for him. I think all the kids did." Despite the school being in a state of disrepair and the summer break allowing students time away, the funeral attendance was something never seen before. Kids from five communities gathered to give their condolences and pay their respects. My stomach flips as I imagine Rita in the receiving line and eventually hovering at the grave site.

"You ruined everything for me," Rita states incredulously, keeping her voice low.

"Rita, I just explained—" Her hand in the air stops my speech.

"My fiancé was taken from me, but I'd come to terms with that loss a long time ago. A reckless act resulted in his death. I'm not talking about Ian. I'm talking about the fact that after years of recovery and counseling to adjust to his loss, I'd finally found myself in a good place. I dedicate myself to helping others through AA and Building Buddies. I have my practice. I refurbished my parents' home, and then I met you. *You* ruined me, not because of what you did or didn't do in the past, but because of what we did together. I gave myself to you, and it felt so different. Even . . . more than what I had with Ian." Rita chokes around the admission, and her eyes blink rapidly.

"You didn't trust me with the truth. If you had only told me . . ." She takes a gulping breath. "I don't know how I'll go back to who I was or rather move forward."

She looks around us, rubbing her hand on the cushion next to her thigh. Confusion fills her expression for a second, and she quietly speaks. "You've even ruined this couch for me."

Next, tears fill her eyes. "But I always recover," she says to the velvety material.

Slowly, she stands and exits the Bean. Carrying a Busy Bean coffee mug in her hand, she takes my heart with her. I stare after her, knowing nothing I say will bring her back to me. Even the truth won't set me free because the truth is still out in the elusive there. I'll never know what happened that night. I only know I've lost a woman who has ruined me just as she feels I ruined her.

[18]

# RITA

The following morning, I meet Scarlett at the Busy Bean Café. I couldn't keep ignoring her, and I needed to apologize for reacting as I had to the information she shared a week ago. She was only looking out for me as a friend. Also, I needed a baby Harley fix.

"You sure you're okay with this?" Scarlett questions as she greets me outside the café. She knows how I feel about the location and the couch I accused Jake of hogging.

"I'm not going to hide," I tell myself as much as reassuring my friend. When Ian passed, I'd fallen into a slump, allowing myself a month to wallow and wane over his loss. Then I picked myself up, or so I thought, returning to work with drinks on the regular when I clocked out for the day and wine before bedtime. By the time I'd made the horrible mistake of throwing myself at a man I can hardly remember and finding myself on the floor of my place, I realized I was still hiding behind a bottle in the shape of Tanqueray or a good red.

Scarlett opens an arm for me, and I step into a side hug from her while she jostles Harley on her other hip.

"Give him to me," I coo, wiggling my fingers for the little man, and Scarlett passes the growing baby into my arms. As I enter the café, I hadn't realized I was using Harley as a shield until I let out a huge sigh of relief that Jake is not present on the favored couch. Taking Harley with me to said sofa, Scarlett steps up to the counter to greet Roderick and a new worker behind the counter.

Once seated on the plush peach fabric, I focus on the baby on my lap, inhaling his sticky, sweet scent. My eyes prickle with a reminder of all I'll never have, but I rapidly blink back the threat of tears. I don't want to cry anymore.

"Tell me everything," Scarlett says as she comes to sit beside me, holding two steamy mugs in her hands. I break into what I'd learned only the night before in this same spot, telling her everything right down to the strange lamp he'd given me.

"A lamp?" Scarlett questions.

"Or a light. I'm not certain what to call it. It's very artistic and obviously handmade, but I don't understand its significance."

Scarlett ponders the gift for a moment before asking, "Do you believe him?"

Focusing on Harley, I answer Scarlett. "I want to believe him. Something deep inside me says there is no way Jake could have done it. He couldn't start a fire. But I just don't know. I don't know him." The statement is more a reminder to myself than Scarlett.

*What do I really know about Jake Drummond?*

I know how his lips taste and his mouth feels as he travels over my skin. I know how he looks when he enters me, his expression always full of wonder at our connection. I know how charmingly he smiles and how he knows it gets to me every damn time he uses it on me. I also know he's been loyal to his family and worked hard his entire life, giving up his own dreams to take care of others.

It hits me that I'd done the same thing for my family. When my father had his first heart attack, I returned for him. When my father became a judge, I took over more of our practice, falling into all the places I am now: a practicing attorney, a Building Buddies supervisor, a woman alone.

"I think you should trust your gut. If it's telling you Jake didn't do it—couldn't do it—then you need to go with that feeling. Find out more information."

"You sound like May," I state, holding Harley's little fists and tapping his pudgy knuckles together.

"What does May say?"

"I should investigate." Scarlett perks up next to me, and I have to level her with my best glare. "Not that kind of investigation."

"What?" she teases, holding a hand to her chest in innocence. My friend might have played a sleuth in the past, but she didn't always do it through proper channels, having used false sources and sketchy connections to report the goods on Hollywood's elite and bad-boy athletes. But this was Jake. "I'm a genuine investigative reporter."

"Was," I remind her. "Past tense and presently mother to one beautiful baby. Isn't that right, Harley? We need to keep snoopynose mommy out of trouble."

Scarlett chuckles. "Well, that's better than some names I've been called in the past." We both glance at Harley, who responds to his mother's laughter with a large, drooly smile. His dark eyes match hers and seek her next to me as I continue to tap his little knuckles together. Scarlett reaches out a hand and strokes her palm over her son's fuzzy head.

"You need to believe in miracles, Rita. Weren't you the one telling me the universe works in mysterious ways, and there are signs all around us?"

"Did I say that?" I softly chuckle, sensing the universe speaks to others, but I have no idea what it's been trying to tell me for the past decade.

"Maybe Jake was put in your path for a reason," Scarlett states, still speaking toward her son while addressing me. "Maybe his presence is more than restoration for him, but restoration for you. He's your sign to move on."

"I have moved on," I snap, a little harsher than necessary.

"But have you really?" Scarlett asks, softening her voice. "I know you submerge yourself in Building Buddies, and you have a successful practice. You're a great supporter of Alcoholics Anonymous. Those are all noble and self-assuring in many ways, but what are you doing for you, Rita? Where's that stud you demanded over a year ago?"

My mouth falls open, but Scarlett raises the hand she's been stroking over Harley's head to stop me from speaking.

"I know you're all independent woman and a man doesn't define you, but . . . don't you miss love, Rita? Don't you miss sex? And before you say Ian was your stud, think again. He was a wonderful man, dedicated to teenagers and higher education, and he was good to you, but he's gone, and you're still here. You're alive, Rita. You need to live."

"I have been living," I remind her. I don't feel dead inside or even numb, but when I consider what Scarlett's trying to say to me, I realize the truth. I've been content, like a steady stream instead of rolling rivers and crashing oceans. I've been moving forward at a trickling pace when I really want to rumble, tumble, and refresh. I want to be happy.

"You know what I mean, Rita, but I'll spell it out just in case. You have before you a second chance to love."

"I can't love Jake," I snap, more defensive than I need to be.

"You can if you want to."

I shake my head and turn my gaze up toward the ceiling, toward the beams painted in chalkboard paint. Little quotes and inspirational sayings are written on the beams, and I stare blindly at the words at first while my thoughts race.

*Could I love Jake?* Despite his past, could I see around all that's happened to him and how he connects with me? In Alcoholics Anonymous, one of our key philosophies is accepting our responsibility in our addiction. We are powerless to the pull and must accept ourselves as we are. But there's also an underlying acceptance of others. No judgments. No prejudges. Accept that others have made mistakes, paid for them, and now must move forward.

When I think about Jake and how dedicated he's been to his work at Building Buddies, I can't help but give him the benefit of the doubt that he is trying to move on. He's been rather accepting of his circumstance. He was convicted of a crime he claims he didn't commit, but he served the time and can't get it back. He could easily be bitter. He could have blamed his nephew or faulted his department, but he didn't do either of those things. He came to terms with his fate.

My eyes narrow in on the beams above me, and I slowly stand, lifting Harley in my arms, to focus on a line of scribble facing the plush peach couch.

"Rita?" Scarlett questions, but I step around the low table before us as if I can see better what's written over my head. Scarlett stands as well, following my gaze, and then her breath hitches.

"It says what I think, right?" I don't take my eyes from the chalk writing.

"It does." A smile fills Scarlett's voice as she turns her attention back to me. I, however, cannot take my eyes off the beam.

"Is it a sign?" Scarlett whispers as I stare at the scrawled letters.

"It's a sign," I quietly echo.

*Don't lose faith in me, sweet.*

* * *

On Monday, I'm headed to the office when another gift sits on my front porch along with another Busy Bean coffee cup. The new piece looks again like a person, a man perhaps, whose midsection is an old metal lantern. Another abstract head is attached with tubing for arms and legs, complete with feet and fingers. The lantern isn't large, and the bulb inside is the size of a dining room chandelier. The inscription on the bottom of this one reads: *You light me up.* When the light is on, a faint heart illuminates to the upper left portion of the bulb. I can't help but smile at the arrangement and the title.

Setting the lamp on a table just inside my front door, I want to leave the light on as a greeting when I return home later but decide against it.

Sitting at my desk, I'm deep in thought, clacking away with knitting needles in hand. The subtle tap of needles along with the steady stitching settles my mind. I'm wearing a summer dress, and the material is tucked between my knees to prevent all the goods from showing as my feet are propped up on the corner of my desk. I'm also wearing an old pair of Converse instead of my hiking boots as the days are warming up.

"You're looking better," May says as she enters our shared office.

"I'm feeling better, thank you," I reply, not missing a stitch. I've had a long weekend to consider all Jake told me about his situation—a crime he didn't commit.

"Did you talk to Jake?" May asks, and I settle my needles for a second. Shaking my head feels like admitting I'm a coward. I just don't know what to say to him.

Silence falls in our office, and I resume knitting. *Knit two purl two.* Suddenly, the clacking of my knitting needles sounds too loud, and I glance over at May, blindly working the yarn.

"What is it, chickie?" My younger counterpart is staring at me.

"He rocked your bedsheets."

"I never said he rocked my bedsheets," I scoff, fighting the sheepish grin that comes with instant images of Jake and me in my bed. There was that time he loosely tied my wrists and then he . . . I bite my lip and glance up at May. "It was a fire pole."

"Ri-*ta!*" My name screeches through the office. "You skipped a few details."

I laugh, not willing to share more. "I'm just trying to keep things in perspective. It was only lust. Good lust at that, but nothing more." However, my heart drops to my belly with the thought. Was it really that simple? Was sex all we had? It wasn't. We laughed. We'd argue a little. We'd kiss a lot. I don't think I've smiled as much in years as I had in a week with Jake. It felt . . . good.

"I don't believe you." May's voice softens, her eyes narrowing in on me, and I stop my knitting and drop my feet from the corner of my desk to face her better.

"What's to believe?"

"I've worked across from you for over five years, lady. Nothing you do is off the cuff other than your remarks. You dive in with intention and purpose to everything, and I don't think Jake Drummond was any different. He means something to you."

"You told me he was my rebound man."

"I never said that." May's voice rises. "I said I *didn't* think he was a rebound. You bounced a long time ago. This is more." Her eyes drop to the sweater in my hands, and her breath catches. "Is that for him?"

"Maybe. He said purple is his favorite color." At least, it's his favorite color on me. I fight the blush on my cheeks at the recall of all the times Jake commented on my purple undergarments.

"You can't knit him a sweater. He'll break up with you."

"We already broke up," I remind her, swallowing back the lump in my throat. I've been telling myself all weekend it was for the best. I can't be with him. *Because of Ian.*

"You can't knit him a sweater without a ring."

I tip my head to lower my glasses and peer over them at my dear young friend. "What?"

"You know the rule. You can't knit your boyfriend a sweater. Knit him anything else but not a sweater. When you get a ring, then you can knit him a sweater."

"Boyfriend? Ring?" I scoff. "I'm a little old for a boyfriend, and no one is talking rings. Besides, we are not together."

My attention returns to knitting this beautiful purple yarn into a sweater, but May has stood from her desk and rounded to mine.

"Rita Kaplan, I forbid you to give that man a sweater. He is your boyfriend or boy toy or man machine or whatever you want to call him, and I will not let you ruin your love life by giving him a sweater."

She holds out her hand like a mother demanding the cookies stolen from the jar before dinner.

"You are being ridiculous."

"And so are you. You like this guy. Let it happen." Her voice softens. "There's nothing wrong with falling in love again."

My sweet chickie had her heart broken once upon a time and then found love in her beau, Alec. This isn't the same thing. Jake and I were not in love. I could easily have fallen for him, but I wasn't convinced I could love someone again. I couldn't risk the shattering of my heart again, and it had shattered when I learned the truth about Jake. It isn't memories of Ian breaking me but the trust I had in Jake. The belief he couldn't do what he'd been accused of doing. Nothing made sense. He was a good man.

*Good people make bad decisions all the time.*

Even I was victim to this statement. People make mistakes, but the harder part comes in forgiveness and acceptance. If Jake had done it, could I forgive him? I consider how adamant he was in stressing he hadn't started that fire. If he hadn't done it, then who did?

I consider how Jake has suffered if it hadn't been his fault. He took the blame in case it had been his nephew, but he wasn't convinced it had been. Only a good man sacrifices himself for someone else. A man who loves his family, who works hard to protect them.

A man worthy of that same love in return.

"Enough about love," I mumble, my feathers ruffling. "I have something else I want to discuss with you." May lowers herself to the seat before my desk at the seriousness in my tone. A forlorn expression fills her face. "Don't look at me like that. This is important but nothing earth-shattering."

"Giving up on love is earth-shattering," she mutters.

"May," I warn, and she holds up both hands in surrender. I swallow hard before I speak. "I've been offered the directorship of Building Buddies, and I'm considering taking it."

"What?" May's eyelids flutter before her gaze focuses on mine, waiting on more.

"As you know, I've been struggling for a while, wanting a change but not knowing what that change should be. And as I've been passing more and more of our contracts and cases to you, I don't really have as much investment in Kaplan and Shipley as I once did."

It pains me to admit the truth, but I just haven't been as busy as I once was, and it's my own doing because I'm not as invested in the Eaton-Bottom cow-sheep dispute or the real estate contracts for so-and-so moving into the area. "You know you were hired on when I was coming out of a low point in my life with the intention that one day you'd take over when I retire."

"You're too young to retire."

Her comment is sweet. I am still young, which is why I want to spend my time devoted to something I'm more passionate about. My flame for the practice of law is flickering. "I'd like to step back and give the directorship more of my attention."

May nods again. "Okay. What would that look like?"

"You'd be in charge here." Her eyes widen, but the gleam tells me she's pleased.

"I've got this," May states, confident and secure in herself. She's been the best prodigy and friend.

My lips curve into a knowing smile. "Yes, you do, chickie."

Now, I just need to speak with Alfred. I have an additional question on my mind for him.

---

Later that day, I stop at the building site after ignoring it for a week. It's a poor display of supervision, and I apologize again to Sullivan, keeping up the ruse that the past week had been busy at work. Alfred is present as I asked him to meet me there.

"Have you considered my suggestion?" he asks after I pull him aside outside the house. The siding is up. Outdoor lighting is wired but waiting on installation from our resident electrician, and I don't know why my eyes fixate on this object.

"I have, but I have a question for you first. Why did you select Jake Drummond for our program?"

Alfred shrugs, looking over at the single-story home. "We have a relationship with the prison system."

"That's not an answer, Alfred." I pause a moment, allowing him to admit more, but when he doesn't, I prompt him. "Did you know his past was connected to me?"

Alfred turns his gaze toward me, slipping his hands in his back pockets. His liquid eyes are difficult to read. "I knew of his crime and the victim, yes."

*The victim?* It was difficult to be impartial. He had a name.

"Ian Sanders was my fiancé," I remind Alfred as if he didn't know the connection. Alfred purses his lips a second before glancing back at the house.

"You suffered a terrible loss, lamb chop," Alfred states, calling me a nickname I haven't heard in years. My father teasingly called me the name when I was young, and a wave of need for my dad washes over me. He'd know what to do. He'd know how to react to everything happening.

"Sometimes, a man has more to repair than a home. In the case of Jake Drummond, the idea of building a place equates to the building he destroyed on an elementary level. Jake also has to amend for the life taken in that building. He needs to show compassion and seek forgiveness, both of himself and of those he wronged." Alfred turns to narrow his eyes at me.

"Did you know that when your father and I started this organization, a few of us didn't even know how to build? We tinkered with tools but hadn't a clue how to construct a house. There were millions of mistakes as we went. Accidents happened. Sometimes people were hurt. But we persevered in learning, bettering ourselves, bettering the homes we built. We had a mission. We wanted to help those in need."

I shake my head, knowing the concept behind Building Buddies but not finding Alfred's point.

"Jake Drummond had a clean record until that night. Not a speck out of place in his past. In fact, it was noble of him to leave college and raise his brother and then his brother's child. He'd been a success in his own right and helped numerous fire departments solve crimes."

I nod to agree with his summary of Jake, but I still didn't understand.

"He made one mistake."

"How do you know?" I'm curious if Alfred knows something more I don't.

"Ever hear the saying measure twice, cut once?"

"Of course," I admit. It's a basic practice in construction to prevent miscalculations before cutting materials.

"Sometimes mistakes still happen." His rummy eyes search mine before he slowly smiles. "But you're a measure twice kind of woman, Rita. You'd double-check all your measurements before you'd cut."

"What's that mean?" I ask, staring at the elder friend of my father.

"You'll figure it out." He pats my shoulder. "And take the directorship, Rita."

With that, he walks away from me, leaving me with even more to consider.

# JAKE

A weekend without work should have been a godsend, but it was hell. I needed to work. I needed to keep my hands busy to settle my mind. Now, it's a new workweek and another day without Rita. At night, I find myself out in the garage.

I'd asked Sullivan if I could have some of the scrap pieces of pipe and wire around the building site.

*"Are you a junk collector or something?"* he mocked. I had waited until I felt a little more confident with Sully before asking permission, but even after the awkward morning he'd nearly caught me with my pants down, I couldn't resist requesting the materials.

*"Something like that,"* I stated.

Sullivan had only grunted in response, watching as I made my collection in an empty box. Maybe he thought I was a thief instead of an arsonist, and I was getting my fix by *stealing* construction castoffs.

As I stand in my garage, the door is open, allowing the warm, early-summer evening air to filter around me. My thoughts return to Rita as I work on another project.

What was she thinking? How was she feeling?

*You set the fire that killed the love of my life.*

Nothing could have hurt worse. She thought I stripped her of her future. Despite her doubts in me, it hurt to think she'd loved someone else. The love of her life—those were strong words. I didn't want them to gut me, but they did. My feelings had been so fierce and fast for her. I often worried I'd misread them, mixing them up with the high of being outside the prison and the desire to start a fresh life. In many ways, I guess I had. Rita certainly didn't feel the same about me, and now, she never would.

The sound of tires pulling into the driveway turns my head, and I freeze with the soldering iron in my hand.

"Rita," I whisper, struggling to find my voice as she exits her crossover and approaches me in the garage. Today, she wears a summer dress and an old pair of Converse. Her appearance is eclectic, and so her.

"I would have called first." She shrugs, entering the space. "But I was in the neighborhood."

Lying isn't something Rita does well, but I accept this bit of dishonesty and hold my breath.

"What are you really doing here?" I set down the hot iron and take off my gloves.

"I wondered if we could talk." Her eyes travel around my shoulder as I've stepped before my workbench. "What are you working on?"

Slowly, I take a step to the side and allow Rita to see my work. An assortment of galvanized pipes, copper tubing, and electrical wires in a variety of shapes and sizes lay organized along the table.

"Are you . . . making another lamp?"

"It's called industrial art, but yes, it can be used as a light source." I rub at the back of my neck, nervous about showing her this side of me. It's another reminder of where I've been.

"Did you . . . make those other ones for me?"

I shrug in response, and her eyes widen behind her red-rimmed glasses. Her head turns back toward the worktable.

"What will this be?" She steps closer to the table and examines what I've started.

I shrug again, not having defined it yet. Soft round bulbs will eventually dangle from the coiled metal tubing, giving the lamp an almost octopus appearance.

"Where did you learn to do this?" Rita asks, her voice full of admiration as she bends at the waist to further examine the beginnings of the structure.

"In prison. I'm sort of self-taught, but they offered classes in metalwork and art, so I gave it a try. I find it soothing, and it allows my mind to focus when my thoughts scatter."

Rita stands upright. "What has your thoughts scattered?"

Lowering my face, I glance down at my feet. If she doesn't know by now that my thoughts all include her, I can't spell it out any plainer.

"You made those other pieces for me, didn't you?" she asks again, her voice softening while full of awe.

"I did." Sheepishly, I wonder what she thought of them.

"Is it me?" The question cracks her voice, and I glance up at her. "The first piece. Was it me?"

"It is. It reminds me of you when we went fishing." *When I kissed you under a covered bridge.* "It was one of the best days of my life."

Her eyes widen before she gazes over at the piece I'm constructing.

"And the second piece? Is it you?"

*A hollowed man with a newly lit heart?* Yes, I'd say that represents me, but I don't. I just stare at her, certain she's about to tell me to go to hell again. "You still haven't mentioned what you're doing here."

She squints at the beginning of the sculpture. "Remember when I told you about my wake-up call to being an alcoholic?"

I remember too vividly. We'd discussed alcoholism, and Rita told me about the night that changed everything for her. I'd never been so angry on behalf of someone else. If ever there was someone I wanted to throttle, it was a man who goes home with a drunk woman and takes advantage of her. Rita assured me she didn't think that's how it happened, but that night scared her. It scared me *for her*.

"I made a mistake, right? A big one." I nod to agree. Things could have gone so much worse for her that evening.

"Good people make bad decisions." She's said it often enough to me. She made a poor choice that night.

"You made a mistake, too."

I lower my head. God, not this again. I can't keep rehashing my past. I can't seem to get away from that damn fire.

"You should have told me."

My head pops up.

"You should have told me the whole story."

"I didn't know the man inside the building was your man, Rita. I swear if I had known there was a connection, I never would have—" *What?* I never would have fallen for her? I never would have touched her? I can't take those things back, and I don't want to. Swallowing hard, I stare at her. "We said no sob stories."

Rita weakly smiles. "I think this is a little different." In silence, we look at one another a minute. "But then again, everything about you has been different."

My breath hitches at the implication. Does she think I'm wrong for her? *Way to drive in the nail.*

"Well, I don't want to be a bad decision for you." Sarcasm drips from my tone along with hurt. I don't need her to keep rejecting me.

"You're everything I never thought I'd need. You've gotten under my skin, and I think that's exactly what I needed and didn't know it. I needed a push. Maybe it was that winning personality of yours." Her voice teases, and my eyes widen.

"I thought it was the smirk." She's constantly telling me I have a curl to my lip that I use against her.

"Maybe it was your fine ass on my couch."

This makes me chuckle a little. "You don't own that couch, sweet."

"But you own me."

"What?"

"I can't let you go," she whispers, and tears fill her eyes. She blinks rapidly, and I step forward, reaching for her shoulders and massaging them.

"What are you saying?"

"I'm saying I can't go through this kind of heartbreak again."

I exhale while rubbing at her arms. "I can't be with someone who doesn't have faith in me."

Briskly swiping at her cheeks, Rita pops her head up and meets my eyes. "I do. I do have faith in you."

"You believe me about the fire?"

"I believe you about the fire."

Suddenly, I'm suspicious although this is everything I want to hear. I tilt my head. "Why?"

"Because I know you're a good man. In here." She taps my chest over my heart. "You light me up." She states the title of my second piece to her. "I just can't believe a man who does such a thing, who has made me feel so alive, could do what you've been accused of doing."

I swallow hard again. My own eyes prickle. *She believes me.*

"I talked to Scarlet and May and Albert, and—"

"Albert?" I interrupt.

"The director of Building Buddies. He told me something that made me pause. You didn't have a spot on your record before that night, right? Not even a parking ticket."

"Well, I might have had one," I mock, wondering where she's going with this.

"So it doesn't make sense. You don't become a criminal out of nowhere."

"I'm not a criminal," I state, squeezing her arms.

"I know. *I know.* That's why we need to know the truth."

"The truth?" My hands slip down to her wrists.

"We need to know who did this to you. We need to help right your name."

I'm caught in the crossfire between her saying *we* and her

wanting to investigate. "It doesn't matter anymore. I've already served the time. I can't get that back. The State isn't interested in the truth. They wanted a fall man, and it was me. They got what they wanted, and I'm almost free. I don't want to go through this again. I don't want to keep looking back at the past."

"I know people." Her tone softens. "Just let me look into things."

I shake my head. "I can't do this." Releasing her, I step back and swipe a hand into my hair. I turn my back on her a second and notice my hand trembling. What would it feel like to have my name cleared? What would it mean? In many ways, I wasn't certain it would change anything. I'd still have gone through what I've been through. I'd still have spent seven years in prison. I can't get that time back.

"I can't do it," I say, turning back to her, my voice low.

"Just one name. The prosecutor? Or the defending attorney?"

"I didn't pick Gordon Howard. He was a shit lawyer." The department assigned him to me, and I took him in good faith he could help. He hadn't.

Rita closes her eyes a second. "I agree. I don't even think he's still practicing. He was a terrible attorney." The fact Rita recognizes his name surprises me. Is there some kind of lawyer club? Then I remember us discussing how she went to Vermont Law, as did her partner, as does my nephew. Vermont is a small state. Maybe many of them do know each other. I'm about to ask her such a thing when I hear the telltale sound of wheels moving down the ramp before the house.

"Hey." Nolan's hesitant voice rings out as he glances from Rita to me and back at her while he approaches us. Things have been strained between my brother and me since our big blowup.

"Hey." The single word is a warning. *Play nice.*

Rita steps forward and holds out a hand to shake his, formal and proper as though he's a client instead of my brother.

"Rita Kaplan," she states.

"Nolan." He sounds like a disgruntled teenager in response to her name.

"No hello beautiful today?" she teases, attempting to dispel the weird tension coming off my brother.

"Not feeling it today, no," he replies a bit harshly. Swiping nervous hands over my jeans, I step forward, preparing to put myself between Rita and my brother. *Why is he being so rude?*

When Nolan doesn't move or say more, Rita glances at me. "I guess, maybe I should be going." Her eyes seek mine. I don't want her to leave. We have so much to discuss, but maybe we've said enough for tonight.

Rita turns to Nolan. "Nice to meet you." Her voice is bright, hopeful even, despite his strange demeanor.

"We already met, remember?" he mutters. My brows pinch at my brother's belligerence, but I redirect my attention to Rita. "I'll walk you to your car."

Stepping forward, I feel the need to protect her from my brother's glare although I know he couldn't hurt Rita. Still, I place a hand on her lower back and usher her to her crossover at the end of the driveway, sensing my brother watching us. As we near her SUV, we pause, and I remove my hand.

"Can I ask you something? Just hypothetically speaking, of course."

"Sure." One brow arches.

"You mentioned that Ian was the love of your life."

Rita turns her head, glancing back at the open garage behind me. "I'm sensing a *but*."

"Do you think lightning would ever strike twice?" Her eyes leap to my face, and she stares at me, giving me those sad blues behind her red-rimmed glasses.

"Hypothetically speaking, of course," she says, chewing at the corner of her lip. "Why?"

"A wise woman once encouraged me to believe in second chances, and it occurs to me that leaves second chances open to a variety of interpretations."

"I suppose, should the opportunity present itself, yes. Love can happen a second time." Rita licks her lips, and I see her fighting a smile.

"So if I presented me as a chance I'd like you to take . . ."

"I'd be a fool not to take the opportunity. Of course. Or are we speaking hypothetically still?" she teases.

My heart races. My palms sweat. I want to kiss her until she says, "But maybe we should slow down a bit."

I falter. How much slower can we get? We've practically stopped. However, I nod to agree. Having faith in me doesn't mean she's ready to jump to loving me.

"Guess I'll be seeing you around the Busy Bean," I tease, trying to keep my voice light when it's the opposite of how I feel right now.

"The Busy Bean," she whispers as if the words mean so much more.

# JAKE

When Rita arrives at the project site the next day, I'm a sweaty mess in the summer heat. Today is sunshine and blue skies and feels prophetic for some reason. Rita hardly looks at me, but I can't seem to look away from her, following her inspection in and around the home. Her laughter travels through the open windows where I'm painting a bedroom. *God, I miss her laugh.* I especially miss when it's directed at me.

It's been difficult to cross the front room in this house and see the covered couch, knowing what Rita and I first shared on the dusty drop cloth that now protects the floor in this room. Memories of all our moments have filled my nights, especially the softer times spent in her bedroom. Rita is a spitfire in bed, willing to try anything, do anything, and it only fuels my desire for her.

As I told her, it wasn't all sex for me, though. I liked spending time with Rita. Cooking in her kitchen. Hanging out in her living room. Watching television with her nestled into my side. I didn't need to be out sowing wild oats after years of confinement. I needed comfort and a home. I needed Rita.

Suddenly, a throat clears behind me, and I turn to find her standing in the doorway of the bedroom I'm painting a denim blue color for the boy moving into this place.

"Looks good in here," Rita states, eyeing the walls and the crown molding.

"I'm not really a painter," I admit. Rita simply nods. Silence falls between us, and I hate the quiet. I want to drop the roller and rush to her, press her into the freshly painted wall, and beg her to go back to who we were.

"Sullivan told me about the light you designed for this room."

It's nothing, really. Just something I thought would be fun for the boy. I found an old catcher's mitt in the garage at home and dipped it in melted copper, preserving it like people used to preserve baby shoes. Adding the attachments to make it a light fixture, it will hang on his wall with a ball-shaped bulb like it's being caught in a mitt.

"Have you ever considered selling your work?" Her question surprises me.

"It's just junk soldered together with a light bulb." I downplay the craft.

"It's art," she states. "You might be on to something." Slowly, she smiles, and her expression shows that faith she has in me. She believes in my ability to turn trash into treasure. To make art. Now I just need her to have faith in me with her heart.

"I'll be headed to the Busy Bean later," she finally states, and I dare to hope it's another start for us.

"Is that a warning?" I tease as my lip curls, and I'm hoping to give her that smirk she claims works at charming her.

"Putting in my claim on the couch."

"Not unless I get there first," I tease.

"Maybe I'll save you a seat," she sheepishly offers. I stare at her as she brushes a section of her light brown hair behind her ear. Gray streaks fill those strands, and I love how she unabashedly shows her age. Her face is still young-looking, and the twinkle in her eyes displays wisdom along with wit. The whole package is a gift.

"I'll be there," I admit, fighting the victory smile that wants to dance across my lips.

Rita Kaplan just asked me to join her for coffee—on the plush peach couch. I just want her to invite me to love her next.

When I get to the Bean later that afternoon, Rita is indeed sitting on the couch, right smack in the middle. I place my order for a dark roast and turn in her direction. The energy between us sizzles to near crackling. I want to spread her out on that couch and let her bare body feel the velvety fabric underneath. I might need to invest in one of these sofas and convince Rita to live with me; however, I curb my thoughts, knowing I'm five steps ahead of a simple coffee date. Not that this is a date, but I don't know what else you'd call an invitation from a woman to join her for this drink.

"Is this seat taken?" I tease because Rita lounges backward, spreading her arms wide to hog the entire piece of furniture.

"I don't know. Is it?" Her head tilts to the side, and I place myself in the space between her hip and the armrest.

"Yes. *She's* taken," I say, holding her gaze. Rita slowly grins and lowers her arms from the back of the couch. Leaning toward her, I cup her cheek and press my lips to hers, keeping it quick and chaste since we're in public.

"We have some things to discuss," she whispers. "But I hate to waste a good cup of coffee."

"Drink fast," I warn her, wiggling my brows before reaching for my own mug and taking a sip of the hot heaven. Rita giggles as I burn my tongue. "Think that's funny, do you? I'll need you to suck on it to make it better."

Her eyes widen. The color matches the bright day outside, and that prophetic sensation returns.

Rita and I will be alright.

Half an hour later, my ears ring with her sweet moans.

"Is this the talking you wanted to do?"

"God, I've missed you," she grunts as I slam into her while she balances on her kitchen island. Her legs wrap around me with her dress at her hips. My hands clutch at her backside, holding her against me while I surge into her over and over again.

"I hated being away from you," I admit before Rita's mouth comes to mine, kissing me hard until our rapid rhythm interrupts. Her hands cup the back of my head as my hips flex to fill her with a hard-on that's been aching for her warmth.

"I'm sorry," she stutters.

"You have nothing to be sorry for." I don't want to talk while we're in this position, so I cover her mouth again with mine, swallowing her gasps as I thrust into her, fighting the release clenching at my balls. Sometimes, I hate how quickly my body responds to her and eagerly wants release because of her, but at the same time, I love it. She does this to me.

"Sweet," I warn because the rush is coming whether I want it to or not. My hand moves between us, rubbing at the spot that sets her off. Her fingers dig into my shoulders as her head tips back, and her legs tug me tighter to her center.

"Yes," she cries out as her body stills. Her head lolls forward, and she covers my lips as I break. I cup the back of her neck and thrust my tongue into her mouth as I go off inside her heat.

As the crest subsides but our hearts still race, I pull back from the kiss and press my forehead to hers.

"Please don't lose faith in me, sweet." My voice remains ragged, breaths coming unsteadily as I close my eyes and will her to trust me.

"I'm not going anywhere," she tells me, and I want to feel that assurance in my bones. I want to believe I won't lose her, but only time will tell where we will lead.

---

For the next week, I'm back in Rita's bed and also in her home. We cook together as we did before, but we also talk about everything. I tell her more about my art and the history behind it.

"As I mentioned, I was just playing around with things but found it soothing. I like to keep my hands busy." I suggestively wiggle my brows as Rita glances up from her side of the kitchen island.

"Had you ever considered the possibility of selling your art?" She suggested such a thing the other day, but I hadn't really considered it.

"You're very talented . . . with your hands." She winks at me, playing along with the subtext conversation. "But seriously. You could sell your work at some of the touristy places in Burlington or even online. What about from the firehouse? You could make it a studio and rent the apartments upstairs."

It's certainly a thought. "That old firehouse isn't cheap."

"Could your brother go in on it with you? Is there something he could do with you?"

Considering my brother, I sigh. "Drummond Brothers Electrical had been a discussion years ago, but I didn't like how Nolan never took anything seriously. Don't tell him I said that, but he hasn't always been very responsible." I hate to admit such a thing about my brother, but I didn't have confidence in his ability to stick with a business plan or dedicate his all to working together. "He is my best friend, while my little brother, but crossing the line into business partners felt like a risk I couldn't take with him."

"I don't think he likes me," Rita states.

"He doesn't even know you," I defend my brother. "Why would you say that he doesn't like you?"

Shrugging, she answers. "Maybe it was that less than stellar greeting he gave me when I went to your house a week ago."

Nolan had been a total dick when Rita showed up at our house, and we had words again about Rita after she left. It wasn't that Nolan didn't like Rita; he didn't trust her. He told me lawyers were snakes with their own agenda, reminding me of that python attorney Parker Avery who prosecuted my case. He added that there wasn't a single thing Rita could want from me, other than some orgasms and great sex. I scoffed at his lack of faith that I could offer a woman something more than my dick.

Sneaking a strawberry from the bowl she's filling, I pop it in my mouth and enjoy the burst of flavor. "He's just being protective of me. He doesn't want me to get hurt."

"And he thinks I'd hurt you?"

I shrug, unable to answer her question without it potentially leading to a fight. Rita could hurt me. It isn't just my past but also my future. I want her to have faith in it like she says she does. I want her to have faith in us, but I accept that we are still raw in our reunion. Although in the words of Nolan, we are having great sex with lots of orgasms.

"I wanted to tell you I've been learning a little bit about myself from the AA meetings." In that discussion we had about alcoholism, when she told me about her past, I explained to her how I was under the influence when I was arrested and my response to said arrest, which resulted in assaulting an officer friend. She also knows that I drank in prison. Sarcastically, I once explained how I could become a ketchup moonshiner if I ever wanted a new career path. Rita listened as I described how creative inmates could be with fruit syrups or the famous condiment to produce alcohol. Getting caught sick off the stuff landed me in my prolonged sentence in alcohol counseling. I'd learned my lesson well enough from that experience, but the prison system thought otherwise.

"There's a lot of talk about God in the program, and I'm not certain what I've done to piss Him off, but a bigger part of the program is learning to forgive myself. Accept what's been done."

Rita slowly smiles. "The Serenity Prayer?"

I nod. "There are things I cannot change. I'll never know who set that blaze. Why the school. Why the timing. I need to accept those things." Rita wants to do more sleuthing into my case, but I just want to leave it alone. I'm almost to the end of my sentence. "But there are things I can change, and that begins the second I'm free of my sentence."

"Why do you have to wait until your sentence is complete?"

I shrug. "I just want to be free of all constraints before I take the next step."

"Am I a constraint?"

The question surprises me. "Why would you ask that?"

"I don't know. Do I hold you back from moving forward? Do you feel like being with me is some kind of purgatory or penance or transition from who you were to who you want to be? Albert mentioned your working for Building Buddies is restoration, both physically and mentally. Do you feel you have something to make up to me?"

My brows crease, wondering where all this is coming from, and I slowly stand to round the island. "Sweet, I'm the same man I was before prison. Maybe a little bitter. Maybe a lot hardened, but I'm still me. Inside." I point at my chest. "I still feel things, want things. I want to be trusted, and I want you. If I started that fire. If I had a hand in your Ian dying, I might feel I had to make something up to you, but I'm confident in my innocence. And you and I have nothing to do with my past. You're like some freak of luck that's finally come my way in seven years."

"It's not just a seven-year itch?"

Taking the knife from Rita's hand, I place it on the counter. I lift her hand, still holding a sweet strawberry, and suck it out of her grasp. "Why would you say such a thing? What's going on in that smart head of yours?"

"I just don't understand why you'd be with me. What are we doing?" Her voice softens, and doubt crosses her face.

"We're enjoying one another," I state, lowering to kiss her. I don't want to keep talking, and I definitely don't want her to start overthinking. We're still on tender ground, letting go of what we've learned and stepping forward to learn more about one another.

Quickly, the kiss turns more intense. My lips slip to her jaw and then her throat as my hands slide into her hair. Eventually, I tug at the hem of her T-shirt, dragging it up and over her head, breaking the kiss only long enough to note the color of her bra.

"No purple?" I pout.

"I thought I'd change it up." She laughs.

I smile, tugging one cup downward to expose her full breast. Her breath hitches as I lower for her nipple, my tongue circling the tightening nub before I pull back with an idea. I reach into the bowl of berries and place a sliced strawberry atop her nipple, perching it on the peak.

"What are you doing?" She chuckles as I lower to nip both the fruit and her sensitive skin.

"Tasting how sweet you are," I tease. "Almost as sweet as this berry."

"Is that why you call me sweet instead of sweetheart?"

"I call you sweet because you said you weren't my sweetheart. As soon as you give me your heart, I'm happy to change the word, although I've become partial to sweet."

Her eyes widen before her smile grows. "You have my heart, Jake." Her hands wrap around my neck, and fingertips rub through my hair.

"Do I, Rita? Do I have your heart yet?"

"Hypothetically speaking, it's getting there," she says, chewing the corner of her lip, fighting a grin.

"And not hypothetically speaking . . ." I whisper, lowering my lips to hers but not giving in to the kiss I want to give.

"It's already yours."

Unable to fight a grin, the corner of my mouth curls upward, and I finalize the distance to kiss her as I wish.

"You have mine as well. Of course," I tease.

"Of course." She laughs again, and I capture the sweet sound with another kiss. "Now, can I show you how well I use my hands?"

"That ego. Your head is so big." Rita continues to laugh and adds, "Please, show me how skilled your hands are, handsome."

I catch one of hers with mine and reach around her for the bowl of berries before tugging her forward. "What are you doing with that fruit?"

"I'm also going to show you how skilled I am at getting drunk off berries lined along your body."

"Oh my." Rita chuckles.

*Oh my, indeed.*

## 21

## RITA

When the law school graduation arrives, Jake sits in the audience with his brother while I sit among the other alumni present. While I'd typically pass on this event, I'm honored to attend because Jake wanted me here. I'll be meeting his nephew today as well as his nephew's fiancée. Having not been back to Jake's house, I haven't crossed paths with Nolan, but I'm hoping for the best as today is his son's day.

As the ceremony ends, people gather in the crowded vestibule and spread to the outdoors while awaiting the graduates to find their families. I stand outside by myself, waiting on Jake.

"Rita?" Turning at the sound of my name, I'm surprised to see Parker Avery. Instantly, I recall that Parker prosecuted the case that involved Ian's death, which means she prosecuted Jake.

"Parker." She walks toward me with a man at her side. He's dressed in the academic robes of a professor.

"Rita, I haven't seen you in years." Parker reaches for me, offering a hug I don't expect. We didn't cross paths much despite us both being lawyers. Parker had eventually been connected with the State, taking on more criminal cases. She often encountered my father as a judge in our area. Her embrace reeks of sympathy from years past, and I grin and bear the pity in her eyes. "How are you?"

Dismissingly, I wave my hand. "Life is good," I say, finding I mean it. Jake and I are working through things together while experiencing terrific sex. *We're enjoying one another*, as he said.

"What are you doing here?" I ask her.

"This is my husband, Lance." He's a nice-looking man with streaks of gray at his temple and sharp cheekbones. A firm hand reaches out for mine, and we shake in greeting.

"Nice to meet you." I didn't know Parker was married.

"Lance has been teaching a course here this last year. What are you doing here?"

"I'm waiting on a friend. His nephew graduated."

"Oh, really? Who?" Lance asks me.

"Rory Drummond."

Lance slowly smiles. "Ah, Rory. Great student. He'll make an excellent lawyer. He's the one I was telling you about." Lance turns to his wife, but Parker is looking at me.

"His uncle is Jake Drummond," Parker states as if I should recognize the name.

"Actually, that's the friend I'm waiting on." I wink at her. Parker's forehead hitches upward, causing her blond hair to shift in her tight ponytail.

"You know who he is, don't you?" Her voice is full of concern and compassion, and once again, the sound grates on me.

"I believe you prosecuted his case a few years ago. A fire, correct?" I meet Parker's eyes, letting her know I'm aware of Jake's case.

"Honey, I'm going to go congratulate some of the students," Lance interjects. "Nice meeting you, Rita." He steps away, but Parker remains.

"You know, I never really thought he did it," Parker states, surprising me once again. "I remember that case. It's one of those that haunt you once it's over. The evidence was so sketchy."

I'd love to ask how she can prosecute such a case, but I know the objective is to prove the guilt of the innocent from her posi-tion. If he was innocent, she'd have no case against him.

"Why would you say that?" I still question.

"There was just something about him. His background didn't match the criminal mind of a pyrotechnic, nor did he have any prior convictions or even complaints within his department. There wasn't a scrape or dent on his record. Factor in the circumstantial evidence of his background, linking it to the crime with no proof, and I never felt good about that case."

I stare at Parker for a long moment, wondering if one day I would have become like her. Hardened to the truth, in the name of winning, not justice.

"Who do you think did do it then?"

Parker shakes her head. "I don't have a clue, but I suspect someone else in the department. Someone lower in the ranks. Maybe someone passed up on being a chief. When budget cuts occurred, those candidates would have been the most upset if they didn't have other income." Parker shrugs. "It had to have been someone who understood fire mechanics and maybe elec-trical work, but that could have been anyone."

*Passed up for being a chief.* I remember Jake telling me Nolan had been up for that type of promotion. It would have been a paid position within the department.

"So you're dating him then?" Parker questions, interrupting my sudden thoughts.

"Something like that," I state, flippantly dismissing a label for us.

*Someone who understood fire mechanics* but *also electrical work.*

*Drummond Brothers Electrical had been a discussion . . . Don't tell Nolan, I didn't trust him to be responsible.*

Parker's brows pinch, and she looks up to notice her husband waving her over.

"It's been great to see you again, Rita. I miss your dad." Her words are like a final stab to my chest. He was respected by those who entered his courtroom, but I miss him a million times more than anyone else because he was my father.

"Yeah. Me too," I mutter as Parker rubs a sympathetic hand down my arm before excusing herself. I watch as she walks away before turning back to the gathered crowd, hoping to find Jake among the mass, only to find Nolan on the periphery a few yards from me, watching me.

*Firemen started fires to save jobs.* The words come back to me in Jake's voice when he explained the judge's reasoning behind a motive for Jake's actions. The actions he didn't make.

*Oh my God.* I didn't like what I was thinking.

# JAKE

"Rory," I call out around the cluster of people. I'd gotten Nolan out of the fray, pushing him to the edge of the sprawl of graduates and families who trickled outside before I headed back through the crowd to find his son.

Rory turns as he hears his name and waves at me. We both work our way around bodies before we connect then I drag his body into a hug.

"I'm so proud of you, little man," I say as I slap his back.

"You know you can stop calling me that," he teases, pulling out of my embrace but keeping an arm around my shoulder. It hits me at the moment how much I've missed this kid, who is no longer little, and how much I've missed out on with him in the past seven years. His graduation from high school and college. His senior moments like prom and parties. His college fraternity weekends for families. His meeting Brynne.

A petite blonde stands off to the side when Rory spins out of our embrace.

"Uncle Jake, you remember Brynne." My nephew's voice is infused with his love for this girl who smiles shyly and offers a hand in greeting.

"I hear we're going to be family again." Clutching her offered hand, I step forward and press a kiss to her cheek. I decide it's not her fault she's a Dunhill and related to Lisa.

"Still the charmer, I see." My back straightens at the sound of my ex-wife's voice. Lisa's still stunning with raven black hair and deep-set dark eyes, but her tone reminds me how ugly she turned. Standing beside Lisa is her older sister, Brynne's mother, Monica.

"Monica. Lisa," I state, a bit surprised at their attendance. "I didn't know you'd be here."

Rory clears his throat. "Lisa and Brynne are close." The unspoken is heard loud and clear. Brynne was raised by her aunt, almost like Rory was raised by me as his uncle. Brynne's mother was a single parent just like Nolan. Connections become clear to me. Rory and Brynne understand one another.

"It's great to see you again," Lisa states, but I'm certain she's lying. Her eyes roam up and down my suit-clad body. "You look good."

Unease washes over me. I'm not playing games with my ex-wife. She wanted to dissolve our marriage. We'd called it irreconcilable differences as she wished, but the truth was she cheated on me with a chief in the department. They had an affair, and I'd caught her.

Glancing away from her, I search for Nolan, who I didn't think I'd easily spot, but the crowd is thinning as people move about the campus for pictures. Rita stands near my brother. The two of them are facing one another, and Nolan wears an expression of irritation. His lips move rapidly while Rita stands before him, hands clasped together near her belly. Her head is bent forward as if she's listening intently or taking a verbal beating.

"Excuse me," I say, mindful of Lisa watching me but keeping my eyes focused on my brother and my girl. Drawing near, I slip my arm around Rita as Nolan clamps his lips shut.

"What's going on?" I question, looking from Rita to my brother, who has a fine sheen of sweat along his upper lip.

"Rita was just telling me about an old friend," Nolan states.

"I wouldn't say she's a friend," Rita mutters, and I stroke my hand up her back.

"You looked pretty cozy," Nolan accuses, and I glare down at my brother.

"Who did you see?" I ask, shifting my gaze to Rita.

"Parker Avery," Rita states, turning her head so I meet her blue eyes through those glasses I love on her.

"Really?" I swallow around the question, recalling Rita's claim to have known the prosecutor of my case. I wasn't aware they were friends.

"She was just informing me how she never believed you were guilty."

"And this just came up out of the blue during a graduation ceremony?" I glance around us, checking how close others stand. "Maybe now isn't the time to discuss this."

"Of course, he's not guilty," Nolan states, a little too loudly. A few heads turn in our direction.

"Nolan, I just said not now." *What is happening here?*

"You don't need this, Jake. If she doesn't believe in you, she shouldn't be in your life."

"I didn't say I didn't believe in him," Rita defends, turning back to Nolan, but now I'm curious what did she say. What have the two of them been discussing?

"You aren't convinced of his innocence, though," Nolan blurts.

"I didn't say that either," Rita states, holding her own against the growing irritation of my brother.

"Nolan. Relax," I mutter, glancing over my shoulder once more to find people watching us.

"If you were convinced, you wouldn't be poking around with the lawyer who put him away."

Rita turns to me. "I wasn't doing that." Her voice remains strong, confident, and I want to believe her. I want to have faith in her like she says she has in me, but something isn't settling well with this situation.

"Almost ready for dinner," Rory says, finally making his way over to us, holding Brynne's hand. The tension around the three of us is thick enough to cut with a knife, but I turn to my nephew and force a smile.

"Ready," I state, noticing my ex-wife standing behind Brynne. Lisa's eyes don't miss my hand on Rita's back which I slowly drop, and Rita turns her head toward me once again, watching my hand fall away from her.

"Who's this?" Lisa snaps, but Rory steps forward to offer a hand to Rita.

"Hi. I'm Rory Drummond." The firmness in his shake, along with the strength in his voice, says he's gone into future lawyer mode. I'm so damn proud of him. My heart is ready to burst, but that also might be my blood pressure rising at the strain around us. Nolan and Rita. Lisa and Rita. I'm noticing a common denominator, and I'm not liking it.

"Congratulations. Rita Kaplan, fellow alumnae as you are now official alumni." She smiles with warmth at someone entering her inner circle. Rory introduces Brynne, and I hold my breath as he introduces Lisa as Brynne's aunt.

"I'm also Jake's ex-wife."

*Jesus.* My eyes briefly close.

"Okay, then," Rita says as if that wasn't awkward as fuck.

"Are you joining us for dinner?" Rory asks Rita, who immediately answers, "No," as I say, "Yes."

My head turns toward her, wondering when her plans changed.

"I'm only here for the graduation. Have a wonderful night with your family," she says, turning to step away from us, but I catch the dark robe she's wearing, distinguishing her as alumni.

"Excuse us," I say to Nolan and the gang, walking Rita a few steps away.

"Hey. What's going on?"

"I think it might be best if you celebrated with your family without me." Rita's quiet voice disturbs me. It isn't like her to acquiesce like she is.

"Tell me what happened? Did Nolan say something?"

Rita lifts her head, eyes meeting mine once more. "This is Rory's day. I don't want to ruin it."

"Ruin it?" I question. "It's dinner."

Rita turns to glance at the gathering of Nolan, Rory, Brynne, Monica, and Lisa waiting on me. "And I'm uninviting myself. Why don't you call me when dinner is over?" She pats my chest in a patronizing manner, and I'm not liking the brush-off she's giving me, especially before my family.

"What is this?" I state, glancing up and down her robed outfit. "Am I not good enough for you? My nephew just graduated from this school. He's one of you." I pause. "Is it that I'm not?"

"Jake," she mutters under her breath, eyeing my family, who is surely staring at us.

"Is that it? I'm not some fancy attorney. I'm the criminal." My voice rises a bit, and I swallow the lump in my throat.

"That is not it," she says, leveling me with a hard stare. "I think it best if you call me once your family meal is over."

I match her stare. In the time it took for Rory's ceremony to finish, something changed her mind about us, and now she doesn't want to spend time with my family. She doesn't want to be with me. *Well, screw this.* My family means everything to me. Nolan has been my number one supporter my entire life. He's been the one person who believed in my innocence. I don't know what Lisa's doing here, but she's a part of Brynne's life, and Brynne is important to Rory. And every hit I've taken, I did so Rory and Nolan could stay together. I don't need this attitude from Rita. Swiping a hand over my hair, I hiss, "Fine."

Only, it isn't fine that my girlfriend is ditching me on such a monumental family occasion, especially when the reason she's leaving me is because I'm not good enough for her.

I don't call Rita after dinner. Instead, I celebrate with my nephew, finally catching up with him after seven long years. After that first awkward dinner, he hadn't been home again, working to complete school and study for the bar, which he'll be taking soon. Rory has grown into such a good man, and I am so damn happy to commemorate this accomplishment with him. I was so proud of him.

Even Lisa was pleasant throughout the dinner we shared at a fancy steakhouse near the law school campus.

However, Nolan was off. He was still his mouthy self, making inappropriate jokes and being the life of the party, but something wasn't right with him, and the beers he consumed did not help.

Eventually, Lisa drives the two of us home as we closed down the bar. I thought I'd be going home with Rita after dinner, so I hadn't driven. I was wrong.

"You look really good," Lisa states to me once more as we arrive at Nolan's and my house. I've helped him out of the car and watched him struggle to wheel himself to the ramp, brushing off my help. "Maybe I could come in for one more drink, and we could talk."

The invitation startles me. Lisa has exited her car, waiting on Nolan to leave us alone. "We have nothing left to discuss." Our divorce mediator handled everything over seven years ago.

"You know I'm still sorry about how everything happened," she says, not letting it go.

"It's over, Lisa."

Stepping up to me, her hand comes to my chest. "But we could start over. A fresh start. A second chance. You look so good, Jake."

My stomach churns at the solicitation. Lisa might be thinking she's seductive, but she's not. I don't need a woman who broke our marriage vows. Hell, I don't need any woman who isn't committed to me, and that goes for Rita as well. Her earlier rejection still stings.

"I'm not interested in doing this with you," I mutter, shaking my head at my ex-wife and removing her hand from my chest.

"I made a mistake. One night, Jake. One time. I made a mistake. Can't you forgive me?"

I'm not interested in rehashing an old argument. Lisa and I both know it was more than one night. It was more than one time. Forgiveness was all I wanted once upon a time. Actually, faithfulness was what I wanted. I wanted Lisa to believe in us as a couple, but she hadn't. She turned her back on me even before everything fell apart.

"I do forgive you, Lisa, because you have to live with the regret, not me."

"What about your regrets?"

"What regrets?" I state, a cold sweat breaking out on me.

"The fire," she whispers, showing her lack of faith in me once again.

"I'm not doing this," I mutter, stepping away from my ex-wife. "Thanks for the ride, Lisa." I turn my back on her and wave over my shoulder. I don't need this shit. Not from Lisa. Not from any woman.

---

"So Lisa looked good," Nolan teases, wiggling his brows over glassy, inebriated eyes.

"Yeah, that ship sailed, brother," I state, pouring him a glass of water in the kitchen and handing it over to him, reminding me of so many nights he'd come home young and drunk, and I'd try to help him squash a potential killer hangover.

"Could go sailing again," he says, lifting the glass and downing the water I offered.

"Not interested in sailing," I say, wanting to cut this euphemism conversation short and get to bed. I'm exhausted.

"Thank goodness that other ship pulled out of port," Nolan mutters.

"What ship?" I snort.

"Rita Captain."

"Rita Kaplan," I correct. "And what happened with you two anyway?"

"Oh, Jakey," Nolan mutters. "The things I could tell you." His eyelids lazily lower.

"Well, there's always tomorrow," I tease, patting him on the shoulder and stepping behind his chair to wheel him to his room. His hand catches mine over his shoulder.

"You didn't need her," Nolan says, and something about his touch and the tone of his voice has the hairs on the back of my neck rising. Stepping back around the front of the wheelchair, I lower to my haunches and glare up at my brother.

"Why would you say that, Nolan?"

"She was talking to that fancy lawyer, all chummy and hugging. They probably laughed about your conviction, saying how easy it was to put you away." Nolan licks his lips, and his lids close once more.

"Why would you say that? Did you hear something?"

"I didn't need to hear anything. She kept looking at me like she knows."

More hair raising. A cold sweat starts next. "Like who knows what, little brother?" My voice is tight while I try to coax whatever it is he isn't saying out of him. I remember having to do the same thing when he was younger. He'd be in trouble at school but didn't directly say what he'd done to cause it. And typically, when trouble occurred, Nolan was the culprit. Softening my voice, lowering to his level, I learned how to speak to my brother to get him to open up. Of course, it was never Nolan's fault. Someone else always made him do whatever he'd done.

"She knows about me. She knows about us."

Having lost me, I pinch my brows in question. "Us?" Immediately, I think back to Lisa. Was Lisa standing near Nolan? Did Rita sense that something happened between my ex and my brother after all? My stomach churns again. The beers I drank slosh around in my belly.

"I just wanted to take care of you. For once, I wanted to do right by you." Nolan awkwardly reaches out from my face and pats my cheek several times until he's nearly slapping me. I catch his hand and crush his fingers.

"Nolan, what are you talking about?"

"I wanted them to know we were needed. The State needed more manpower. We needed you." His eyes widen in emphasis, coherent for just a moment, but I'm the one confused.

"What are you talking about?" I repeat.

"The warehouses. We needed their attention. They needed to see how important we were. Firemen put out fires."

"Nolan," I hiss, eyes rapidly blinking as fear courses through my veins. "What did you do?"

The mystery of those three warehouse fires comes back to me. Electrical tampering. Chemicals nearby to ignite the flame further. The judge's voice as he sentenced me, saying he'd seen it before. Firemen setting fires to save a department.

"Nolan," I whisper, my throat thick. He shakes his head from side to side, his face lowered.

"I never thought they'd catch me."

"They didn't!" I suddenly shriek. "They caught me. They thought I did it."

Nolan's head shakes more vigorously. "I messed up."

"Tell me you didn't set the fires? Tell me you didn't burn down that school?"

I'm going to be sick. For all the guilt I felt over a crime I didn't commit, my heart races faster as I think of Rita.

"They weren't paying attention. The empty warehouses weren't enough of a sign for them."

"A sign?" I question, not understanding his thought process.

"I needed to go bigger. No one cared about the warehouses. I needed to go somewhere where they'd take notice. Someplace with more meaning."

"The school," I whisper.

"An empty school."

"But the school wasn't empty," I remind him, tightness filling my voice.

"I didn't know," Nolan says, finally lifting his head, tears in his liquid, red-rimmed eyes. "I didn't know."

My fist clenches in his shirt, tugging him forward in his chair. "What the hell did you do?"

"I just wanted you to keep your job. I wanted that promotion to chief. No one was going to get hurt." My eyes drift to his legs, paralyzed in the chair where he sits. Bitterly, he laughs, following my gaze.

"When I came out of that coma, you were arrested. I had faith in the system. They wouldn't find a thing." A tear slips from Nolan's eye. "You'd get off. There wasn't any evidence it was you."

Releasing my brother, I fall back on my ass to the cold kitchen floor and stare up at him in his chair. A shaky hand swipes over my mouth. "But there was evidence."

Circumstantial but substantial evidence.

"The images at the school were me. The wire cutters were mine."

Suddenly, I recall the tools submitted as evidence for stripping wires, intended to shorten them. As a case was built against me, the tool was discovered in the garage. They belonged to me, but I hadn't used them. My brother had.

"Nolan, why . . ." Why didn't he tell me? Why didn't he come forward? Why did he do this? Although he'd just explained himself, I still cannot comprehend what he'd done.

"I went to prison," I remind him, my voice hardening. His head snaps up, eyes wide but spilling with liquid.

"I know. I'm sorry. I'm so sorry." A sob cracks through the room before my brother falls apart, shaking uncontrollably with guilt and tears.

My blood runs cold. I have no comfort for him. "You're sorry?" I bellow, slapping a hand to the linoleum flooring. Nolan's fragile body shudders.

"I was so messed up. Hurt and on drugs at the hospital. Then you were gone, convicted, and I didn't know what to do. Rory told me how he thought it was his fault, and you told him not to tell anyone. I said the same thing. I couldn't have my son go to jail for something I'd done. And then I couldn't admit it myself because I couldn't leave my son without a father. I couldn't do to him what had been done to us."

His body shakes harder, the tears falling faster. I don't even know what to say. I'm vibrating with confusion and anger, hurt and betrayal. *My own brother.* Sadly, I knew Nolan justified his actions in his head. It was never his fault. He had his reasons. He had his convictions, but this time, I had enough.

Scrambling up off the floor, I stumbled in my dress shoes. I was still wearing my shirt, rolled to the elbows, but my tie was loosened. My coat had been removed hours ago. Fumbling through the hallway, I attempt to climb the stairs, tripping on them and banging my knees on the risers. I wasn't drunk. In fact, every drink I'd had earlier turned to ice in my veins.

My own brother.

The little boy I'd become a father figure to.

The child I'd protected from bullies.

The teenager I'd moved home for.

The man for whom I'd given up my life.

Stumbling up the stairs, I find my truck keys in my room and slip back down the steps. My legs hardly hold me. My knees give out once, and I fall to the steps again, slamming my ass this time on the hardwood. My heart races too fast. My ears ring.

I owed my brother nothing, and I'd be damned if I lost one more thing because of him.

**23**

# RITA

A sharp rattling on my front door wakes me from a fitful sleep. My room is pitch black, and it takes me a second to gather my wits. Throwing off the blanket, I can't imagine who would be at the house this late and assume it's either an animal bumping against the door or someone trying to break in. After grabbing the baseball bat I keep under the bed, I head down the hallway. I'm not afraid to use this thing. I'm certain I could get in one good swing although my hands sweat along the handle. As I press myself against the wall of the staircase, lowering for the first floor like I'm the one sneaking into my home, I see that a forehead rests against the frosted glass while knuckles wrap on the wood as if separate from the body, creating such a ruckus.

Tiptoeing down the staircase, I feel goose bumps scatter over my flesh. I'm only wearing a low-cut T-shirt nightdress which hits at my kneecaps. Not the best body armor, but then again, an intruder wouldn't be knocking on the door. Still, the bat remains raised as I reach the front door, and call out, "Who's there?"

"Sweet." Sounding strained and off, I'm almost surprised I heard his voice through the glass. Quickly, I set the bat to the side of the door and release the locks. Once the door is opened, the man on my front porch hardly looks like Jake. He sways. His shirt is wrinkled. His tie disheveled. An overwhelming hint of cinnamon wafts between us. Gum is the first attempt to hide alcohol on someone's breath.

"Are you drunk?" I snap. Jake does not confess to having a problem. He's told me all the ways he's been accused of having an issue but remains adamant he does not. I know all about closet drinking, thinking you're fooling others when you aren't. I'm also not convinced Jake really does suffer from alcohol addiction as I had.

"I'll admit I've been drinking." His voice remains controlled, but his hands reach for the doorframe as if he'll pitch forward if he doesn't hold on to something. "I didn't know where else to go."

The low tenor of his tone has me reaching for his tie and tugging him forward. He stumbles into the entryway, and I close the door behind him.

"Sweet," he whispers, but it isn't a drunken slur or even a seductive taunt. The sound is a broken man.

"What happened?" Before I've even finished my question, his arms are around me, dragging me to him and pressing my body against his. His arms wrap around my back, and he holds me like he doesn't ever want to let go. Hesitantly, my hands come to his lower back. His weight falls against me, and I can hardly hold him up.

"Let's sit down," I state, but Jake twists his head which lays in the crook of my neck. Gently pushing at him, I separate us enough to lead him into the front room while holding his hand. As we near the couch, Jake reaches for my waist, slipping his arms around me again. We lower as one before he tips back. My hands rest on his biceps, pressing at him to release me, but he isn't letting go. As we flatten to the couch, my legs twist awkwardly beside his hip, dangling off the furniture while his upper body holds mine down. He scoots so his ear lands near my heart. With his arms still snug around my back, and my spine arching over them under me, I feel Jake shudder. A strange vibe rolls off him.

Slowly, I relax from the temporary fear of him and give in to the presence of his body blanketing mine. My hands slide up his arm, and my fingers massage the back of his head.

"What happened, handsome?" I ask, keeping my voice low. Skittish of his reaction, I remain still other than my racing heart and stroking fingers. Jake only shakes his head against my chest, and then I feel the tremble of his body. The definitive sound of a sob and the utter collapse of this man. His arms tighten as his face presses into my skin, and he cries.

"Oh my, honey," I say, staying quiet and tender as I rub the back of his head and stroke my other hand over his upper back. Without additional words, I let him cry out whatever has upset him. My heart rips in half and half again, knowing whatever has broken such a strong man had to be something bad. Something very bad.

Time slows as Jake cries against me until his body relaxes. His weight turns heavy, and I assume he's fallen asleep. Still stroking his head and rubbing up his back, I lean forward and press a kiss to the top of his head.

"I'm sorry." His hoarse voice startles me.

"You have nothing to be sorry for." I don't speak louder than a whisper as if I'd disturb the remainder of the empty house.

"At the graduation. I overreacted."

Ah, the moment where he was calling me out for thinking he wasn't good enough. I didn't wish to get into the altercation I'd already had with his brother, who accused me of being friends with the enemy as he called Parker. I can't say I'd call Parker the enemy as she was only doing her job, which involved proving Jake's guilt. However, I had to agree with Nolan a little bit. If Parker believed Jake was innocent, she should have requested an audience with the judge to discuss her suspicions.

Still, I had my own suspicions now.

"What happened tonight?" Something must have occurred after Jake left for dinner. Shifting slightly on me, I sense the dampness on my skin and the scoop neck of my nightshirt. Hardly lifting his head, Jake uses his tie to wipe at both.

"Nolan." His voice cracks on his brother's name, and he shivers all over again. My arms tighten around him.

"Tell me," I quietly encourage.

"Nolan did it, Rita. He set the fires. In the warehouses. In the school." My heart drops to my stomach. I feel sick and press at Jake's shoulders to get a better look at him, but Jake returns his vise grip hold on my waist, keeping himself tethered to me.

"What?" My own throat clogs at the revelation. "How?"

"He didn't want me to lose my job. He wanted a fire chief promotion. It's exactly as the judge thought, only it wasn't me. It was him." There isn't bitterness in Jake's tone as much as shock like I've never heard—incomprehensible shock.

"How do you know?" I question, allowing my hands to flatten on his shoulders as if I'm tugging him to me, keeping him against me. As if I need his strength to support me.

"He told me. He was drunk, and we were fighting about my ex-wife—"

"Lisa," I interject.

"Yes. She was there tonight."

"I met her, remember? She's very pretty." The surprise at finding his ex-wife present did nothing to quell the nerves I'd already felt after the altercation with Nolan. Lisa was a raven-haired beauty, and I was a mouse compared to her. We looked nothing alike, and I'm certain our temperaments didn't compare either. Judging a book by its cover, she was all beauty and makeup, while I was hiking boots and knitting nerd. I recall the slow release of Jake's hand from my back once she uttered those words: *I'm also Jake's ex-wife.*

"Don't," Jake says, finally lifting his head and twisting his neck so he can look me in the face despite the dark room. "Don't even think of her."

I nod but still wonder what he means by she was there tonight. Had she joined them for dinner in my place, or was she always intended to be present? There wasn't time for the sudden pang of jealousy I felt. Jake had larger issues with his brother unless those issues further included Lisa. Jake told me his suspicion that his wife came onto his brother after Jake was incarcerated.

"Tell me more about Nolan." I swallow back the bile at simply stating his name. Jake shifts his feet as if kicking off his shoes before he lowers his head once more, returning his cheek to my chest. He speaks to the quiet, dark room.

"He admitted to it all. Setting the fires at the warehouses, hoping to gain attention from the State."

"Warehouse fires?" I interject, and Jake quickly refreshes my memory of the initial investigation he was under regarding the vacant warehouses.

"Nolan hoped to make a statement that fire departments were necessary as is. When that didn't gain the attention he'd wanted, he went for the school. He swears he thought it was empty. A vacant building so no one would get hurt."

"But someone did get hurt," I interject, clenching my teeth with the statement. Not only had Ian died but Nolan was permanently disabled as well. I wouldn't even admit to the irony of the situation.

A sense of sad relief comes over me as I wasn't certain how I'd tell Jake of my new suspicions. After my conversation with Parker and then Nolan's dismissal of me, I was confident—but without evidence—that Nolan could have set fire to the school. Accusing him, though, would have been similar to what happened to Jake. I didn't have any proof Nolan committed a crime. It was all circumstantial.

"I know," Jake whispers, squeezing me tighter. At this point, I was an uncomfortable human body pillow to Jake, but I didn't complain. I needed to know more.

"So, what happened next?"

"I couldn't believe what he said. It seemed impossible. Like what was he thinking? What did he hope to accomplish? How could he do such a thing?" Jake pauses for air as his voice rises. "I have so many questions. Nothing feels like it makes sense right now. I want to believe I imagined it."

My hand swipes down his back. "But you didn't, did you?"

Sensing his eyes close, he rolls his head against my chest once more. "My own brother," Jake mutters. Defeat fills his voice. Heartbreak and irreparable hurt linger.

"What will you do?" My mind races as there aren't many options. Jake already served the time for the crime he didn't commit. A crime he'd been adamant all along that he never did. To know his brother went along with Jake's arrest, allowed him to go to prison . . .

"Why didn't Nolan come forward?" I ask before Jake has a chance to answer my first question.

"He was in a medically induced coma when I was arrested. He says by the time he came around, I was already in jail. He didn't speak up for fear that Rory would be found out with those damn fireworks. He also didn't want to lose his son. He thought I'd get off."

Jake lifts his head once more. "I understand his thought process around Rory. As sick as it sounds, I might have done the same thing if Rory had been mine." But Jake doesn't have a son. It's something we've discussed. His wife hadn't gotten pregnant in the time of their marriage. Jake believes it was partially responsible for their issues. Lisa's infidelity had been another part of their problems.

I shake my thoughts of her, returning to options for Jake.

"You can go to the authorities. Tell them the truth."

Jake perches up on an elbow, wedged between my body and the back of the couch. "I don't know what to do." He shakes his head. "I just . . . can't think about this anymore."

I understand. There's so much to consider, but the pile-up from Nolan's confession alone is weighing Jake down. He's gone to prison for a crime he didn't commit, while his brother had known the truth all along.

"Why didn't he ever tell you? Admit his part in the fires before."

Jake shakes his head again. "I don't know, and I don't have space to think. I'm just . . . spent tonight." He lowers his head once more, and I'm reminded of his cinnamon scent when I opened the door.

"Are you drunk?" I ask again, worried that his own state of mind is clouded by more than this revelation.

"Stone sober, sweet. The gum was not to disguise anything but just take away the stench. I didn't want to upset you."

My arms tighten around him again, holding him in place against my body. Jake slips one arm out from under me and slides his hand along my outer leg, lifting them both to lay across the couch cushions. He shifts himself, so my legs spread, and he settles between them, keeping his upper body over mine. His head remains near my racing heart, and we hold one another for a while longer in this position.

Time passes although I'm uncertain how much before Jake shifts, rubbing his nose against my skin above the scoop neck collar of my nightshirt. Slowly, he begins kissing me along the ridge of material.

"Jake?" I whisper.

"Don't talk," he quietly states, opening his lips to suck at the path he's made. He shifts a bit, and his mouth moves to my neck before his tongue comes forward. He licks down the column of my throat to the edge of my low-cut nightdress. As his tongue moves down my skin, his hand slips upward, covering my breast over the material.

"Jake," I groan as he squeezes me hard through the soft covering, bringing my nipple to a sharp peak.

"I need you, sweet," he mutters into my skin. It's wrong, I want to say to him. It shouldn't be like this—when he's so broken, so desperate—yet I can't deny him the comfort he seeks, reminding myself of that fateful night for me. How badly I wanted to recapture the sensation of another body over mine. How strongly I wanted to join with another. I had hoped to get lost in someone else. Of course, the circumstances were different. I was drunk out of my head, unfocused, and uncertain of what I was doing.

This is Jake.

"I stopped drinking hours ago," he states, looking up at me once more to assure me of his mental state. As our eyes meet, he leans upward, joining our lips. At first, the kiss is slow and sad. His mouth is swollen. His cinnamon flavor invades my tongue. Quickly, the kiss grows more desperate. Jake fists his fingers in my hair and deftly moves us until he's sitting upward and I'm straddling him.

"What is it with you and couches, Kaplan?" he teases before nipping at my lower lip and forcing my mouth open to continue kissing. My hands cup the side of his head as we continue to explore with eager tongues and unquenchable lips. Jake breaks first, pressing me back only enough to work a few buttons on his skewed dress shirt. The tie is already loose at the neck. He tugs everything over his head from the back collar, giving me his firm shoulders and flat chest to explore. My hands wander down his pecs while fingers comb through the fine hairs on his chest.

His hands fist in the material of my nightdress and gently tug it upward, revealing my body in a slow tease of exposure until I lift my arms and he removes it completely. His face is eye level with my naked breasts, and he cups one, leaning forward to suck hard at the swell. Instantly, my back arches, forcing myself deeper into the warmth of his mouth. My fingertips dig into his shoulders to balance myself against his hungry suction. Popping free of one, he moves to the other, swirling his tongue around the nipple before dragging his teeth to the nub. The contrast of lapping tongue and sharp bite causes me to squeak. Jake returns to my mouth.

With our lips still joined, his hands slip into the sides of my underwear, and he presses at my hips to momentarily stand. When we can't remain joined by lips, I break free, and Jake lowers my panties. He keeps me upright a moment, skimming his hands over my naked thighs, along my hips, and over the small swell of my stomach.

"You're so beautiful, sweet," he whispers, choking on the compliment before leaning forward and sucking at my belly. One hand slips lower, cupping between my thighs as his mouth sucks at my loose abdomen. My fingers fall into his hair once more, combing through the locks while his fingers stroke over slick skin. Without warning, two fingers slide into me, causing my head to loll and a moan to escape. Jake takes his time to drag them to the edge before filling me once more. He works me back and forth, and the motion is like a slow-release drug, taking its time to sedate me, relax me. I make sounds I've never made before as one arm wraps around my backside to keep me balanced. He licks and sucks over my stomach while his fingers work their magic.

Quickly, my legs tremble, and my knees break. I warn Jake with only his name.

"That's it, sweet. Come alive for me," he says. My body is hyperaware of being alive at this moment, being treasured by this sad man before me. Tonight should be about him and his loss, what he's learned, but I sense taking from me, doing what he's doing brings him the distraction he needs. Once I break, he rushes forward, forcing his face between my thighs and lapping at the release. I'm still standing, and I'm not certain my legs can support me as his tongue is wicked torture. He works hard to bring me to the edge once more. My hips rock. My pelvis thrusts. I'm right there when he stops.

I hiss, but Jake softly chuckles. Leaning back against the couch, he unbuckles his belt and removes his pants, shoving boxer briefs and all over his knees. As they fall to his ankles, he guides me by my hips to climb over him. Holding his stiff shaft upright, I position myself on the tip, and we both groan at the sensation of his hard skin against my damp folds. Slowly, I lower over him, bringing him into me. Once seated to the hilt, I pause, and our eyes meet.

"Thank you," he whispers up to me, tipping his head back for my mouth once more. We return to kissing, keeping this still position for only so long before Jake moves my hips up and down his hard length. With hands on his shoulder, I aid myself in the movement, rocking with greater speed, quickly rebuilding the lost orgasm from his mouth on my clit moments ago. In this position, I feel both wild and sensual, taking what I want from this man but also giving to him what he needs. He needs me, and I marvel at how I'm in a position I never thought I'd be in again.

I'm in love with him.

The emotion overwhelms me as I rock where we are joined, keeping him deep within the warmth of my body. Moving faster, rubbing my clit against him in a manner that quickly ignites the tension, I break apart once more. When I lower my face, my hair curtains our heads, and Jake captures the silent scream of my orgasm ripping through me. I struggle to kiss him in return, unable to catch my breath. As my body slowly melts into his, his arms wrap around my back.

He shifts, keeping us attached, and I laugh at the unexpected movement as well as his strength. I'm flipped to my back with him over me, our position similar to that first night on a dusty covered couch. This couch is certainly more comfortable and more functional. Jake grabs each of my hands, lifting one and then the other over my head. Sliding his fingers between mine, he balances over me, moving his hips in that manner he has, reminding me again of how he can dance. He thrusts, and he sways. He surges, and he teases.

"God, Rita," he hums like I'm a prayer of gratitude. Then he stills, pumping into me. His forehead comes to mine as he squeezes my fingers until I lose circulation. We remain joined as he rides out his own release. His body stays tense, keeping some of his weight off me until he can't balance any longer. He collapses briefly over me, breathing into my neck, inhaling my sleep and sex scent. A soft kiss comes to my lips, and tears fill my eyes. A sudden sense of ending slips down my body like a silk cloth falling to expose my raw skin.

"Let's go to bed," Jake mutters, pressing up over me like he isn't exhausted or distraught. He slips out of me quickly and stands, lowering a hand for mine to pull me upward. Silently, I follow him to my room, walking naked through the house until we reach my bed and fall into one another once more.

# 24

# RITA

After our second round, we lay as we did on the couch, only with a little more room in my bed. Jake sprawls over me. Head above my breast. Arm over my waist. One leg trapped between mine. He dozes, as do I, but I can't quite sleep. My mind races with options for Jake and his brother. Will Nolan turn himself in? Can Jake be set free from his sentence? Most of all, can he ever forgive his brother?

I honestly don't know how to feel about Nolan. I want to be sympathetic to his condition and his fate, brought on by his own reckless actions. On the other hand, Nolan's thoughtlessness for the safety of others, including the fact other firemen could have been harmed or died in any of the blazes he set, feels unforgivable. Once again, I call up what I've learned within AA. There are things I can change and things I cannot. I need to use wisdom to know the difference, not judgment or prejudice. Forgiveness for Nolan would take time if he were my brother. I wonder as I have in the past if there are circumstances that are beyond forgiveness. Has Jake reached his limit?

He stirs over me, rubbing his nose against my chest as he did earlier. I smile to myself as I stroke my hands over his head and down his neck, smoothing my palm along the firm skin of his back. His body is a wonderland, firm and tight. He's so different from what I've experienced before. I lean forward to press a kiss to the top of his head, and Jake stiffens. The final sensation from earlier returns, and my shoulders tense.

Jake places a hand on my belly, covered by the sheet. The heat of our naked bodies has kept us together for the remainder of the night.

"I need to go," Jake whispers, fisting the material over my stomach as he speaks to my lower body. My head shifts on the pillow, glancing toward the window where the dawn of a new day is slowly filling the sky with pinks and yellows.

"It's still early. You could stay." Where will he go? Would he return home? Is he prepared to face Nolan?

"No, sweet. I mean, I don't think I can stay in Vermont."

My head shifts again on the pillow, and I gently curl my fingers into his hair, tugging his head upright. His eyes struggle to meet mine.

"What do you mean?"

"I'm done here. If I ride out my sentence, there's nothing left for me here." The comment stings.

Slowly, I remove my fingers from his hair and swallow the thick lump in my throat.

"What will you do about Nolan?"

"What can I do? I can't turn in my own brother. I can't do that to him." His eyes finally seek mine, but I can't look at him. Will he really leave? What about me? What are we? What is he doing with me if he only plans to walk away?

And what about his brother? Nolan cannot just walk free, not that he can walk. He isn't even free, either. He's been carrying this burden in him. Or maybe it wasn't a burden after all. Nolan had certainly made up his mind how things would play out. No one would get caught, and when Jake did, he assumed Jake would not be found guilty. But he was, and then he was sentenced to prison in Nolan's stead.

"Don't look like that, sweet."

"How am I supposed to look?" I snap, struggling to keep my emotions in check. I'm angry—angry like I haven't been in a long time. How could Nolan do such a thing to his brother? How could Jake be so calm and continue to protect him?

"This isn't an easy decision to make. I don't want to leave you."

"Then don't," I whisper, licking my lips and continuing to choke on the swell of my throat.

"But I can't stay. Not with Nolan here. Not with my history. I want to be free, Rita. Can you understand that? I don't want this following me everywhere I go."

I nod with understanding I don't have. "No matter where you go, you'll need to disclose your imprisonment."

Jake sighs. "But it will be easier without the rumors and knowledge of what happened. I simply have to admit to a crime."

I want to believe it's that simple, but life will always be complicated for him. This scar is permanent, and it isn't just the prison sentence marring Jake's heart. The truth that his brother committed the crime and Jake paid for it has made forever-lasting damage.

"I don't know how to get over this . . . this . . . sense of betrayal." Jake glances up at me, and this I understand.

"I once felt the same way," I remind him, thinking back to when I learned about the fire and Jake's part in it. Jake's *assumed* role in Ian's death. Betrayal is a good word for my emotions, but I moved past it. Perhaps it was my faith in Jake. That sense that he couldn't have started a fire, and he would never intentionally hurt someone. In fact, Jake hadn't done anything wrong.

He lowers his head once more, his forehead meeting my covered breast.

"Where will you go?" I ask as if I support his decision, which I don't.

"I don't know." The roughness to his tone gives away his frustration. He shifts off me and easily turns for the side of the bed. Slipping out from under the sheets, I have a fine view of his smooth back and firm backside. His body is a testament to beauty but looking at him hurts my heart. He's walking away from me without a glance back.

A part of me screams to fight for him. Tell him how I feel and what I want. The other part of me feels his defeat as it wavers off him like a hazy fog, seeping outward from his existence and shrouding us both. He pauses at my bedroom door, placing a hand on the doorjamb before turning his head to glance over his shoulder.

"You're the best of women, Rita Kaplan," he states, and I fight the sob rolling up my chest. "I'll never forget who you are." Jake steps into the hallway without a full glance back at the bed, and I roll to my side, clutching the sheets to my chest. Understanding and heartbreak riddle my insides, and I turn my face into the pillow to hide my tears as I cover my ears to the sound of Jake leaving my house and my heart.

---

Jake is still under obligation to serve his parole without risk of violation, so being true to this arrangement, he returns to Building Buddies when I check in with Sullivan on Monday. In the meantime, I have a call in to both Jake's parole officer and Parker Avery.

I am potentially overstepping my bounds with Jake and his parole officer, but I didn't know how else to get Jake to see reason. From a personal perspective, Nolan's confession isn't mine to share as it was hearsay through Jake. On the other hand, I had an obligation as Jake's supervisor through Building Buddies and our relationship with the prison system to disclose information I feel would be beneficial regarding our ward. The same went for damaging information, which was why Jake had been concerned about our first kiss. Reporting that kiss could have been a strike against his parole.

Sensing that our night together had been Jake's farewell, I

didn't approach him about the possibilities before him. First and foremost, Jake could be exonerated of the crime if Nolan confessed. His record could be wiped clean and his status restored, although technically, the damage had been done to both Jake's reputation and his mental health. The confession from his brother was another crushing blow. If Jake didn't turn his brother in or if Nolan refused to confess, Jake would live forever with the stigma of being a convicted criminal, and he'd continue to live with the knowledge he hadn't done it when he knew who had. His brother was the culprit.

By the time Ryan James returns my call, I am too worked up to think straight.

"As his parole officer, can't you prompt him to talk to you?" I encourage.

"Rita, if you know something, you should just tell me. I can't help Jake if I don't know the facts."

"But it's not my place to tell you what I know. It should come from the source."

"Is that Jake?" Ryan's question stumps me as Nolan is the one who would have to confess. "It's obvious you have a relationship with Jake Drummond. Maybe you can convince him to come forward with this new information you think he has."

I had to be as vague as I could without giving away any hints of what I now know. I wanted answers without exposing either Nolan or Jake. I wanted to free Jake without damning his brother.

I had to fight for Jake the only way I knew how at the moment. He needed the truth exposed to set himself free. After a long talk with my law partner, I had a plan, and thankfully, May agrees. Things could be tricky, but I am determined for Jake. I'd already lost a man I'd loved once before, and I recovered. I survived, as Scarlett said. I would risk Jake's hatred if it meant giving him a future he deserved by wiping out his past. I would recover again, as I once told Jake. I always do.

On Thursday, Jake is called by his parole officer to attend a meeting. At Building Buddies, we allow release for such appointments, so this part of my plan is easy to orchestrate. The harder part is when Jake arrives to find me present after days of silence between us. I'd reached out to check on him with no response. I was hoping he'd change his mind about Nolan, about leaving, and about us. I wanted him to come back to me, but I needed him to decide we could work something out together.

Confusion is written on Jake's face as he enters the small meeting room and takes a seat beside his parole officer instead of me. Across the table from us is Parker Avery.

"Okay, Rita," Officer James begins, waving out a hand as he tilts his chair in my direction.

"It's come to my attention that my client has information that could exonerate him of his crime."

"Rita," Jake hisses two seats away from me. I don't look at him. Instead, I focus on Parker.

"Before revealing this information, I'd like to know what Mr. Drummond's options are?" I'd already discussed a few things with Parker in a vague, hypothetical sense, but I need her to explain the facts to Jake.

"First, if we can obtain a written confession from another party, there's no reason not to present the information before a judge. I'm certain the conviction on Jake would be overruled, and a full pardon would be granted."

"Rita, what are you doing?" Jake hisses again, and Parker's eyes drift to Jake, but mine focus forward. Looking at him might break my resolve. I need to remain impartial to him despite the emotional connection between us, but after several seconds of silence, I can't fight the pull. Glancing at him, I beg him with my eyes to trust me. Instead, I see more hurt and more betrayal etched in those lovely blues of his.

"What if the new information is sensitive and my client doesn't wish to share?" I turn back to Parker.

"If this were the court, he'd be held in contempt for concealing evidence," Parker warns me.

"But this isn't court," I reiterate, so Jake is clear. "This is an informative meeting of Mr. Drummond's options."

Parker again addresses Jake. "Then Mr. Drummond would complete his sentence as currently stated by the State's sentence. You had a ten-year sentence and were released in seven on good behavior with a six-month parole as a contingency to re-acclimate you into the workforce."

Jake huffs, disagreeing with that assessment. His position as a worker with Building Buddies isn't job potential. We can give him a reference for his skill and his dedication to quality work, but the referral will come with the information of why he worked for us. He's in a restorative justice program through the prison system.

I have one more question for Parker. "If another party were to come forward and accept responsibility for the crime, exonerating Mr. Drummond of all grievances against him, what would happen to that person?"

"Jail," Parker states immediately. Even seats away from Jake, I feel him go rigid.

"What are other options?" I ask.

Parker glances at Jake. "Taking into account the time lapsed since the crime and the circumstances, it is possible another party might be placed on probation. But this isn't an answer or a guarantee I'm speaking of. We're talking very hypothetically here, Rita," Parker warns.

Ryan James steps in at this point and swivels his chair to Jake, noting Jake's indignation. "Is there something you'd like to share with us?" With Ryan's back to me, I glance over his shoulder to find Jake staring across the table, eyes not necessarily on Parker but the wall behind her. He wants to be free. He wants to be cleared of the scar on his record and the dirt on his name, but the way Jake holds himself—stiff and tense—he's going to protect Nolan at all costs. It's written in his body language. His loyalty is something I love about him, but in this situation, I'm not liking it.

"I have nothing to share." His elbows rest on the table, and his fingertips steeple, pressing them against his lips.

"Jake," I whisper, and Ryan turns his chair back in the direction of Parker.

"Are you certain?" Parker prompts. Parker admitted herself she never felt right about how Jake's case was handled or sentenced. When I reached out to her with the possibility of information to exonerate him, she was willing to listen. The warehouse fires were considered inconclusive so only the high school is on Jake's record along with Ian's death. I didn't want Jake to continue to suffer with these facts when it isn't his cross to bear. He hadn't committed a crime, but he still held the guilt that someone had, and now he knows who.

Jake nods in answer to Parker, still steepling his fingers. Parker glances at me. As we had spoken before this meeting, I warned her that Jake might actually resist sharing information. She'd also told me that if he didn't speak up, she couldn't do anything to help him. "Then if you'll excuse me, I'm finished here."

I wait for her exit before turning to Officer James. "I'm sorry I dragged you here," I say to him. Ryan turns from me to Jake and back.

"It was worth a shot. I can't make you talk, but I would have offered up something," Ryan says. "Then again, it's your life, man, and you're so close to the end of this sentence."

"Am I free to leave?" Jake asks, sounding a bit belligerent toward his parole officer.

"Free to leave this room, yes," Ryan states, and Jake hastily stands without a glance back at me.

"Well, that imploded," I state, scoffing at my failed attempt to right a wrong for the man I love who doesn't love me.

Ryan shakes his head. "We see things like this all the time. Fear of giving up someone else. Retribution if he did."

I sigh as I doubt this case is that devious. What could Nolan possibly do next to his brother? Ryan slowly rises and then turns to shake my hand.

"It was worth a shot," I mumble.

Ryan narrows his eyes at me. "Why do you care?" His question isn't intended to be derogatory. He's simply curious, and I have to wonder myself. Why did I invest the time and energy into this risk when Jake clearly doesn't want to be set free? He wants to serve his time and leave his brother behind, just like he'll leave me.

# 25

# JAKE

As I exit the meeting room, I'm fuming. *That insufferable woman.* Anger nearly steams off my body. Walking away from Rita's bed the other morning had been difficult enough. I wanted nothing more than to stay as she invited, but I needed to get my head clear and organize a plan. I needed to take steps to move forward, as she was always stating. I needed time to recover from what Nolan had done to me.

Still, I don't know why Rita has to be so meddlesome. She should have asked me what I wanted to do. She should have talked to me. Then again, I'm the one who hadn't answered her texts. I'm also the one who told her I was leaving Vermont. I had to get away from this place, and that presently includes her. Huffing out into the hallway and down a corridor, I see a familiar wheelchair and a woman next to my brother.

"Nolan?" My heart races double time at my brother in his seat. "What are you doing here?" I don't want him anywhere near this courthouse or attorneys. Maybe he was onto something when he called them all snakes. Rita certainly had her own agenda for calling this meeting, but I can't see what she'd gain.

"I got a call from this beautiful woman saying I was needed here to discuss your case." Nolan looks over at the brunette next to him and winks. She shakes her head, and I'm certain she's just endured minutes of my brother's ruthless flirting.

"And you are?" I question her as she stands.

"May Shipley." She holds out a hand to shake, and slowly, the name registers.

"As in Kaplan and Shipley," I clarify, knowing the answer. I haven't met Rita's law partner, but I have heard her name often enough from stories Rita told me.

"Yes." Behind me, I hear the soft clack of heels on tile, but I don't turn around. I sense Rita's presence before I see her.

"And you're here with my brother because . . .?" I allow her to fill in the blank because I clearly do not understand what is happening.

"I'm here to offer your brother legal representation, should he need it."

Nolan's head cranes from May to me. "Why would I need legal representation?" His face blanches, and his voice squeaks.

"No reason," I state, my voice terse. I step around my brother, ready to push him forward for an elevator, but he stops me.

"What's going on?" he asks, looking from May to me and then to the woman I'm certain is behind me and behind this shit show.

"Nothing," I mutter again. "I'll explain when we get home."

Nolan's eyes widen, noticing how I don't turn to face Rita. I simply nod at May and excuse both myself and my brother. Once inside the elevator, Nolan's hands twitch in his lap.

"You're scaring me," he mutters, watching the elevator count down to the first floor.

"Not here," I mumble. I'm holding it together by a thin thread, and I can't risk exposing Nolan or myself in this courthouse.

Nolan and I arrived separately, which means I need to wait until we get home before I implode.

"What were you thinking?" I'm yelling at him before he even exits his car in the driveway. My truck door slammed so hard, the sound still echoes in the yard.

Nolan stares up at me, half in, half out of his vehicle. "I was there for you," he states like it's perfectly natural. Like he's always been there for me.

"Nolan, stop doing me favors, okay?"

"What the fuck?" he snarls up at me.

"That was a ruse. Rita wanted you to turn yourself in."

"That bitch," Nolan huffs. However, his defensive tone turns my allegiance.

"She's not a bitch. She did it for—" The truth slams into me. *She did it for me.* She wanted to free me from my sentence, but she shouldn't have gone about it how she did. She should have talked to me, asked me what I wanted to do.

"I told you attorneys were snakes."

"You watch your mouth," I bark at Nolan, pointing a finger at him. For the first time ever, Nolan stops and stares at me like he doesn't recognize me. I hardly recognize myself. That's been the problem for seven years. I don't know who I am anymore, but I can't do this. I can't keep protecting Nolan.

"Rita . . ." I pause, realizing I'm not exactly laying blame where it belongs. "*I* could have turned you in, Nolan. If you confessed, my sentence could be wiped free. I could walk away with the conviction struck from my record."

Nolan's face turns white once more.

"I could go to jail," he whispers as if he never understood the depths of the consequences. He committed a crime. He killed an innocent man. He could have gone to jail seven years ago.

*Rita.* Oh God, my stomach clenches for her all over again. She only wants justice. She wants the right person to pay for taking the love of her life from her.

"I'm not turning you in, Nolan. I'm not offering you up or pressing any kind of charges, but you're still going to pay for what you've done."

"How?" His head lifts, panic in his expression.

"I haven't decided yet, but I'm going to find something." I pause, taking a deep breath. "In the meantime, I'm moving out."

"Why?" His eyes widen.

"Because you don't need me, Nolan. You're self-sufficient here, and frankly, I don't want to live with you. No offense, little brother, but right now, I'm having a hard time looking at you."

"Because of Rita," Nolan bites, color returning to his face.

"Yes, because of Rita. Don't make me choose, Nolan, because it's going to be her." I can hardly believe the words leaving my lips, but it's true. If I thought I'd stay in this godforsaken area, it would be for one reason only. *Rita.*

"Just like you chose Lisa."

"What?" I glare at my brother, uncertain what he's said.

"You picked her over me."

"What are you talking about?"

"You left me behind."

I stare at my brother. *Unbelievable.* "I was in love. I married her. I didn't leave you. You were an adult by then, Nolan. Capable of taking care of yourself. In fact, you needed to fucking grow up." Jesus, he'd been twenty-three when I married Lisa. *Why is this coming up now?*

"I don't want to be left behind."

Staring at my brother in his chair, I should feel sorry for him. I want to feel something for him. He's my brother. I love him, but right now, I hate him. He did this to himself. I coddled him too much by filling in for our father, compensating for our mother, and even taking over when he wasn't fit to father his own son.

"I'm not leaving you behind, Nolan, but I need separation from you."

"Where will you go?" he asks, and I glance up at the garage, full of my supplies and scraps, waiting for more sculptures to be made.

"I don't know yet," I state, turning back to Nolan. "But I need to do something for myself."

Rita appears at the building site the next day, and I'm counting the minutes until the weekend. I need time away from everywhere and everything. If this had been a normal job, I'd have called in sick, but I can't. I keep to myself, ignoring Rita, which is difficult in the small house. The project is nearing its end ahead of schedule.

As Rita slips into the newly laid out kitchen, I step out the back door and round the house for the front yard. I've been tiling the backsplash but need air. Standing beside my truck, I take deep, gulping breaths, hanging onto the edge of the bed. Just having Rita in the same room sets my heart racing, and a cold sweat running over my skin. I want to throttle her while wanting to pull her to me.

Despite the crunch of gravel near me, I don't look up but keep my head between my outstretched arms.

"I wanted to apologize." Rita pauses. "I thought I could help."

Slowly, I lift my head but look over the truck bed instead of directly at her. "What's that saying? You were out of line, counselor."

No sound comes from Rita, not a snort or a laugh, so I turn to face her, finding her sad. She's almost as sad as when she learned the truth about me, or what she thought was the truth. Either way, I'll always have a connection to her beloved's death. It wasn't me, but it was my brother who took that man from her.

"He should pay somehow," Rita states.

"That isn't your decision. He's my brother." My voice rises, and Rita turns her head. "I could never turn him in. He's in a wheelchair, for God's sake. He's suffered enough."

"Has he?" Rita asks, turning her attention back to me.

"This isn't like you, sweet." Her nickname comes out bitter on my tongue. "You aren't vengeful like this."

Rita shakes her head. "It wasn't about Nolan. It was about you."

I nod because deep down inside, I know.

"I want you to be free of the constraint you feel. Be free to do as you please." She swallows, and I visibly see her throat roll. "Be free to move about the country at will. That's what you want, right? You want to leave this all behind." She waves out a hand, implying the build.

"I don't know what I want, Rita." She flinches at the harshness in my voice, but I'm still upset. "You should have spoken to me, not tried to ambush me. Or Nolan."

"I tried to call you." She pauses. "And would you have listened? I got the message loud and clear the other morning."

I could argue that I wasn't brushing her off. I was separating myself from her. I needed to let her go. We weren't going to be good together. My brother would always be between us. Rita had loved someone else, and she wasn't going to get over him for someone like me, with connections to his death. Nolan would be a barrier between us.

"I don't need your help."

Rita rolls her lips inward and turns her cheek to me. "Fine." Her arms flap outward, and she slaps her hands to her thighs. A slow second passes before she turns back to me. "Fine. But you have a job to complete here. Once it's done, we can move you to another location, away from here, to complete the remainder of the months on your parole. I won't be a supervisor on that site. I'm taking over the directorship role."

In all the chaos, Rita hadn't told me.

"Congratulations," I say, finally looking over at her in her jeans and Building Buddies T-shirt. Seeing her hurts for all she could have meant to me and all she does. As I told her, she's the best of women and maybe under different circumstances, I could admit I'd fallen in love with her.

Staring at her, I swallow my pride as I do need her help in a certain matter. "I would like to ask a favor."

Rita straightens.

"I want you to give Nolan a job somehow. He needs this restorative justice program. I demanded he seek therapy, and he needs something constructive to do for redemption."

Rita's mouth falls open but then shuts. Her arms cross over her middle, and she looks away from me, then back. It's comical to watch her arguing with herself in her head. She's cute, but I fight the urge to laugh. I hate how once she's in my presence, my attraction to her is just as strong as ever. I've stewed for days and had the past twenty-four hours to be really angry with her, but seeing her fight control of herself, I want to wrap her in my arms and kiss her senseless.

But I won't.

"I'll see what I can do. I'm not certain how to go about finding him something without explaining his guilt, though."

"Try. Trying is all I can ask. At this point, we've all suffered enough, Rita. It's time we each move on as best we can."

Without another word, Rita turns on her heels and leaves me still gripping the edge of my truck. I hadn't realized how hard I was holding back from reaching for her until my fingers ache as I peel them back from curling against the metal.

Suddenly, she spins back to face me, and I still, afraid I will reach for her after all.

"You asked me to have faith in you, and I did. I only wish you'd had the same faith in me."

With that, she turns again, giving me her back, and walks away.

# RITA

It wasn't easy, but I found something I thought Nolan could do for Building Buddies. It took more than a week to consider my options and make a decision. As Jake suggested, I should have spoken to him first before planning the meeting with Parker Avery. In the same breath, I knew Jake might not show if I simply told him what I thought. I'd lost Jake in my bet that things would work. I'd known it was a risk. Lesson learned. I should never gamble.

Still, I found myself at his house with a proposition for Nolan.

"Is Jake here?" I could have called, but I thought it best we discussed what I'd come up with face-to-face. Nolan stares up at me through the screen door.

"He isn't."

It was a Sunday, and I expected Jake to be home, maybe working on a lamp in his garage, but the closed garage door gave no sign of him. In the heat, he'd surely have it open.

"Do you know when he'll be back?" I ask, finding this kind of conversation tedious.

"Actually, I don't know where my brother is. He left here a week ago. Said he was moving out. I thought he might have moved in with you."

"Me?" I ask. "Why would he move in with me?"

Nolan shakes his head without answering. Licking his lips, he looks away from me, and I cross my arms, feeling the tension between us through the screen barrier.

"Could I come in? I'd like to talk to you."

Debate plays out on Nolan's face, but eventually, he acquiesces, tipping his head to the side. I help myself to open the door and enter the small home. The place is clean but very much a bachelor's pad, complete with a slouchy couch and a flat-screen television taking up most of the wall. I help myself to a seat on the cushions while Nolan rolls into the room. He waits on me to begin.

"Jake asked me to do something for him which involves you. As much as he wanted me to speak with him before I did anything in regards to you, perhaps I should just lay this out for you, as it does pertain to you."

Nolan huffs at my run-on sentence. "What could big brother possibly want me to do?" Bitterness rings in Nolan's tone, and after all I've sensed his brother has done for him, it's undeserved toward Jake.

"Nolan, it's obvious we don't care for each other. I don't know what I've ever done to you, but I know what you did. Period. Jake told me everything."

If Nolan knows this truth, he gives nothing away, but a slight tic near his closed jaw hints he didn't know how much I knew.

"I'm not here for your confession, although I certainly believe you need to confess to someone. It must have been hard to hold that secret in all these years."

Nolan huffs again, turning his face away from me, giving me belligerence. "Lady, you have no idea what you're talking about."

"I know enough," I state, but I don't wish to go into my own story. "I'm here because I care about your brother. I care about him a great deal, and he asked me for a favor. I'd like to offer you the redemption you need."

Nolan scoffs. "Redemption?"

"You should have gone to jail." My voice cracks, and I swallow against the prickle in my eyes. "You let an innocent man go in your place. Your own brother."

"I don't need your *damn*ation," he bites, narrowing his eyes at me.

"I'm not here to damn you," I state, reminding myself why I'm here. I will not pass judgment. "I'm here to offer you a job of sorts."

Nolan's brows lift as if I must be joking.

"Jake would like you to enter a restorative justice program similar to his parole. Without officially being on parole, I can't make you attend, nor can I place you in a program without revealing your guilt."

His mouth opens, but I hold up a hand to stop him.

"I've also found you a criminal therapist."

"I'm not seeing a shrink."

"She's not a shrink. She's a therapist who specializes in guilt. She's different from a criminal psychologist. She isn't profiling you. She's here to help you."

"I don't need—"

"Yes, you do," I cut him off. "And your brother asked me to find someone for you."

This is addiction 101. You cannot help those who won't help themselves, but sometimes a strong intervention is necessary, and the push someone needs to get over their hurdle.

Nolan remains quiet for a second, glaring at me with eyes similar to his brother's but harder, tougher. It's unfair as his brother is the one who lost out on time, and he isn't nearly as hardened as the man before me.

"I need an assistant for my new position as director of Building Buddies. We have social media to maintain and a website to update. We host two fundraisers a year, and I need help organizing them. I know nothing about parties, and I'm told you do." My eyes narrow but a slight grin forms on my lips.

Nolan smirks, and I recognize the trait amongst brothers. "You wouldn't be paid. This is service."

I let that sink in.

"Finally, I want to organize a youth group that works on projects during summer breaks. My fiancé was a high school principal." I pause, letting the information settle although Nolan must already know my personal connection to his crime. "He used to bring a group of teens together for a project every year, and they'd help us build a home for a family in need."

"I can't build anything," Nolan states, sarcasm filling his voice as he taps his chair.

"Maybe not, but you can supervise. You can organize, and you might even be able to instruct. If nothing else, I'd hope you could encourage young minds to get involved in their community and help others."

Nolan's quiet for a long minute before speaking. "What if I don't want to do this restorative bullshit?"

"Then you've shown your brother you don't love him as you should for all he's done for you."

Nolan's face hardens once more, but his eyes soften just a touch.

"I'm not going to defer this decision to Jake. This is my offer. If you want it, here's an address to report to tomorrow. If you don't show, I'll have my answer, and I'll tell Jake he'll need to look elsewhere for you."

Quickly, I stand and cross the room, but Nolan's chair is in a position that blocks my exit. His eyes follow me as I near him.

"Why would you do this?" He pauses. "Why would you give me this job, this service?"

Taking a deep breath, I exhale before stating the truth.

"Because I believe in second chances. Good people make bad decisions all the time. And because I'm in love with your brother."

I step left, hoping to go around Nolan, finding there's just enough space to squeeze past the chair. As I attempt my move, Nolan catches my wrist to stop me beside him.

"He didn't move in with you?" The question is the first sign of reluctance I've heard from Nolan.

"Did he tell you he was?"

"No. I just assumed he was going to your place. When he moved out, he told me he picked you."

"Picked me?" I scoff. I hadn't spoken to Jake in days.

"He said he'd choose you every time." It sounds sweet, but it's completely untrue. However, I didn't wish to argue with Nolan.

"Monday," I warn, dread filling me that Nolan won't show, and Jake will know how his brother feels about him.

# JAKE

It's another Monday, and we have one week left to finalize this house. I'm not part of the final touches inside, so I'm commissioned to work on the landscaping. A ramp has been made to accommodate the owner's son, who has multiple medical concerns. His room is my favorite. The special lamp I made for him worked, and it was hung near his bed. The interior decorator really liked it and commissioned me for a few other lamps and lanterns.

I'm already working outside the house when something catches my eye, or rather, someone working a wheelchair up the new driveway.

"Nolan?" I stand to face my brother before glancing across the property to Rita, who's planting flowers where we've already secured new bushes. Rita stands from her kneeling position and removes her work gloves. She swipes her hands on her jeans and walks over to Nolan.

*What the hell?* I tug off my own gloves, dismissing Sullivan's glare, and cross the yard to where Rita has approached my brother.

"Nolan, what's going on?" I address him first, finding it strange that he'd come to the work site. I'm also a bit concerned as he sought me out here of all places. I don't need my family drama mixing with my parole.

Nolan sheepishly glances at me before looking up at Rita. "I'm here to accept your offer, if it still stands."

Rita slowly grins, chewing at the corner of her lips for a second before straightening her expression to look stern. "You're late."

Nolan lowers his eyes and sighs before answering. "I was lost."

My head is so busy moving back and forth between the two of them I'm not certain what to focus on. The fact Nolan is here. The fact Rita is smiling. *Just what the hell is happening?*

Reaching out a hand to Nolan's shoulder, Rita responds. "We've all been there."

Again, my gaze is moving from one of them to the other. "I don't understand," I state, but neither of them looks at me.

"Let's get to work," Rita says to Nolan before glancing over at me. "Jake, get back to work." Her demand is soft but still commanding before she addresses Nolan once more.

"Let's step into my temporary office." She chuckles as she tips her head toward her crossover and leads Nolan toward the vehicle. I'm frozen in place on the pavement, watching my brother wheel behind Rita. Her head twists to make certain Nolan follows her, and then her body shifts so she can look at me as she walks backward.

"*Thank you,*" I mouth to her.

"Anytime, handsome." Rita salutes me with two fingers at her forehead before lowering her gaze to my brother and offering him another smile.

Watching Rita interact with my brother for a moment, a presence comes to my side.

"She's good people," Sullivan states beside me, pride filling his voice, along with desire. I haven't missed how Sullivan tracks Rita, just as I do when she's on-site.

"She's the best of women," I mutter, having stated the same

thing to Rita once. I don't deserve her, and Nolan certainly doesn't deserve her kindness either.

A half hour later, Nolan starts to wheel away from Rita, and I drift over to him. "What's happening?"

Nolan explains the job offer Rita's given him. Rita has stepped up to listen and occasionally nods at Nolan's explanation.

"Does this arrangement have a time limit?" I question, glancing up at Rita, shocked by all I've learned. The social media work Nolan can easily do from a computer. The fundraising efforts seem like something Nolan would be good at organizing, and the youth group, which is a bit of a surprise, could really do Nolan some good.

"This isn't a sentence," Rita clarifies. "It's effort. Nolan will get out of it what he puts into it."

"And Nolan can speak for himself," he interjects, narrowing his eyes up at Rita. Rita softly chuckles and shakes her head at my brother. They aren't friends, but I can see she's trying. She'd done more than a friend might do. She did what I asked, and then she took it one step further. She's put her faith in Nolan, too.

"Rita says you'll be leaving the area," Nolan mentions, changing the subject.

"I explained how you'd like to move out of state, but I can't place you on our sites in New Hampshire yet. We have a new project up in Gaskin," Rita clarifies.

"You're really moving away?" Nolan questions, his voice lowering with regret.

My eyes leap up to Rita. "I'm undecided."

Her lips purse, ignoring my comment, and she pats Nolan on the shoulder. "Well, Nolan, it's good to have you here."

"Yeah, I need to get going. I have that meeting next." Nolan sets his hands on his wheels, but I step before him. My hands lift, stopping my brother's retreat.

"What meeting?" I ask, fear creeping over my skin. Is this another setup for Nolan to turn himself in? What is Rita playing at?

"Rita found me a therapist."

Slowly, I lower my raised arms. "Why?"

Nolan looks up at Rita once more and then back at me. "I need someone to talk to." Shame fills his voice as he twists his lips, but there's nothing shameful in seeking help.

"I-I'm proud of you for this."

"Yeah?" Nolan's head lifts higher, and he visibly swallows before glancing back at Rita once more. Then a shield drifts back over his pleased expression, and he stiffens his jaw. He's scared, and I don't blame him. It's difficult to accept he's done wrong. "Okay. I'll see ya around."

I step out of Nolan's way, and he rolls past me to his car. For a few minutes, I watch him work his way down the drive and then open his door, maneuvering himself with the aid of the door. Everything in me wants to rush forward and assist him. Wants to take over and help him. Protect him.

"He's going to be okay," Rita states, and I turn back to her, squinting in the bright sunshine.

"How do you know?" The question seeks reassurance. Will Nolan find what he needs? Will he not feel as if he's been left behind? Will he repent what he's done? Will he find forgiveness for himself? The questions seem endless, and genuine concern still exists because he is my brother.

"I believe in second chances. This is his." Rita gives me a weak smile before turning around and returning to her crossover, where the passenger door remained open. A laptop sits on the seat along with a file box on the floor. Rita needs a real office, and I might know the perfect place for it.

As the week comes to a close, the project receives its final touches. Saturday is the big reveal for the family and Rita has invited me to join them even though Saturday isn't a mandatory day for me. I was expecting a large bus blocking the building like those emotional extreme makeover shows or maybe a big barrier, separated by the fixer-upper hosts. In prison, we watched a lot of random television. But the truth is, Jackie and Bob park down the street and are guided to the house with hands over their eyes. It's a bit comical but also exciting.

The couple stands side by side clutching hands. Their son sits in his wheelchair while their daughter stands beside him, covering his eyes with her hand. He chuckles as he keeps trying to swat it away, and his sister demands her hand block his sight. Sullivan Vance is present along with Alfred Jennings, the officially *former* director of Building Buddies. Nolan is here as well.

"Jackie and Bob, are you ready to see your new home?" Rita even sounds like a television host, announcing the big reveal, and I find I'm actually holding my breath, hoping they like what they'll see. I hope this house will recover all they've lost and offer them a future. I hope it brings them peace.

My eyes don't leave Rita as she tells them to remove their hands. The air actually stills around us a second before Jackie bursts into tears, and Bob wraps his arms around his wife. The joy on their faces, along with the relief, is almost too much. My heart swells, and my eyes prickle.

Rita rubs a hand up Jackie's back. "Would you like to go inside?" Her softened tone encourages the couple to move forward. Sullivan holds the keys to the house, and he hands them over to the stunned couple.

Nolan has been watching the whole process with rapture. Something settles over his expression, softening it a little bit, and I'm wondering if he's thinking the same thing as me. This is a family. This is their new home and a second chance for them. Whatever the future has in store for them, they'll weather it together.

"I'll race you," Nolan suddenly teases of the young boy in his wheelchair, sounding like a kid himself. The little girl squeals beside her brother before she reaches around the chair and pushes her brother forward. They each take off, but Nolan holds back, allowing the kids to feel like they're winning. The laughter coming from all of them is like a fist clenching in my stomach—a happy fist—one that wants to hold on tighter.

Bob gives gratitude to Rita, but Rita shifts his praise. "Sullivan and Jake did it all."

When Bob steps over to me, I anticipate his hand, but instead, he reaches for me, pulling me in for a back-slapping hug.

"Thank you, man," he mutters over and over again. "Thank you from my entire family." My eyes burn, and I rapidly blink away the threat of tears.

"It was no trouble," I admit, uncertain if Bob knows anything about my history. This wasn't a project but a sentence. Then again, standing here watching all of them, pride fills my insides. At this moment, it has become so much more.

Jackie steps up next. Her tear-soaked face is wet as she brings me in for a hug, burying her face in my neck. She begins to sob again.

"Thank you so much." She draws back to pat my cheek once before holding my face a second. Looking me in the eye, she repeats herself. "Thank you for everything."

The damn threat of tears breaks on me, and I quickly press at my lids, drawing my fingers over them to the bridge of my nose.

"It was nothing," I state.

"It means everything," she says, turning to include Rita.

"We owe you everything."

"You owe us nothing," Rita states, her voice confident and reassuring. This seems to encompass Rita's entire attitude. No one owes anybody anything. We owe what we do to ourselves first. Service to others second.

As a couple, Jackie and Bob are led by Sullivan to the ramp where their son has beaten Nolan up the incline. Nolan is giving the daughter a high five. As I watch their interaction, I accept that this is all I ever wanted in my life. A family. A home. I had those things in a slightly unconventional manner. I've definitely been missing them in the last decade.

"You did this," Rita says beside me. "You did good here," she adds, still glancing at the house. Her hands are tucked into the back pockets of her jeans as she nods at the place. Pride fills her voice along with appreciation. She loves what's been done here, and I have to agree I do as well. It feels good to give Jackie and Bob this fresh start. It feels good to build something and see that, like anything, there is a beginning and an end. The thought has me staring at Rita. Some things are not meant to end, though.

"Is that a compliment?" I tease. The last week has been difficult. Rita has been here full time, but we haven't had a moment alone together. I have so much to say, so many apologies to give her, but I've been stumped as to where to start.

"Yeah, but don't let it go to your head, handsome. It's already big enough," she snarks back, giving me an easy smile.

"You still think I'm handsome?" I joke, falling easily into our old banter.

"You already know I do," she says, her voice lowering, reminding me of all the tender moments between us.

"Would you let me buy you a coffee? To celebrate."

Observing her red-rimmed glasses and her light-colored hair blowing in the breeze, Rita wanted the same things I did at one time. A spouse. A home. Maybe children. If I could restore anything for her, it would be these things, and I chew my lip waiting on her answer to my invitation.

"Sure," Rita says. She shrugs and squints back at the house. "Why not?" Her casual response has that fist in my belly unclenching a little bit, but a new tightness fills me instead.

"Meet you on the couch," she teases, implying our spot at the Busy Bean.

"Actually, I was wondering if you could ride with me. I have somewhere I'd like to show you first."

# RITA

*Never let 'em see you sweat,* my dad used to say when he'd coach me on how to handle a courtroom if I had to enter one. So, I was trying my best not to let Jake sense the hesitation rolling off me as I climbed into his truck. We'd been together in his pickup plenty of times, and maybe that was the first part of my fear. The memories of making out with Jake in this front seat were overwhelming.

The harder part of being in his truck, though, was the confinement with him. His scent of sawdust and cinnamon overpowered everything in the cab, and my thighs clenched like the fragrance was an aphrodisiac. My attraction to Jake had not waned despite his exit from my bedroom or even his anger in that courthouse. If anything, over the past week, his attention on me working with his brother only doubled the magnetism. I felt him watching. And sometimes, I thought it might be apprehension. He didn't believe in my intentions to help his brother, which made me better understand his desire for another person's faith.

I wanted him to have faith in me.

I consider myself a decent person, but that confidence has been tested, and I wanted to prove to Jake I believed in his brother. Good people make bad decisions all the time. I'd had to come to terms with Jake's decision not to turn in his brother because it was his decision, not mine. And then I had to agree to help Nolan when parts of me screamed he didn't deserve it. I went to an AA meeting every night that week to remind myself we all deserve a second chance. Each person has moments of poor decision-making and the consequences that follow. If forgiveness isn't an option, we'd all be damned.

"Where are we going?" I question as we bypass the turn-off for Colebury and head in the direction of Hampshire.

"As I said, I'd like to show you somewhere first."

To my surprise, we pull up before the old fire station. Jake pauses, and I turn my head to stare out the window.

"Do you trust me?" Jake asks, and I swivel in my seat to face him.

"I never doubted you." Once I got over that initial hurdle of Jake's sentence and then learning what happened from his perspective, I never felt a moment of distrust in him. I believed in him. I'd even wanted to believe in an us, but that seems like a lifetime ago.

Jake nods before opening his door. "Wait a second?"

I remain in my seat until he comes to open my door. A small thrill rumbles up my middle. Then he takes my hand, and a tsunami of apprehension fills me. Anticipation mixes with hesitation, and for a moment, I feel sick. I don't want to read too much into him touching me.

Jake leads me to a smaller door in the larger garage opening. Quickly unlocking it with a key, we enter the vast space where dust dances in the dim sunlight streaming through the windows, and a few items are scattered in the once empty truck space. Jake releases my hand and steps to the side, flipping a switch.

Miniature Edison bulbs on strings illuminate the dark space. The crisscross effect is almost romantic until I lower my gaze for the large workstation covered in scraps of industrial items and light bulbs.

"What's this?" I question stepping forward to admire a collection of lamps Jake has designed using old pipes and wires. Examining each piece, I lower to one in particular. It's man-made entirely out of copper conduit with that abstract cylinder head becoming a signature of Jake's work. On the chest is the smallest of bulbs shaped like a heart. He looks like the Tin Man from *The Wizard of Oz* only he's copper and missing a funnel for a hat.

"I'm calling him *Man Enlightened*."

I stand upright and stare at the creation. "He's beautiful." The piece is solid but looks delicate, and still, my fingers itch to touch it.

"He opened his heart to possibility."

I glance over my shoulder, wondering what he means. "What possibility?"

"Love. Second chances. New directions."

Slowly, I smile and return my attention to the structure. "So, you've bought the place?" I glance up and over our heads at the vast room.

"I did," he says, and I sense the smile in his tone. Gazing at him, he looks upward. "This will be my workshop. I plan to renovate the apartments upstairs and rent them out. One is mine. Maybe eventually I'll do something else with this space." He shrugs, implicating the lower level, and then he lowers his head, meeting my eyes. "For now, I want to keep it just as it is."

Blushing, I turn away from him and peer at the fire pole still intact. A surge of memory and desire ripples up my middle.

"It's a work in progress here. Just like me."

My attention draws back to him. "Aren't we all?"

He matches my smile. "I have one more spot I want to show you." For a second, I'm thinking he's planning to take me upstairs. Show me his apartment. Take me to his bed. Instead, he leads me into the lobby area of the old firehouse. There, an old metal office desk sits, freshly scrubbed and painted a deep metallic gray. The wooden desktop is refinished, perhaps new, and a vase of fall flowers sits on the corner. Beside it is a skein of purple yarn and two knitting needles.

My brows pinch. "Do you knit now?"

"I was thinking the new director of Building Buddies might need an office, and as she loves to knit to help her think, well . . ."

His voice drifts as I stare at him. Then the desk. Then him again.

"What?" The word is more of a choking sound.

"I suppose you might keep your office in Montpelier, but I thought, as you were making a change, maybe you'd prefer someplace new. New-*ish*. And we could—"

He's cut off from the rest of his thought as I've thrown myself at him, landing my lips awkwardly against his. He's still and stiff underneath mine, and I realize I've made a terrible mistake. I read into this gesture more than I should have. Quickly, I release him, but just as quickly, his arms fasten around me, and my body is flush with his once more. His mouth latches onto mine, and it's the kiss I've been longing for since he left my bedroom.

His mouth moves against me, soft yet demanding. His hands slide up my back, and one cups the back of my neck. Jake breaks the kiss but rests his forehead against mine.

"I'm sorry I walked away."

I want to tell him I understand. I want to assure him I accept his reasons, but I also don't want to keep looking backward.

"As long as we're walking forward together, that's all that matters." Pulling back from him, I need to see his eyes. I need to know I'm not alone in my thoughts. "Are we going forward together?"

"Does lightning strike twice?" Jake suddenly asks me, swiping my hair over my ear.

"Yes. Yes, it does. It strikes and strikes hard."

"Hard, huh?" Jake teases, meeting my eyes again before his lips close over mine once more. His hand at my lower back presses me against him, letting me know how hard he is for me. "I'm in love with you, sweet. I love you."

My breath hitches as I pull back from the words said against my mouth. "I love you, too, Jake."

Our mouths come together once more, and then he leads me upstairs to show me his new apartment, the waiting bed, and how hard he is.

# RITA

*Two weeks later*

Jake and I are sitting on our comfy plush peach couch. We don't technically own the thing, but it's our spot, and I snuggle under his arm as we sip the dark roast heaven on a lazy Sunday morning. The Busy Bean Café is . . . well, busy. Our resident writer sits at her table, typing away. A new barista has arrived. The place is abuzz with subtle activity, but Jake and I remain quiet, in our own little world on this old furniture.

He tips his head and absentmindedly presses a kiss to my temple. We treasure the weekends as Jake travels up to the Gaskin area for his latest Building Buddies project. His parole doesn't end until November. As I'm the new director for Building Buddies and staying on as a consultant at Kaplan and Shipley, my future employment and passion goals seem set on a new path. For Jake, the plan is to hire him as a supervisor for Building Buddies. He wants to continue working as well, finding his own passion in constructing houses for those in need. He'll also work on building up his industrial art following. The interior designer who works closest with Building Buddies has commissioned him for several more pieces on top of her first order, so Jake has plenty to get him started. He'll take his time to revamp the old firehouse, he says. Maybe one day he'll turn it into a bed and breakfast, but he's in no rush to make a decision.

We had a long talk about Nolan, and I've had much to consider in order to come to terms with Jake's decision. He hasn't asked Nolan to turn himself in, and Nolan hasn't offered. Jake doesn't want to risk his brother going to jail. It's still possible Nolan wouldn't have. His current physical condition, topped with the time that's lapsed from the crime, could have garnered him parole or probation. Still, it really wouldn't have been different from what he was doing now—working in a restorative manner, seeking therapy, and taking steps to better himself. Topped by his physical condition, Jake believes his brother is suffering enough. I still think Nolan should come clean to free his brother's name and maybe his own conscience, but Jake stands firm that it doesn't matter. He's already lost the time. He can't get it back. We've decided to take to the grave what Nolan did. We are the only three people who know the truth and maybe his therapist.

Nolan continues to work for me, struggling some days in frustration while other days he's a champ. I don't know how the old Nolan was, but this new one seems to be digging into his assigned role, accepting his fate, and working on himself. Jake suspects his brother has a girlfriend or a woman annoying the crap out of him, but Jake hasn't asked. Their relationship has lots of restructuring to be done before they are solid again. For now, they are each polite when they see one another and reflective when they are apart.

I lift my mug and take a sip. My gaze wanders upward to the chalkboard-black beams overhead, and I scan the various quotes and sayings. Slowly, I sit upright, staring over my head.

"What?" Jake asks, his voice concerned at my cautious movement. My eyes squint as I've misread the words. I read them again. Slowly, I stand on shaky legs, focusing on the recognizable scrawl.

"Rita, what is it?" Jake asks, his concerned tone turning to a knowing sound. I shift around the low table before us to read the words once more.

Suddenly, I snort, loud and obnoxious, before covering my mouth and closing my eyes. The words light up behind my lids, emblazoned for my mind. *Is this happening?*

Jake's hands come to my shoulders, rubbing over them.

"Sweet," he whispers behind me, and I vigorously shake my head. "No?" he questions. "You won't do it."

Jake spins me so I face him, and I lower my head, embarrassed to be teary-eyed in a public place. He bends his knees a bit and lowers his body, so I'm forced to meet his eyes.

"You won't marry me?" The question in his voice is part teasing, part honest concern.

"Aren't you supposed to be on one knee or something?"

He chuckles at my inappropriate response. "Well, I was, but you were taking too long to turn around, and now you're saying no, so what does it matter. I was hoping you'd notice that beam while we were on the couch."

"I was on the couch," I remark, but now I'm standing, facing him in disbelief.

"Yes, but it's been up there for weeks."

"It has?" I turn my head, glancing over my shoulder at the words scribbled on the beam facing the couch.

*Will you marry me, sweet?*

"When did you put it there?" I ask, still not fully accepting what it asks and the importance of this moment, which I'm totally botching up by asking all these other questions.

"The day we gave the house to Jackie and Bob. I offered to buy you a coffee to celebrate." He pauses, and I fill in the rest. We'd spent the rest of the day making up by having sex and talking and having more sex. Then I started knitting in bed, showing him how to weave the yarn, and he distracted me with more sex.

When I realize that this question has been laying out in the open for two weeks, and I've missed it every time we've entered the café, I want to kick myself.

"I'm not saying no," I squeak, worried I've ruined this perfect moment.

"Is that a yes?" he teases.

"Can you repeat the question?" I smile.

"Of course," he teases. First, he spins me around and points at the beam again. I laugh as he slips his hand into mine and tugs, so I twist to face him. Licking his lips, he reaches into his pocket. Then he lowers to one knee, and I hear gasps and the scratch of chair feet against wood around me. But all I focus on is Jake on one knee before me, holding up a beautiful diamond ring and looking at me with faith in his eyes.

"Rita Kaplan, you beautiful woman, will you marry me?"

Tears of overwhelming joy flow down my face, and I quickly swipe at them, finding my voice before I answer.

"Yes. A thousand times, yes."

And with a plush peach couch and an entire coffee shop as witnesses, I accept Jake's ring and agree to a future—a second chance—of love, hope, and faith in one another.

THE
END

# A LOVE NOTE FROM THE AUTHOR

When the opportunity to write in Sarina Bowen's World of True North arose, I nearly fell off my comfy chair. It's an opportunity I'd been wanting to exist – and then *voila!* It was here. As an avid reader, True North is one of my favorite series about family and friends, small towns and community, love, romance and sexy bits.

When I applied to write Rita Kaplan's story, I had lots of thoughts. First, Rita is 'my age,' meaning older-ish, kind-of, sort-of, and as the stage was already set for her to retire one day from her law practice, a midlife re-evaluation seemed like the perfect moment to move Rita along. Forty isn't old, but as I found with myself, forty and a half did bring about some re-assessment of my life. In Rita's case, she had conquered her addiction and was devoted to service for others. Building Buddies was born, and a one-eighty from her previous career began.

Which leads to Jake . . . as a former middle school teacher, restorative justice is a huge form of redemption in school districts, and it got its start in the prison system. Much of what we learned about the process involved studies done in more extreme cases – criminal activity – and the result of those cases in helping re-establish good people who had made poor decisions. Restorative justice can include rebuilding a physical object to make amends for damage done to property. My love of television shows for extreme home makeovers and fixer-uppers added to my ideas for Jake's parole. But there's also an element of restoration to the individual in restorative justice, as in rebuilding the offender. In Jake's case, it was difficult because he hadn't actually committed a crime.

Like many of us in the middle of our lives, though, we're a fixer-upper, in need of an extreme makeover, or maybe just a new couch to plant our backsides on and drink some coffee.

Wherever you're at, I'm hoping there's a stud in your life or at least a plush peach couch and a decent café to daydream in. May your forties (and beyond) be fabulous.